Copyright ©

All:

The characters and events portrayed in this book are fictitious. Any similarity to real persons, living or dead, is coincidental and not intended by the author.

No part of this book may be reproduced, or stored in a retrieval system, or transmitted in any form or by any means, electronic, mechanical, photocopying, recording, or otherwise, without express written permission of the publisher.

To make a request, visit: www.hollygreenland.com

ISBN-13: 979-8-66-129852-2

Original cover design by: Adrian Hastings
Additional design by: Lynsay Biss

MURDER ON MATERNITY

An Emily Elliot Mystery

Holly Greenland

www.hollygreenland.com

CHAPTER ONE

Greetings Ms Tate,

Everything's on the up for you, right? Wrong.

Time to find out how it feels when you aren't number one.

How does a little murder sound?

Keep an eye on Newton Hill on the 4th of this month.

Have fun!

Your friend,
Mr Naughty

It was that little letter, fewer than fifty short words, that changed everything.

But let me fill you in a bit first. This story really began back before the letter. When my ordinary world collided with Tabetha Tate's.

Hold on. I'll back up just a little further. To

when I was in the first beautiful months of pregnancy.

I can remember it so clearly. The cool spring air, the bulbs peeping through the ground, the birds beginning to nest. It all seemed so right, like I was part of this wider story of life. I really felt like Super Woman. Stroking my lovely rounded belly to get seats on the train, explaining to anyone who'd listen how I'd carry on as I always had when the baby arrived.

People told me I was glowing. And I was. I was growing a person inside me for goodness sake. I was a walking miracle. So, I did my light exercise, ate responsibly, didn't drink for the longest time since I'd turned eighteen. Well okay, sixteen. It felt beautiful.

I fantasised with growing intensity about what sort of mum I'd be. I had visions of myself as an earth mother; all nursing chairs, amber necklaces, recycled baby wipes and cute organic cotton baby-grows with teeny little flamingos on.

There I'd be at the window, waving Dan off to work, while rocking the baby in a mini-Emily outfit. Then heading out to walk by the river with my sleeping little bear in the sunshine, before catching a yoga class during nap time (even though I'd never made a yoga class pre-baby). No thoughts of work, no stress, just time to bond and enjoy the most special time of our lives.

Then the third trimester hit; the last three

months of pregnancy. Suddenly I was up for hours in the night, my skin dulled, and the baby started to sap my energy. I mean I could literally feel it pulling the energy from my limbs and mind to fuel its squirming and rolling and kicking. My hips began to ache as they were pushed apart by the growing being inside me. Like a tiny alien desperate to burst out.

Then Josie, one of the girls from the office, brought her wriggling, squealing little boy in and I realised I was terrified to take it.

'Come on Emily, it'll be you soon!' Ian from HR jeered from the side-lines and I felt I had to pick it up or risk looking completely heartless.

But as I looked down at its angry little face, like a scrunched-up invoice, I realised I didn't have the slightest idea how to even hold a baby, let alone change, feed or entertain it. That night I gave in and signed up to NCT's three-week intensive course, presumably set up for people like me, in denial until the last second.

If you haven't had kids, there's no reason why you should even know what NCT is. Let me enlighten you. It's basically a match-making service for middle-class, prospective parents.

It's also where you go to put your first nappy on a second-hand doll, discuss post-baby sex with near strangers, and find out the shocking secrets about labour. Like, you have to do ninety percent of it at home, no hospital, no doctors, nothing; or that there are three whole different stages including a giant placenta to birth (or was it just me that had no idea?)

My mum had carried on and on about what lifelong friends she'd made at NCT and how I'd struggle without them. But I resisted, for a while. I laughed with my non-parent mates when I was pregnant. Why do these silly women make new friends purely because they are becoming a mum? Ha!

Oh, poor stupid pre-baby me. Now I know you need new friends, because your old ones are going to disappear. Not forever, but for a while. And to be fair, who would want to spend every girlie meet up with a screaming baby tagging along? Other people's children are dreadful. And mid-morning on a Tuesday in some chain cafe, with your friend's boob out, isn't the ideal meet up if you have a job and enjoy a large glass of Pinot. Like I do. Like I *used* to. No, mum friends are a requirement those first few months.

So there we were, baby arrival minus four weeks, slightly panicked, very uncomfortable and heading into our first NCT class.

It was Fay I gravitated to first. She was one of those women with a slightly too loud, practical voice, like a primary school teacher trying to take command of a room. She was mid-thirties and it turned out, like me, she worked in marketing, but in a local firm.

I could feel my pulse quicken as she asked me about my view on hypnobirthing and the 'pain-diminishing power of pressure points'.

'We're quite relaxed about the birth, aren't we Dan? It's all natural really, isn't it?' I replied breezily, trying not to let on I had no idea what she was talking about. I'd done everything I could not to think about the birth at all.

'Well, if you're planning to go natural, you'll probably want to consider perineum massage, if you haven't already started of course,' she said, smiling. 'Tim's been doing mine morning and evening for the whole of the last trimester. It's really very easy, you just need some massage oil and about ten minutes of hand manipulation from the inside. It's great for limiting vaginal tearing. Let me take you over to him, and he can give you the details.' She took Dan by the hand and he looked back at me with desperate eyes as she led him across the room.

I took the opportunity to introduce myself to another mum in a smartly pressed shift dress over her neat baby bump, her hair smoothed back in a tight pony.

This was Priya. She arrived clutching a clear plastic wallet with all the NCT letters and information packed inside, along with check lists of questions and topics to tick off.

Unlike me, she had a large family with loads of nephews and nieces nearby. She picked up the dolls confidently for bathing, while wincing a little at the clang as mine flopped back at the neck, its head knocking hard on the edge of the baby bath. I could see even then she'd be the one to WhatsApp the group with developmental milestones, or to coordinate library rhyme-time outings.

The next mum was Nina. She was from Bulgaria originally and now lived the next stop along from St Anne's. Nina had that soft, comforting, motherly way about her already. All cashmere scarfs and flushed cheeks ready for kisses. When she spoke about her baby or stroked her belly, I could see tears of excitement rise in her eyes. She shared how she had been waiting for her baby for years after trying to get pregnant with her husband, Alek.

It made me feel a bit guilty. I'd become pregnant within hours of discussing babies with Dan. I mean, literally hours. Which at least proved that fretting about contraception and picking up the morning after pill in my twenties hadn't been a total waste of time.

The final group member was Shelley. She was a skinny little thing. At first glance her tightly pulled back hair and rough makeup distracted from her pretty features hiding underneath. And her great big eyes. She had clearly been forced on the course by her mother who came as her birthing partner. She was due first and just about ready to pop, with her bump high and perfectly round like a football tucked up her jumper.

Poor thing was twenty going on fourteen and behind those big eyes you could tell the depths of teenage angst were still bubbling away. She had a voice at once shy and surly and only spoke to give her name and due date in session one. Every word had the tone of an insult. But it was her mum, an angry sort of lady with a creased face, who took charge.

Around twenty minutes into the first session, as my competitive side came out with a pop quiz, I glanced up and saw a dark bob flash past, heading to the spare seats on the other side of the room. I didn't look any closer, instead putting my head down ready for the next question.

It had been sold as a 'fun ice breaker' but the quiz was already frightening the life out of me.

'Question three: what is the likelihood of defecating during labour?' asked Jen, who ran the class, with a big smile on her face.

I realised later that dark bob was Tabetha. She didn't try to speak to any of us. Instead she hung back, listening quietly, bolting as soon as it was over. I didn't think about her again.

It was the second session, about a week later, that I got a proper look. I'd managed to get an earlier train from work, so it was just me waiting in the community centre reception for Dan. She came in flicking through something on her phone and sat opposite me on one of the sick-coloured sofas. Like train seats, they had a pattern chosen to disguise spilt food and bodily fluid from the various AA meetings, baby groups and OAP coffee mornings passing through.

Even with her baby bump she looked like she was heading into a Shoreditch bar. I wondered if she may be having a 'surprise' baby. Maybe it was a total assumption, but she didn't give off the glow of someone who just couldn't wait for the baby to arrive. In fact she looked like she'd prefer to be anywhere else.

She was tall, a lot taller than me, with long, slender limbs, almost non-existent boobs and that dark-dyed bob I'd seen flash past the week before.

She was almost flapper-like in shape and her short, sharp haircut just accentuated that 1920's look. She'd pulled a man's shirt on over her bump, looking comfortable but still effortlessly trendy. I tried the same with one of Dan's right at the end of my pregnancy. I left the house feeling great but was appalled when I caught a glimpse of myself in a shop window; a six-foot shirt with greying armpits on my five-foot frame – gaping across my pregnancy double Fs. I looked less like I was heading to a Shoreditch bar and more like the local needle exchange down the clinic.

Tabetha was sort of androgynous, but the way she moved and the twinkle in her eye when she eventually looked up verged on flirting. We caught eyes, but she still didn't speak. Finally, she dropped her phone into a large neon yellow bag at her feet and sat back into the chair.

'Are you here for NCT?' I asked after the silence was too awkward to bear. She responded with an almost imperceptible roll of the eyes, quite the opposite to the joyous, bubbly 'hellos' from the mums the week before.

'I know, right?' I said, rolling my eyes in return. For some reason I felt like the cool kid at school had shown me some attention for the first time. I suppose I'm a sucker for the eccentric trendy.

'Sorry, I have to take this,' she spoke with a hushed, husky tone as she pulled her phone back out and up to her ear.

'Got it?' she asked into the handset, then nodded. 'Thought so. I'll be out of action for an hour or so now. No, just a... thing. But message if anything progresses.' Her voice was low and quiet.

'Work,' she said simply, putting the phone into her pocket.

'God, tell me about it,' I replied, even though I'd pretty much checked out at my work already.

Suddenly there was a bustle at the door and the other mums came in chatting and laughing, with partners dragging a little behind doing some awkward man-bonding.

'Come on in ladies and gents,' called Jen from the door to the room. As I entered, I could see knitted breasts laid out on every other seat, along with a range of ethnically diverse dolls.

'Dad's turn to have a go at breastfeeding today!' she smiled brightly as we walked in, which was when I realised Dan hadn't made it.

'Tabetha, Emily, you two pair up for now,' she

called, as we took our seats.

While some of the other pairs seriously got down to business, trying different holds and asking about how long to wait before burping, I worked on getting a grip on who Tabetha was. I tried to get her talking, or even to laugh, but she barely said a word. She followed Jen's instructions quickly and efficiently, then took any quiet moment to check her phone and fire off messages.

One bleep elicited a barely audible 'for fuck's sake' and she headed out of the room to make a call, while Jen came over to talk through how to manually hand pump milk in case the baby didn't latch straight away, helpfully adding another terrifying activity to my new-motherhood list.

Just before the end of the session Tabetha snuck back in as the local health visitor, a mousy woman called Tilly, talked us through some of the more scientific parts of birthing. I focused on trying to take in all the information, nodding seriously as Tilly talked through what would happen as the baby arrived.

She was a typical healthcare pro, talking comfortably about all things bodily that my instinct was to ignore and certainly not discuss in a big group. She pointed expertly at giant pictures of babies' heads coming out of a range of different women's lady parts. I'd never seen so many vaginas. Or any now I come to think of it. And these weren't drawings, they were actual photos.

I looked around the room, but it seemed to just be me who found it hard not to smirk at the words that I would have found hilarious in a real-world conversation – 'nipple', 'vagina', even 'cervix' made me wince.

As I looked away from Tilly again, hoping she hadn't spotted my reaction, I caught Tabetha already looking at me, and as if she'd been watching me for a while. That twinkle had returned in her eye and she gave me a brief half smile as Tilly said 'labia' proudly while happily describing the four types of tearing. Four types? At this point I decided to zone out.

As I grabbed my bag at the end of class I realised Dan had missed the entire thing, kept late at work yet again. Since I'd been pregnant and had been coming home earlier myself, I was much more aware of just how often I was sitting waiting for him. We'd been together nearly ten years. We'd always kept our own lives, alongside our time together, it worked for us that way. But I could feel something shifting.

I took a deep breath, turned to Tabetha, and asked if she wanted to stop at the pub on the way home, genuinely not sure what she'd say. She looked one more time at her phone and said, 'fuck 'em, go on then.'

I felt a bit nervous as she came back to the table from the bar with our sad little Diet Cokes. After a painfully long thirty seconds, where neither of us spoke, it was me who broke first. She was obviously better at coping with silence than I was.

I opted for the classic first date question, 'So, what is it you do?'

I'd already painted a picture of who she was. A senior designer, I'd thought, working at an agency in town, developing striking identities for music and arts brands. She came up with the big ideas, a creative maverick, quiet but innovative. Hence all the phone calls. They probably had a big pitch deadline today. Maybe she'd had a fling with the MD and this baby was the result. Not planned, but she'd make it work. She was just one of those women.

She looked at me and replied, very casually, 'I work in CID, I'm a homicide detective.'

I was shocked. Her cool factor had just risen again.

I loved anything with a mystery. Those gritty British crime dramas were my favourite, set in a London that never really existed or some crappy Yorkshire town which would never make the news in the real world. But I'd happily get stuck into a tacky true-crime special on some obscure digital channel too. It felt sick to admit it, but the weirder and gorier the better.

Dan was the only one who knew about my interest in murder. It was sort of at odds with the bubbly, positive work persona I'd carefully cultivated, and which had drifted into my home persona too. He thought I was a bit strange to get such a kick out of one person killing another one, but it was fascinating. Alien and familiar at once.

I couldn't wait to ask her all the gory details. But like a horse whisperer trying to build her trust, I decided to hold back so as not to freak her out just yet. 'That's an unusual job. How did you get into it?' I asked instead, as casually as possible.

She shrugged, 'I became a Police Officer, and worked my way up.' I was surprised it sounded that easy, but she was extremely matter-of-fact.

'Are there many female detectives then?' I asked.

'Not enough. I was mentored on this god-awful diversity scheme that was going to change the world of policing. But, apparently, I'm still the only female DI in the County. It's the same for everyone though. Getting ahead is down to bloody hard work really isn't it?' I nodded sagely.

Before I could dig any further, I spotted Shelley, the young girl from NCT, come bustling into the pub looking behind her. She looked like she'd been crying.

'Oh God,' I said, under my breath, disappointed we might be interrupted. Tabetha looked around to see what I'd spotted then back to me. 'An argument with that uptight mother of hers I guess?' I said. 'I should check she's okay.' I started to step up reluctantly.

'No, it'll be the boyfriend. Just leave her,' said Tabetha turning back and taking a sip of her drink. I didn't feel like I should just ignore the poor girl, and was deciding what to do when sure enough a young bloke, the hood of his dark jacket pulled up so I could barely see his face, followed her in.

He grabbed her arm and leant close to her face to say something I couldn't hear over the noise of the bar, but I could see his tight eyes as he spat the words in her face. They spoke back and forth briefly, faces close and words hard. Then suddenly she softened just a little, put a hand up to his cheek and kissed him lightly on the lips. He shook his head and looked away but the urgency had left him now. Almost as soon as it had begun, the argument was over, and she followed him back out.

'Yep, you're right, they've just gone.' I sat back down. 'And that's why you are the detective!' I said with a laugh.

'It's just about watching people, that's all. There's no trick to it.' She took another sip of her drink.

'I've always liked the idea of being a detective,' I said truthfully. 'It must be fascinating getting into the minds of people who have the guts to see through some dreadful crime. I can't imagine the people you must meet, the secrets you uncover.'

'Very few people surprise me actually. Most are the same underneath. You recognise the different types quickly after a while. It's like picking out a card from a pack. There are different hands, but the characters tend to be the same. Soon you get pretty good at the game.' I don't think she intended to, but this felt close to a boast and I couldn't help but push her a little.

'What about me then?' I asked. 'What card am I?'

'Well you're an eight of hearts aren't you,' she said without missing a beat, 'not quite royal, but somewhere towards the top.' I wasn't sure whether to feel offended or pleased.

'You're obviously intelligent, fairly creative. You've probably chosen to work where understanding and getting on with people is important. Communications, marketing, publishing? Something with clients you need to keep on side.' She looked at me and I realised I was sitting open mouthed.

I closed my mouth as she continued: 'And you're obviously a people watcher too. It probably helps you change your behaviour depending on who you're with, which keeps those around you happy. Although sometimes people aren't as good back to you as you are to them. Not hard to pick that up after your partner didn't arrive today.'

'Oh, he was just kept late at work,' I said, suddenly feeling a bit defensive on Dan's behalf. She nodded as she took another drink then sat in silence again.

I couldn't argue that she had me pretty much spot on. I felt a bit cross that I was so transparent. But it wasn't her fault, I'd asked her the question after all. I shook myself out of it and broke the silence.

'Okay, you got me, I work in marketing, I love watching people and I do try to keep everyone happy!' I laughed a little. 'I'd always thought I would make a pretty good detective though. Police dramas, detective novels, true crime, all of that, it's a bit of an interest of mine.' She still sat quietly, so I continued.

'I mean, the idea that someone who is in other ways just like me might turn around after breakfast and stab her mother in the neck, or hold her lover under water in the bath until they turn blue, or snip the cords on her partner's parachute; who wouldn't be fascinated by that?' I asked.

'The thought that your next-door neighbour, your best friend, the guy at the desk next to you, someone you'd trust with anything, might be a closet sociopath, you know? No empathy, no guilt, ready to manipulate anyone. Ready to kill someone that gets in their way. And they exist, right? We know that. Hidden in plain sight.' I looked up and Tabetha was still watching me intently.

'Maybe it's because I can kind of understand

it, you know? On a darker day. Like, maybe you can't bear to look at the face of your bully of a husband one more time. Or, maybe the thought of being poor another day is more painful than knocking off your parents for the cash. Or, maybe your silly girlfriend has gotten pregnant and you realise you are never going to be able to leave her now,' I waved my arm in the direction Shelley had headed and laughed. 'I'm kidding of course,' I said quickly.

'But everyone has a last straw, right? I suppose what you see is the result of that. Then you need to work out what that last straw is each time. And trace it back to the killer.'

I could see Tabetha's face had changed a bit now. Her head was leaning to one side, owl-like, and her eyes were tightly focused on me.

'What is it?' I asked, feeling self-conscious, like I might have a bit of wasabi pea stuck in my teeth.

'You're interesting, aren't you? Maybe a spade, not a heart,' she said.

I laughed awkwardly.

'You probably would make a good detective.' She broke into a half smile; finally a peek behind the mask.

We stayed in the pub for two more drinks and carried on chatting. Well, mostly me chatting, she wasn't overly talkative. But when she did speak, she was direct and no-nonsense. I liked that.

From that point on we'd catch each other before class, after class and on the odd occasion in that same pub on the way home.

Dan was relieved I'd made a mum-friend already, so was quite happy to head off home for some 'he time', whatever that meant.

I expect he thought we were talking about babies, but for some reason that barely cropped up. Instead we talked a lot about her work, a bit about mine, and generally discussed the murky underworld of murderers, crime lords and serial killers. Heaven.

It was a final pre-baby hurrah, although I hadn't realised it at the time.

CHAPTER TWO

Everything changed on the nineteenth of July when baby Nellie arrived, just a day after I'd finished work. I should have been relieved, but I'd had some personal admin planned for those missing two weeks. The wrapper was barely off the box set and she arrived.

It was a hot, hot day when she decided to make an appearance. The sun was bright, and the air felt close. It was a day to be in the garden, laid out on a towel with a book and a cold G&T. Ideal for a twelve-hour labour.

It really was an awful, terrifying, painful mess. Nothing like how I'd imagined. Even those NCT pictures of vaginas with heads poking out couldn't prepare me for how animalistic and raw the whole thing was.

'You said in your birth plan you wanted to stay mobile Emily,' said one brave midwife about four hours in when they'd finally checked my paperwork. 'Do you want to move around now?' she asked.

I took a break from the gas and air just long enough to scream 'bugger off!' in her general direction, then settled back down with my eyes closed praying it would all be over soon.

Poor Dan recited our hypnobirthing mantras from the book Fay had lent us, using the soothing voice he'd practised at home; 'I am present, I am doing this, *we* are doing this', 'my body is opening and ready to birth my baby'. I tried to pretend he wasn't there.

Then, when I was starting to feel desperate, it all happened, moving within five minutes from, 'don't push yet' to, 'oh, there's the head, get pushing!'.

I listened to the gentle trickle of the taps filling up my longed-for birthing pool, while I pushed out the baby on some towels in the corner like a dog on a pile of old newspapers. One leg up on the midwife's shoulder; hand gripping tightly to the gas and air. This was not how I'd planned it. Maybe I should have realised that would be a common theme from now on.

Anyway, Nellie was out. I breathed a big sigh of relief as I heard her first scream. It was relief that she was here safe of course, but mainly that labour was finally over.

I pulled Dan towards me as the nurse took her for a quick check-up and with my nose almost touching his, spoke as clearly and directly as I could: 'I am never doing that again.'

One thing I did learn from NCT was just how important skin-to-skin was, and when I held that tiny body next to mine it was amazing and terrifying. I looked down to see the bright pink little person, covered in soft downy hair. I'd been waiting nine months to meet her but was surprised to find I didn't recognise her at all.

And when Dan took her for his own skin-to-skin time it was amazing and strange to see him transformed into a dad in seconds. He had that soft-focus look of love in his blue eyes as he kissed her soft head.

Just 24 hours later we were sent home to start our new family life and it felt surreal.

I thought that I couldn't wait to get out of the hospital, with that awful nauseating smell, something like when a guest sprays air freshener after using the downstairs loo, creating that dreadful mix of sewage and Ocean Breeze. But it was when I got home, and it was just up to me and Dan to keep Nellie alive, that the fear really set in.

The first six weeks was a dark, bloody, murky blur of cracked nipples, sleepless nights and overwhelming fear. It is insane that people are allowed to take babies home with no experience whatsoever, purely because said babies came out of their vaginas.

I look back now on those first few weeks and think about how naive I'd been BC (Before Children). Even with my NCT warnings. I had imagined I'd adapt straight away when the baby arrived, that instinct would take over, that somehow a new me would emerge. Maybe that's the reality for some first-time mums, and that's great for them (I don't mean that, I hate those mums), but it wasn't for me.

I was still the old me, and the old me was beginning to feel very frustrated. I'm a people-pleaser I suppose, and my baby couldn't even smile, let alone complete a positive appraisal. Without regular affirmation of my success, for the first time in my life I began to feel that I was a failure.

In my day job my over thinking, my obsessive attention to detail, my compulsion to deliver at all costs were my greatest strengths and could be indulged hourly. There was no denying my Myers Briggs results when to my horror my comparison 'celebrity' was Margaret Thatcher. I liked to be in control, and in the office that was ideal. As a mum it made daily life almost unbearable. A baby could not be controlled.

It must be different for everyone, but for me it felt like all the parts of my life that'd I'd carefully chosen and had built around me to fit my own ideal way of living had been taken away.

Now my daily life was basically a 24/7 baby shift. The same repetitive tasks over and over and over again, with little interaction with others and absolutely no thanks. This was combined with the fear that if I did any one of those little tasks incorrectly, the person I now loved most in the world may die. And it would be all my fault. Although Dan was doing his bit, for some reason I felt the responsibility heavily on my own shoulders. Or placed it there perhaps.

What scared me the most was that looking at every other parent around me, I seemed to be the only one who felt that way.

I mean, I knew people found it hard. But no one else seemed to be feeling the sort of general, life altering panic at what they'd taken on, or missing what they'd lost.

The whole gang from work came around in week one in little groups, carrying bags of muffins, bath bombs and baby clothes. They held the baby, breathed in her soft hair, marvelled at the new little life I'd made, then skipped off home or to the pub without me. It didn't feel fair to Nellie, or our guests, to use that time to talk about me and how I was coping. Or not coping. So, I didn't.

I hadn't heard much from any of my mates since. Part of me was relieved. I wondered if hearing about their world, my old world, would just cement what was in the back of my mind. That maybe having a baby hadn't been such a good idea.

That was me after the birth. After the BC years.

Then, following a six-week motherhood baptism of fire, and when I'd started to think that I'd begun something of a life sentence, a message came from Fay at NCT. She was inviting us to hers to 'share our experiences and support one another' (loosely translated as baby-comparison session number one).

Immediately I thought of Tabetha. She didn't respond on the invite, but I hoped she would be there.

When the day arrived, I'd been holed up in the house for almost a week. That morning as our new 5am alarm call sounded – Nellie squeaking with more and more urgency – Dan turned over.

'Do we have to go today?' he asked with a whine, his eyes still closed. 'I've hardly seen Nellie all week, can't we just have a lazy day at home, and all snuggle up together?' he said, nuzzling my neck.

I took a breath so as not to snap back immediately, but he interpreted my silence as considering the option. 'Coffee, TV, baby, you and me?' he spoke using his most persuasive voice, sitting up and running a hand through his dark bed head.

As I got up to get Nellie from her basket, he tried to catch me for a kiss but missed and caught me with a stubbled cheek instead. I walked straight out of the bedroom door to start the first feed of the day, calling back, 'You're not getting out of this one I'm afraid. I need to get out and you are going to dad-bond, whether you like it or not'.

Fay's house was a 1950's bungalow, decked out in Ikea furniture punctuated with pastel baby paraphernalia, as all our houses probably were now. A pile of muslins here, a bouncer there, a changing mat tucked behind the shelves which housed all the books you'll never have time to read again. The house was immaculate, and the scent of Jo Malone candles filled the air. You'd be lucky if I even got the Febreze out of the cupboard at mine right now.

Tim helped us in with the buggy. He looked just a little greyer than he had at NCT. In fact all the dad's did. It might have been the lack of sleep, but more likely the lack of sex, or perhaps simply the shock of realising just how much their partner did for them before a baby took precedence.

Priya and her husband Anil arrived soon after us. Their little boy, Shay, was quiet and content over Anil's shoulder while Priya circled the room gathering advice and handing out little thoughtful gifts of inscribed egg cups for each baby. I'd only just remembered to grab an old packet of Bourbon biscuits before coming along.

Nina had been so excited throughout the whole course, but now looked run ragged as she arrived late with a bit of baby sick on one shoulder of her inside-out cardigan. It turned out Alek was off on a business trip and she'd been parenting alone for the past week. She was holding her baby, Leah, tight. Endlessly leaning her little head back to put her cheek next to her tiny mouth, possibly to check she was still breathing, then showering her with soft butterfly kisses on her forehead.

Shelley had been dragged along again; but was trying to disappear by tucking herself into a corner, mostly staring at her phone playing Candy Crush while absentmindedly rocking her large baby in one arm. Being the first to give birth, her little one looked like a monster compared to Nellie. Every now and then her mum tried to persuade her to talk to the other parents but with no luck. The old me would have felt like I should go and speak to her and draw her into the group, but I just couldn't find the enthusiasm, and I didn't want to miss Tabetha if she arrived.

I parked up Nellie in the corner and decided to risk a drink as I'd just finished a feed. My heart rose at the familiar glug as I poured a small(ish) glass from the bottle on the kitchen side, then headed into the living room.

A lot of people had said to me since giving birth, 'I bet you can't remember what you used to do with your time?' But I can, I really can. Wine, telly, chatting, laughing.

I was relieved when I heard the doorbell go a final time and Tabetha's low voice drifting through from the hallway. As I saw her glance into the room, straight away I could see that in comparison to the rest of us she looked glowing, invigorated even.

I couldn't imagine how she was doing it solo. The idea of waking up every day and knowing that you and you alone were responsible for another life frightened me. Not to mention getting up in the night with no one beside you.

Having said that, maybe that is better in some ways than listening to a snoring husband while you breastfeed for the third, fourth, fifth time that night. But having anyone there was surely better than no one.

She didn't seem to have changed at all post-baby. Even from afar she had that still, confident air about her that I had become used to. It could probably come across as aloof, and maybe that was why the other mums seemed to avoid her a bit. But it didn't bother me.

My only real concern then was whether she was as interested in catching up with me as I was with her.

I needn't have worried. Tabetha parked up a sleeping Luca and made her way quickly towards me to sit on the arm of my chair.

As she sat, we could hear Nina dissolving into tears, and I could just make out the words 'cracked to buggery' between sobs as the other ladies hugged her while the men moved towards the other end of the room, quietly dissolving into the wallpaper.

'You made it to the other side then?' asked Tabetha deadpan, and I nodded while I took a large gulp of slightly too sweet Zinfandel.

'Only just,' I said, with raised eyebrows.

I could feel that lovely warming sensation of a large gulp of wine sliding down my throat. I was feeling closer to my old self already.

Tabetha reached into her large handbag at her feet and pulled out a new bottle, twisted the lid and offered it in my direction.

'One more won't hurt,' she whispered.

I glugged down the rest of my glass. It had been a while and I felt like I deserved it. She topped me up and filled an empty one from the side table, before clinking glasses with me and taking a deep mouthful.

'I've got a new recommendation for you,' I said, ready to get back to our old chats. 'The whole premise is the wife is found dead at the bottom of the stairs, but...' I paused for dramatic effect, 'did she fall, was she pushed or was the whole thing a big set up?'

'Sounds pretty simple, I'm guessing there's more to it?' said Tabetha taking another large mouthful of wine.

'Oh yes, bloody hell this family are weird. The evidence that turns up you just wouldn't believe. I'd love to know what you think.' I set the challenge, and was already looking forward to hearing her views when we next met.

That had been the best part about our meet ups, hearing Tabetha's take on a show I'd been watching, or a case in the news.

Tabetha nodded but then went quiet and her smile slipped. It looked like she was considering something. I'd learnt to give her a second of silence before jumping in.

Finally, with a nod, she put her glass back

down and leant again into her bag. 'While I've got you to myself, there's something I think you might be interested in,' she explained, as she started to pull out a bundle of papers and a notebook.

'Hang on, are those work papers I see? Remember what Tilly said about taking a proper break...' I rolled my eyes with a tut as I reached out to take a single sheet of A4 paper she was passing in my direction.

She smiled that twinkly smile again, reserved for special occasions, and replied, 'Well, you decide to take your first break from work in fourteen years and immediately a tasty murder falls into your lap.'

I genuinely felt a shiver down my spine as she said 'murder' in such a casual way.

But before I could respond, a scream cut through the music and I was brought back into the room in an instant.

CHAPTER THREE

Heads turned instinctively towards the high-pitched note shooting through the air.

'Emily!' someone called out with urgency. I put down my glass as I jumped up to run into the dining room and peered into my Bugaboo. Nellie's face was scrunched up like an overripe tomato as that all too familiar scream sounded out.

I picked her up and awkwardly tipped her over my shoulder, stepping back with a sigh to look through into the living room longingly. Tabetha was sipping her wine as she started to put the papers back into her bag, while Fay came to take my place in my still warm chair.

I patted Nellie's tiny back in time to *The Wheels on the Bus* which was blaring out of the speakers. As she wailed into my ear, I could feel an almighty fart in my cupped hand, and the scream dropped an octave.

It seemed like an age as I rocked Nellie back and forth to at least stem the screaming before heading back into the crowded living room which now looked like a youth club disco;

boys on one side, girls on the other. Dan hadn't wanted to come, but I could see him now talking closely with Priya's husband and drinking a bottle of beer enthusiastically. It was probably healthy for all of us to get out.

As Nellie quietened to a soft sob crossed with hiccups, I went back to where I'd been sitting. Fay was chatting with Tabetha, who was looking down at her glass of wine.

'I was just asking Tabetha about constipation. Have you had any problems with your bowel movements?' asked Fay before taking a sip of her drink.

'Um, I... well I did have a bit of trouble, but I'm okay now,' I blustered.

'Lucky you! God, I spent hours on the loo weeks one to four. Some of my stitches actually burst!' she said with a laugh, although I couldn't think of anything less funny.

'Oh wow,' I responded quietly, not sure what to say.

'Then they gave me these really strong laxatives, and that did the trick. They were very convenient actually, now I know exactly when I'll need to go, first thing in the morning.'

'That's great,' I murmured, unsure what the appropriate response should be.

'Of course, it's gone straight through me and into poor Jack. He's still doing these explosive poos, and the smell is awful, you just can't get rid of it!' she continued, as Tabetha stood in silence.

'In fact, have you met him yet? Let me grab him from Tim.'

As she moved off to find her baby, I looked at Tabetha who blinked hard.

'Let's pretend that never happened,' I said as I settled back into the chair to rock Nellie off to sleep.

'Right, back to it – did you really say murder?' I asked.

She nodded in silence, smoothing her hair from her face and glancing around the room. I'd never seen her so animated. Something had really gotten her excited.

'Work have told me to stay out of it as much as possible. I'm off on maternity, blah blah blah, but it's impossible.' She looked like she was asking for my permission to continue.

'Well, what happened?' I asked, raising my eyebrows. I had to stop myself from looking behind me. Suddenly I felt like we might be being watched. I wondered for a split second whether MI5 could listen in to a baby monitor.

After a brief pause, she held out the paper again. 'You tell me.'

It looked innocent enough. Before I read the words that is.

And there it was, that first letter from a killer.

I read it several times over.

Greetings Ms Tate,

Everything's on the up for you, right? Wrong.

Time to find out how it feels when you aren't number one.

How does a little murder sound?

Keep an eye on Newton Hill on the 4th of this month.

Have fun!

Your friend,
Mr Naughty

The writing was large and round, it looked almost cheerful. The lined paper could have been ripped from any old notebook you find in WHSmith's. A note tossed on the side to let your partner know you've headed out to the shops and would they put the pizza in the oven.

I turned the photocopy over and found that on the reverse someone had made a copy of the envelope it had arrived in too. I could see what must have been Tabetha's address in that same round writing with a first-class stamp and blurry postmark with yesterday's date. It looked completely normal, with nothing to suggest anything sinister was inside.

'Interesting, right?' I could hear Tabetha was smiling as she spoke. I turned it back over slowly and read the note again before responding.

'Newton Hill, that's where the community centre is, isn't it? At the end of St Anne's if you follow the road that runs along by the river,' I said.

'That's the one. It's just where the high-rises start as you head into town.' She nodded.

I sat in silence, trying to think of something clever to say, until eventually Tabetha asked, 'Well, first impressions?'

'Ummm,' I bought myself a few seconds more. 'I mean it can't be about a real murder, can it? Is it a fantasist or something?' I asked. 'Like with Jack the Ripper, well the letters they thought were from him anyway,' I tried to explain my thinking. 'Turned out they were just some lonely recluse enjoying the police attention.'

Tabetha gave me a look and I shut up as I spotted Anil heading over, he was wearing what looked like his party shirt, a chintzy proud new-dad look. He offered around a tub full of decorated cupcakes that could only have been made by Priya; each one with a tiny baby animal balanced precariously on top of a mountain of pink or blue icing. Tabetha took one for each of us as I smiled and said, 'Ah, how cute.'

He looked like he was anticipating a conversation, which was fair, considering this was a reunion. But I was impatient to continue my discussion with Tabetha. I gave her trick of just standing in silence a go. Eventually he gave up, saying, 'Well, great to see you ladies,' in a very polite British way as he went.

'Mmm, a fantasist, could be...' Tabetha said

once he was far enough away, absent-mindedly putting the cakes on the side.

'I mean – you've always said this kind of thing just doesn't happen in real life,' I said. She made another little noise but didn't speak. I tried again. 'But it's written specifically to you. Someone trying to scare you, someone with a grudge?' I asked.

'Maybe, maybe,' said Tabetha reaching to take back the letter. I wasn't giving the reaction she'd hoped for.

'You don't think so though?' I asked. She didn't respond as she picked up the cupcake and took a bite with a grimace.

'What did your work say?' I asked, half thinking she might not have shared it with them.

'I showed it to our Chief Superintendent. He thinks the same as you, someone looking for attention. It's quite common to have weird letters sent into the office, they don't usually make it up to the DIs. Like you say, it's the fact it came to me directly that seems weird. He reckons maybe someone saw my name in the paper after the promotion. It's pretty rare to get the role this young and being a woman too of course. Shocking,' she smirked.

'They probably didn't know I'm on leave.' As she said the word 'leave' she made that little bleurgh face of hers again.

'I've passed it onto my maternity cover. He's going to keep an eye on the location. But, you're right, it's probably nothing.' That could have been the end of it, but I could feel she wasn't happy with the conclusion.

'You think there's something more to it?' I asked, a little bubble of excitement rising up.

'I don't know. There's something about it that's got to me. The tone, or the timing, or... Maybe it's just being off work, being a bit bored, making it seem more interesting than it is.' It was the first time I'd heard someone call motherhood boring. But it struck a chord.

She took the letter off me and tucked it back into her bag with the other papers.

'Is there anything more you can do?' I asked.

'I've already pulled some strings at work. They found nothing unusual about the paper, nothing to take from the post mark, except it was probably sent locally, which doesn't give us much. I've been asked to forget the whole thing for now.' But I could see from her face that that was not going to happen.

'Well,' I said, picking up Nellie from my lap where she'd started to squirm again and popping her back into her favourite position over my shoulder, 'Monday is the 4th, so you don't have long to wait.'

Just then Fay came back over with Jack. 'Right, here's the little stinker, hand your one over, we can do swapsies!' she said to me.

I stood up to swap babies, feeling some relief that even from here I could see Jack had also lost the top of his hair, giving him the appearance of a shrunken monk.

'She's adorable Emily, and she smells delicious, lucky you!' said Fay. And with that, the conversation turned to breastfeeding, naps and bedtime routines.

My conversation with Tabetha was closed, but my mind ran with the possibilities of a murder and what Monday might bring.

CHAPTER FOUR

Miss Tovey flicked off the telly. She wasn't even sure what was on, she hadn't been watching. Her mind had been other places as usual.

She pushed her glasses back up her nose, picked up her phone and flicked open the notes to a list of names and addresses.

Clicking on one, she looked at the map as it popped up on the screen.

The address icon blinking, she clicked: 'Get Route'.

She looked quickly, then turned her attention to a pile of papers on the side. She flicked through until she got to the right one. She wanted to be fully prepared for tomorrow. She didn't like surprises.

It was Sunday the 3rd.

CHAPTER FIVE

I didn't have to wait long to catch up with Tabetha again. We'd all agreed to meet up every Wednesday at the Costa in town for a debrief about the previous week.

I'd been climbing the walls since Dan had left for work and was ready and waiting with my Americano ten minutes early. I'd given up on decaf as soon as I'd realised that sleeping was out of the question now.

I checked my watch, a little surprised I was the first there. I was soon to find out I'd been lucky so far. Leaving the house with a baby could often take three or four times longer than planned. A last-minute exploding nappy here, magically appearing sick all down your just washed top there; or missing wipes and hidden muslins.

Usually one mum doesn't make it at all, cancelling with a distracted message to say it's just been impossible to make it out the house. As if it's some sort of Crystal Maze challenge, and once the timer goes, you're locked in.

As noon ticked over, and I tried to slow

down drinking my coffee, I was pleased to see it was Tabetha and Luca arriving first to join me. She propped her sunglasses onto her head and smiled hello. She was wearing a dark denim playsuit over a plain black T-shirt covered with bright green crocodiles, looking more relaxed than I'd ever seen her. I adjusted my own Mothercare breastfeeding top, wishing I'd thought a bit harder about what I'd put on that morning, and set down my coffee.

Before she reached us, I glanced into the buggy to check Nellie was still asleep, hoping there'd be time for a bit of a real-life chat first.

Tabetha dropped into the seat opposite and parked up a sleeping Luca.

'So, the 4th came and went?' I said with a bit of a smile before she could even say hello. I couldn't wait to get into it. She nodded with a brief smile.

'Okay, I may have got a bit over excited,' she said, 'I really felt like there might have been something to it, but it does seem like a hoax after all.'

'I guess even you can't always be right,' I said. She gave a nod that was intended to show relief, but something in her dark eyes said disappointed instead.

'And there was me thinking I could be the Hastings to your Poirot!' I smiled.

She nodded again. 'It would have been fun, wouldn't it? And something to keep my brain

ticking over too. Luca just eats, sleeps and craps.'
I laughed in recognition.

'Probably for the best,' I said. 'Anyway, ideally for my first big case I'd be hoping for something a bit more *The Bridge* and a little less Agatha Christie. You know, dead body weighed down with bricks washed up by the river, or a corpse discovered by kids tied up in the basement of a disused warehouse. Something a bit gritty.'

'There are lots of ways to describe St Anne's. But "gritty", I think we can agree, it is not,' Tabetha replied.

I always described St Anne's as 'Outer-London' to my friends who were still trying to make it work financially in town. But it was full on suburbia really. In fact, we'd recently been upgraded to Surrey by an ambitious council. It's a market town, not fashionable, but affordable. And with the Thames running through and a forty-minute train ride into Central London, you could still just about kid yourself you hadn't really made that move out.

'We're maybe a bit more *Midsomer Murders*? Or perhaps *Morse* at a push?' I agreed.

'God, I hate those shows. Bodies dropping like flies. People killed by out-of-control lawnmowers, or scythe-wielding milkmen on summer solstice.' Tabetha rolled her eyes.

'My ideal crime would be something small. Quiet. Something people might miss if they didn't pay attention. An old man found in his chair looking out on the communal gardens at a care home. Dead within the hour with three old boys and the nurse all watching *This Morning* nearby. All swear they didn't move.' She took a gulp of coffee.

'I'd happily make do with a bit of *Midsomer* around here,' I replied, 'anything to liven things up. What about a home-made poisoned dart shot through the window of a stately home killing Lady Fitzwilliam as she writes her new will?' I considered the formula for a second.

'Then there's the second murder, and the third. You can't beat a good steady body count – preferably at least one between each ad break.'

Tabetha was about to respond when her phone went.

'Sorry, I better get this, it's work.' She picked up the call.

I tried to busy myself with checking on Nellie, but I couldn't help listening in. A real detective was on the other end of the phone for God's sake.

'Hi Guv, don't you know I'm on leave?' Tabetha answered with a smile. But quickly her face changed. I tried to work out what the phone call was about just from her side of the conversation.

'Wow. I can't quite believe it...

Is everyone in agreement...?

Sure, yes I'll stop by. Look, I really am happy to help in any way I can...

No, I know. I'm not saying I'll work on it myself. I just mean I'm happy to give an opinion, or...

Yes. I understand totally. We can discuss the letter, and then I'll keep out of it.'

She put the phone down.

'I'm going to have to take a rain check on that coffee. They found a body in Newton Hill yesterday.'

'A body?' was that shock or excitement I could feel in the pit of my stomach?

'Yeah, and it's at the community centre. Like you said, it's just where St Anne's and Newton Hill cross.' She shook her head in disbelief. 'A woman in her sixties, Cheryl Nolan. Found yesterday, the 5th, but they've now placed time of death the previous evening, so my cover has flagged up the connection to my letter. The victim worked on the reception.'

'So we might have met her?' I asked, shaking my head. No poison dart or Lady Fitzwilliam. Just some old lady in the community centre.

'They've got someone they want for it. Sounds like her husband is the local drunk and people have heard him threaten her before. But because of the letter, they want me to stop by, obviously. And now we know it's at the community centre, that just seems too strange a coincidence.' She shook her head again.

'Oh my god. I can't believe it,' I replied.

'I'm going to head there straight away. I can walk from here.' She started to get up and grab her bag, then looked to the buggy as if she'd forgotten she even had it with her. She turned back to me. 'Could you come along to keep an eye on Luca while I pop in? He should still sleep for a while.'

'Of course, anything I can do to help,' I answered, trying to sound casual. I felt a fizzing starting at my head and running around my body at the idea of heading to a police station. The adrenaline was kicking in and I hadn't felt that for a while. 'We can text the girls on the way,' I said, getting up – perhaps a bit too eagerly – to leave.

'At least it sounds like just a domestic though,' I said, trying to sound like a real detective sidekick, as we started out of the coffee shop.

'Yeah,' she murmured, without conviction, as we left.

We power walked to the police station in about twenty minutes and both babies were still sleeping, the rocking of the buggy always seemed to help. It was exciting walking straight through and up to the offices. Like heading backstage after a gig to see the band. A few people smiled and waved at Tabetha as she walked through.

A fuzzy looking middle-aged lady with glasses propped on her head came running over to peer in at the babies. Tabetha made a 'shhh' sign with her finger to her lips and the woman mouthed 'sorry' as she pantomime-crept up the last few steps.

'Oh, gorgeous,' she whispered, 'I wondered when you'd come by to show the baba off.' She looked up at me with a big smile on her face to introduce herself. 'I'm Kim, I work here with Tabetha, are you...?'

But before she could finish, Tabetha stepped forward and pulled her buggy further into view. Pointing in at Luca, she said, 'This one's mine, Kim.' Then indicated back at me, 'This is Emily, a friend of mine from... baby stuff. Are the guys waiting for me?'

Tabetha obviously wasn't in the mood to kick off some big baby chat. Although to be fair, I couldn't really imagine a time she would be, particularly at work. That was one of the reasons I hadn't taken Nellie in yet. Mixing those two worlds just seemed impossible.

'They're just finishing off back there I think.' She took the message and smiled in at the babies again before starting to back away. 'Nice to see you both, and these two cuties.'

As we moved forward again a broad, tall man with a well-groomed goatee headed towards us shaking his head.

'How did you orchestrate this, Tate? Just couldn't keep away, could you?' He had one of those deep and creamy voices that demands you listen. It would absolutely be Morgan Freeman playing him in the movie. He gave Tabetha a warm but practical half hug and I could see her wince a little. She wasn't a hugger. Then he quickly led her into a smaller room towards the back of the office, glancing at me with a brief smile.

I wasn't given any instructions, so followed them in, where a younger man was sitting at a table looking at an iPad. I parked up the buggy in the corner and checked in on Nellie still asleep as I sat down quietly on a spare chair. Tabetha casually pushed Luca up alongside me without a look back, as if she was leaving her bike propped up outside a shop. She was in work mode now.

'You remember Toby? Of course you do, you met during the handover,' said the Chief Superintendent. The younger man stood up. As he did, I could see he must have been six foot at least and looked like he kept himself fit. Brooding evenings at the gym or running in the rain after a hard day catching criminals I imagined. But even he seemed small compared to the presence of his boss beside him. He leant over to reach his hand out towards Tabetha.

'Yep, hi,' said Tabetha curtly, shaking Toby's hand. I thought I spotted a slight nervousness behind his charcoal grey eyes as he greeted her. She was a tough act to follow. He gave a brief wave in my direction before taking his seat.

'We just wanted to keep you in the loop in case there's a link to that letter of yours,' said the Chief Superintendent.

'Thanks, I appreciate it. So, what happened – lady in her sixties you said?' asked Tabetha. Seeing her at work she seemed even more calm and in control than outside.

'That's it, a Mrs Nolan. She was a receptionist at the community centre,' said Toby referring to the iPad. 'She was a bit of a local champion for the neighbourhood, it sounds like. She did all sorts, you know, meet and greet people coming and going for classes, topped up the kitchen, that sort of thing. Her nickname was 'Mama' in the centre, apparently. The really caring type,' he shook his head just a little.

'She was found the morning of the 5th when the next person on shift went to open up at 7am and found it already unlocked. Or rather it hadn't been locked the night before. She was on the floor behind the reception desk in a little tea and coffee area. It looked like she'd been bending down to put something in the cupboard and was struck on the head from behind.' He slid a photo over to Tabetha.

'We think the murder must have taken place around twelve hours before she was found. The last class, some baby yoga thing,' he said with a slight eye roll then looked awkwardly in the direction of the buggies and carried on, 'well, it finished at 5.30pm. Then a Mr Norman Brown passed through around fifteen minutes later,' he consulted his iPad again, 'and spoke with her briefly. She should have locked up by 6pm, but we have another witness who passed through at a little after, when he spotted the light was still on. Some people use it as a cut-through to get to the estate at the back. He didn't look behind the counter and assumed the place was empty so not much there. But at least it helps with time of death.'

'Anything taken?' asked Tabetha.

'Nope, nothing obvious anyway. Her bag was still behind the desk, tenner or so in it, a couple of rings on her fingers. Although they wouldn't have been worth much,' Toby replied.

'And the clear front runner at this point is the husband, right?' asked Tabetha pushing the photo back over to Toby.

'Yes, we've already brought him in. He's not said much yet, but he will,' said the Chief Superintendent stepping in. 'It seems he was a bit of a bastard to put it mildly,' he continued. 'They separated about five years ago, but he's still hanging around and stays at the house on and off. People say once or twice he's even been in the centre boozed up and ranting at her. More in work than out of it, but not really settled, if you know what I mean.'

'Any kids?' asked Tabetha.

'No, although she was a bit of a mum to everyone, that's why 'Mama Nolan' I guess. She has a nephew nearby who checks in on her at her flat every now and then.'

'So how does the letter fit in do you think?' said Tabetha looking between the two men.

'I don't know,' said Toby. 'It might not be

linked at all, but it does seem like a strange coincidence. You sure you don't have a connection to Mrs Nolan?'

'I might have seen her once or twice in the centre. I went there for a baby course not long ago. But I don't recognise her from the photo,' she explained.

He took out a copy of the letter from his own pile of papers. It was the same as the one that I'd seen. He put it out in front of Tabetha and his boss.

'*Mr Naughty*. Mean anything to you?'

She shook her head.

'I just can't see some sixty-year-old drunk signing off like that,' said Toby.

The Chief Superintendent nodded. 'My best guess is the two aren't connected at all. In fact, I'm hoping for your sake, Tabetha, that they aren't. The last thing you need right now is to be caught up in something like this. I think it'll be open/close – a good old angry-husband-kills-poor-innocent-wife murder.' He laughed a little, but I had a feeling Tabetha wouldn't agree.

'And there was nothing else strange about it at all? Nothing unusual at the scene?' she asked.

Her boss shook his head. 'Nothing. No poison-pen note to you with a cryptic clue that I'm squirrelling away. There were only three items on the side. A cold cup of tea, a baby guide, looked like it'd been left by someone from the baby karate or whatever it was, and...,' he looked into the air to remember.

'Her packet of fags wasn't it?' asked Toby.

'That's right, ten Benson Lights. And that was it.'

They stood in silence for a minute while Tabetha looked back at the crime scene photo, her eyes searching for something to stand out.

'Right. Well, if it's not sparking any links for you, I guess the party's over I'm afraid. I'll walk you back out,' said the Chief Superintendent. They looked over to me in the corner as if I'd just reappeared and I stood up starting to jostle the two buggies towards the door, one with each hand.

The others walked ahead, beginning to talk about other things. As I passed the table I looked down and couldn't help but look at the crime scene photo.

The poor woman was lying awkwardly on her front, body twisted, and one arm outstretched. Her face was to the side and her eyes open. I leant in closer. She had very fine grey hair and wrinkles lining her eyes and around her mouth. It's funny how you arrive into the world wrinkled and go out the same way. When Nellie popped out, she looked like a little old man curled over in his chair, dementia muddling his mind. Eyes wise and vacant at the same time.

I tried to work out what the old lady's personality was from the photo. But her eyes were blank. It was the first time I'd seen death, but it was clear in an instant that nothing is left behind. It was just a body. An empty shell.

Had she ever been beautiful? It was hard to tell. Why is it men often become distinguished with age, while women appear to melt away? In fact, that's not totally true when you think about it. Just some well-worn cliché favouring men again. Most old men look bloody awful, in fact most men do whatever their age. It just doesn't seem to be as important to everyone when a man looks a mess.

It's money that usually makes a difference I suppose. A rich old man or a rich old woman both look great. But this woman wasn't rich, just getting by. She looked like one day she'd woken up, looked in the mirror and thought, okay that's that then. Let's pin my hair up and move all purchases to Bon Marche.

I probably wouldn't have looked twice at her in the street. When does that happen though? Sixty-five? Fifty-five?... Forty-five? Surely not. I was already getting used to the fact that people stop me to look at the baby now but look straight through me. So maybe thirty-five. If you have kids.

It was like something of me as an individual had gone, perhaps the bit of me that was used to build Nellie inside me. I'd given it to her.

This woman hadn't had kids they'd said. I wondered why. Perhaps she hadn't wanted them. Or she couldn't have them. Maybe she'd spent her whole life wishing she did. Maybe that was what had made her the community centre 'Mama'?

'Need a hand,' the Chief Superintendent had turned back into the room and was looking over me, his eyes a little tight.

'Sorry, uh, yes,' I stuttered turning around to find both buggies still sitting in the corner, 'yes, please.' He picked up the photo and slid it into a file in his hands, then took Luca's buggy and wheeled it out ahead of me and Nellie. He pushed with the confidence of a seasoned granddad.

I followed behind, as he caught up with Tabetha and Toby. As we walked, I could hear the three of them chatting. He was asking how things were going and remembering what it was like when his kids were babies.

We got outside, and he deliberately closed the door to the police station behind himself as he waved us off with a big smile, calling out. 'You're to think no more about it, okay? This time goes so quickly, don't miss it.'

Tabetha smiled with a vague nod and a wave as we headed down to the pavement and back towards town.

'Right, the community centre first I think,' she said, setting out towards the bus stop across the road. '409 should do it.'

I followed without a word.

CHAPTER SIX

The community centre was a typical nineties building, with large glass walls and ill-fitting blinds. They were probably bunged up once people realised that those lovely bright glass walls meant anyone walking past could look straight into the AA meetings.

It felt strange returning with a baby, when the last time I'd been here it had been just me. When the baby had existed in my tummy and my imagination only. The air felt different too, without the bustle of people coming and going. There was just a young-looking police officer at the door, watching as people passed by.

Tabetha spoke to the officer, 'DI Taylor here?' she asked casually holding up her ID card. The officer looked at the prams but answered without much pause. 'No one from local's about now, they've just headed back to the station. SOCOs all gone too.' He started to move in front of the door a little.

'We're off duty, obviously,' said Tabetha nodding towards the prams, 'but I've got a particular connection to the case, so they reckoned we should stop by to take a look.' She spoke with confidence and started to walk towards the door. The officer didn't move and looked again between the two of us. 'Never seen a working mum before, Officer?' Tabetha said, letting a little venom creep into her voice.

'Sorry, of course, come on in ma'am.' He moved from the doorway and we walked into the centre. I was surprised he'd let us in, but then no one wanted to risk sexism these days, and it seemed to confuse men as to what was right or wrong now. This time it had worked to our advantage.

The body was gone of course, but Tabetha went straight to a set of police files on the reception side. Flicking through, she picked out a blue file and opened it, scanning the page with a satisfied noise.

I turned in a circle to look around the space, but nothing jumped out. The chair; the desk; an old computer, the screen dark; a pile of course booking sheets and promotional flyers. Through a door to the side I could see the little kitchen from the photo back at the station. Some numbered markers left by the police were laid out on the floor, one to six.

I turned back to Tabetha who had picked up a small navy leather handbag and was peering inside. Marks and Spencer's c.1998 I'd guess. It was looked after carefully over the years, but still a little cracked at the edges. A treat from wealthier times, or a present from her nephew one Christmas perhaps. She put the contents back in and took a second look at each item as she did. A small purse, a bundle of receipts held together with an elastic band and a folded flyer with details of the local health visitors and their surgery times.

Tabetha hung the bag back up on a hook on the wall next to a well-worn black coat. She reached into the pocket and pulled out a used tissue and a dummy. I could imagine the old lady picking it up from the centre floor at the end of a busy day. She shook her head as she removed some latex gloves she must have put on when we arrived and, putting one inside the other, bundled them up and stuffed them in her pocket.

'Come on then, let's get out before they come back.'

She returned to her buggy and started to turn towards the entrance as a voice spoke with a laugh, 'Too late!' We both looked round quickly.

'Hi Mike, Toby asked me to pop in and take a look,' Tabetha said, a bit too casually.

The little man had a round face, with sandy hair and a gap in his large teeth giving him a hamster sort of look. He was smiling broadly. 'Oh he did, did he? Funny, I thought I was told that you weren't to get involved?'

'I just wanted to take a quick look,' said Tabetha. 'Any thoughts?'

He shook his head as if to indicate he

shouldn't share the information, but then smiled and carried on regardless. He was enjoying having the upper hand.

'Well, definitely blunt force trauma. But no weapon left I'm afraid. Something weighty.'

'Any idea what it could have been?' Asked Tabetha.

'I'll need to do some tests back at the lab, but if we were in a domestic setting, I'd have said at this point an iron or one of those metal doorstops would have done the job. Could be almost anything heavy though. From behind, no resistance, not that much force needed.' It was fascinating watching people talk like this. Like they were discussing papers for a board meeting or notes for a pitch. This was just work to them. I wanted to be a part of it.

'So, it could be a woman?' I asked quickly, taking a chance. He looked at me a little surprised, as if it was the first time he'd realised I was there. As he nodded, I tried to keep the smug feeling off my face. Ten years of *Midsomer Murders* was finally coming in handy.

'Yeah, a woman, a man,' he said with a shrug. 'Either way she was taken by surprise, you know, from the way we found her. Bending down to reach into the low cupboards probably. No defensive wounds.'

Tabetha made a little clicking sound with her mouth. Mike spoke again.

'Look, I know it's hard to keep away, but

you better go. We're all missing you, of course,' he said dryly, 'but Toby is okay, you know. He's hardly Mr Personality, but he's very experienced, he'll get the job done. You don't have to worry; we're in safe hands.'

'Okay, okay,' she said with a polite smile. I got the feeling she wasn't that keen to hear how great he was. Not yet. It was hard when you had someone keeping an eye on your role. You want them to be good... but not too good. 'Look, thanks for the info.'

We headed out of the door just as Nellie squeaked from the buggy. I'd almost forgotten she was with us. We hurried to the playground just down the road and grabbed a spot on one of the benches. I unclipped the baby and settled her on my lap to start a feed. Luca was wriggling quietly in his buggy, so Tabetha took the opportunity to grab him too. Sitting together in the sunshine feeding our babies, we discussed the grisly murder.

'Well I'm pretty sure of one thing. It's very unlikely to be the husband.' Tabetha spoke first.

'How come?' I asked.

'Why would he hit her from behind? There's no reason I can see that he'd be creeping up on her to kill her. People who kill their partners almost always kill them in that moment of passion,' she said.

I thought back to the endless murders I'd seen played out and the motives that came back again and again. 'Unless maybe they can make some money out of the death, or they are trying to escape a dangerous relationship?' I suggested.

'True, but I can't see that tallying here, she clearly had no cash, and didn't look like she'd hurt a fly. No, most likely, if it was the husband, he'd have been face to face. It begins with an argument, a movement, a look even. But something would have kicked it off and she'd have been looking right at him, not bending down for a bloody teabag.' She shook her head. 'No, this is a real murder.' She emphasised 'real' and I could hear just the teensiest bit of glee in her voice.

My stomach dropped and I could feel a tingle run up my back and neck and down my arms until my fingers shivered.

'My guess is, she was finishing off before lock up, pottering about, and someone crept in and whacked her straight on the back of the head from behind. Pre-planned, weapon brought with them, no hesitation, whack!' She was looking down at Luca feeding as she spoke and managed to keep a warm smile on her face for him while she set the scene for me.

'Poor woman,' I said. We sat in silence while we finished our feeds. I could hear a couple of kids playing in the playground, some sort of pirate game along the climbing frame: 'Ahoy, ahoy'. Cars were lazily driving past behind us.

Tabetha tipped Luca up and over her shoulder and gave him a gentle pat to clear any wind, while I sorted my bra with one hand, Nellie resting on my arm. Her eyelids fluttered as she drifted back to sleep.

'Bus over to the nephew do you think?' Another rhetorical question from Tabetha as she popped Luca back in the buggy and pulled out her phone.

We walked down to the bus station, with Tabetha stopping every now and then to send a message, until eventually she said, 'Number 42. I'll follow the route on my phone until we get there.' Where she got the address from, I have no idea.

We hopped off only ten minutes later and crossed the road, walking just a little way along the street. Tabetha started to slow as we got to a generic, boxy, red brick semi. A youngish stocky man in scruffy jeans and a jumper was looking up from the outside at a piece of guttering hanging off from around the edge of the roof. He had paint on his clothes and dusty hair. His hands looked like they would catch like sandpaper on your skin. His face was lumpy, with dark-stubbled beard and watery blue eyes.

He was frowning as he turned towards us and it took a few seconds before it clicked that he'd perhaps been crying.

'Hi there, are you Ben? Ben Nolan?' asked Tabetha.

'Yes, who are you?' he already seemed on edge.

'I'm from the centre, I take a baby class there,' she said, indicating the buggy. 'I wanted to pop by. We've just heard about your aunt. We're in total shock,' she said. She had a way of talking which wasn't really lying. 'We just wanted to stop by and say we are so sorry.' She stepped forward again.

'Oh, um, thanks,' he said. 'Look, sorry, but I have a job on in a minute.' He was trying to close the conversation, but Tabetha didn't move away.

She looked towards the door and took another step forward. Like a Jedi mind trick, he headed towards the door, with us following. It was difficult to turn Tabetha down.

'You can pop in, but just for a couple of minutes,' he said as he unlocked the door and we moved inside. The house was a bit of a state, it looked like it was in perpetual DIY mode. It always seemed like people who worked in building or decorating lived in unfinished houses themselves.

He collapsed into an armchair. 'I only saw her a couple of days ago. I can't believe it,' he said with a sniffle.

'We can't believe it either. We all used to call her Mama Nolan, didn't we Emily?' she said towards me and I nodded, even though we only knew that from the police meeting.

'Yeah, everyone did. I mean, she was my aunt, but she was more like my mum.'

'Who would do something like this? It's just awful,' said Tabetha, shaking her head, and leaning into the buggy to click out Luca, even though he wasn't starting to squirm.

'They think it's Pat. He was always messing around, disappearing, treating her like crap. Even when she finally chucked him out, he was still hanging around.'

It still shocks me that women stay with these men. Dan could be useless, but I never had to wonder if he would come home at the end of the night, or whether he'd be in the mood to push me about a bit. It almost made me laugh to imagine. If anything, I sometimes wish he was a bit more fiery.

'Thank god they got him. And so quickly,' said Tabetha.

'Oh, don't get me wrong, he was a bastard. But I don't think he actually did it,' he said.

I looked wide-eyed at Tabetha, but she didn't react. She had thought that was too simple and it sounded like she was right.

'He liked a good show, but one word from her and he'd be back in his box,' he said.

'Well I hope they find whoever did it quickly if it's not him. But who else could it be?' Tabetha asked, getting up to reach for a tissue in a box on the mantelpiece to wipe Luca's nose and then sitting back down with him over her shoulder.

'Look, if I knew who did it, I'd be round myself, but...' he looked down, 'I can't think of anyone. No one.' I believed him.

Tabetha had obviously got what she wanted,

as she quickly started to put Luca back into the buggy, fussing about with the nappy bag and giving his face another wipe.

'Well, we were so sorry to hear about her. She used to talk about you. Is there anything we can do?' she asked.

'Um, no. Funeral stuff will be put up at the centre. You're welcome to come.' He looked at his watch and then jumped up and started to usher us to the door. We'd overstayed our welcome.

He nodded a quick goodbye as he jumped into a grubby white van in the drive and pulled away.

Once he was down the road, Tabetha stopped and leant into the bag beneath her buggy, pulling out a framed photo. She must have taken it from the side when she'd grabbed the tissue for Luca.

'Wow, you didn't?' I said, but she didn't respond. She just stood staring at it.

I moved next to her to take a closer look myself, and could recognise Mrs Nolan straight away, even though it must have been taken thirty years ago at least. It was a wedding photo and a smiling Mrs Nolan was standing next to the man himself. I looked closer, wondering why she'd stayed with such a brute. Just looking into his sparkling eyes, all chiselled jaw and broad shoulders, I had my answer. They'd been a good-looking couple in their day, and maybe that's how they still thought of one another.

He aimed his jaunty smile straight to camera, with his fag tucked away in his hand, as she looked up at him smiling broadly. You could tell he just had that thing that some men have. A cheeky twinkle that seemed just for you and that a lot of women can't resist, no matter how bad for you it is in the long run. It sounded like he'd lost that charm now, but maybe she could still see it behind his eyes. Maybe that was why she'd not been able to fully let go.

'Well what do we think, is he in the frame at all?' Tabetha asked, almost to herself.

'Well if he's been heard by almost everyone openly threatening her, I can't see how he can be ruled out,' I said.

'That's true, but Ben seemed pretty confident that he'd never really hurt her. In fact, it sounded like she held her own too,' she said, looking at the photo again.

'But she was attacked from behind, right'?' I asked, 'so she didn't have a chance to fight back, even if she wanted to.'

'True,' she looked at the photo again, 'but like I said, if it was him, they'd have been face-to-face, I'm sure of it. There's more to this, I know it.' She sounded pretty certain.

'So, who next?' I asked.

'She only had one other living relative, a brother who's been in Spain since the nineties. They've already spoken to him. He runs a bar and was there all afternoon and well into the evening. Plenty of witnesses. Fortunately for him.'

'And what about Ben, do you think he could be involved in any way?' I knew the answer already.

'Good question. He seemed genuine, but people can be good liars when they need to be. I can't see what he'd gain, but we'll keep an eye on him.'

'Dead end for now though?' I asked, disappointed.

'No, it just means we've missed something, that's all. And if it's at the scene, we need to go back now, or it could be gone for good.'

CHAPTER SEVEN

When we got back to the crime scene it was pretty much forty-eight hours after the death itself. Getting off the bus we had a clear view of the community centre on the other side of the road. Standing back like this I could see it was more worn out than I'd realised, like Mrs Nolan's handbag. A good investment, but over time nothing can stop it wearing around the edges.

In fact, the whole area looked on the edge of run down, now I looked a bit harder. Litter lay strewn across what was probably a neat front garden area a few years ago. But half the shrubs were dead, and the dog poo bin had a build-up of black bags on the closed lid. I suppose it looked like lots of places in the local area... well lots of places without upper middle-class residences anyway. It was probably due a refurb a few years back, but council cuts meant loads of those sorts of projects had been cancelled, or indefinitely delayed.

It made me feel a bit guilty. In St Anne's the local council had just put up some lacklustre new sculpture by the river; two swans flying together in bronze. It must have cost a good few thousand pounds. Who decides where money is spent locally is anyone's guess.

There was a small crowd standing in front of some railings by the pavement next to the crossing. They were chatting and looking into the building. News must have spread. There was a sense of excitement in the air as their chatter rattled over to us. I started towards the crossing, but Tabetha caught my hand first.

'No, let's try something else,' she said and turned to look at the run-down shops behind us. The parade was made up of an off licence, a William Hill, a fish and chip bar called 'Jims' (no apostrophe), and on the end a typical smallish corner shop called 'Broadway Food and Wine'.

'Right, let's head in here. Just pick up something, anything. I'll do the rest.' I followed Tabetha into the shop and started wandering the two small aisles, looking at the shelves.

It was my kind of shop, different items every month, always something unusual to pick up for a quick lunch. I investigated what was ambitiously described as the 'Fresh Food' cabinet and the selection of frankfurters and chicken-based vacuum-packed meatballs was startling. I suppose they needed to cater for all the different communities in the area. The section was completed with a few brightly coloured blocks of cheese, some bubble-gum-pink-coloured mousses which I would absolutely buy and several types of misshapen pasties.

Unsurprisingly, I could hear the woman at the till chatting with a female customer about the murder as I moved on from the fridge and scanned the aisles. Both women were probably in their early fifties and the customer had a wheelie trolley with battered corners and various patches holding it in one piece. It looked like they went everywhere together. I got the feeling the two women were die-hard locals, they spoke like gossips at the bar in EastEnders and probably knew all the local characters.

'It's frightening to have a family around here these days,' said the shopkeeper shaking her head. The woman she was talking to, made a noise of agreement.

'I'm glad mine are all grown up already. We didn't have to worry about this sort of thing,' she said. 'Some of those young yobs around here, you never know what they're up to. Steal her purse, did they?' She asked the woman behind the till. Now the fact that the victim was an old lady, the main suspect was an old man, and no young people had yet been implicated in any way, seemed to have no impact on their view.

Was it a universal truth that older people always worried about the state of the youth? It seemed to me it was old blokes that were drunk and asleep on the benches, shouting offensive things at young women walking past. It was couples in their fifties and sixties at home gardening in happy retirement as the younger people joined a world of work which probably wouldn't end until they hit seventy. And it wasn't the 'young yobs' who'd made the terrible environmental, economic, political decisions of the last few decades. But they'd be the ones feeling the effects.

My mother continually moaned about seeing young people (that's anyone aged up to forty) on their smartphones. I don't know what she thought they were doing that made her so cross, googling porn in the Tesco queue?

'And to think, he could have even popped in here first?' said Tabetha joining the conversation. The women looked a little taken aback and eyed her up and down suspiciously. Seeing the buggy, which Tabetha was pushing backwards and forwards gently as she spoke, they softened quickly. There was something safe about a mum.

'Or after he'd done it?' continued Tabetha. Her accent and posture almost seemed to change as she spoke to them.

'God, I suppose you're right,' said the shopkeeper. She hadn't thought of that before.

'I heard they're looking to talk to someone from the area. Tall, young bloke, with a ginger beard wasn't it?' Tabetha asked.

'Really? Saima, Saima!' called the shop assistant behind her. A younger woman appeared. 'Yes mum?' she said.

'This lady says they are looking for a tall man

with a ginger beard for the murder of that poor old woman over the community centre. Was anyone like that hanging around last night?'

The younger woman shook her head. 'I'm pretty sure I'd have remembered someone like that coming in. There was no one that stuck out last night. But, like I told the police, the evenings are always busiest aren't they, people going home from work, so...' She drifted back into the office where a TV was on.

'If only they had CCTV or something,' said Tabetha shaking her head.

'Oh, they do, but it wasn't working apparently, hasn't been for a while. In fact, the old lady had told the council a few times, but they never got it fixed.'

'Bet they will now!' said the customer.

'They came over here to see ours,' explained the shop owner proudly. 'But it just points at the door and into the shop, so I doubt they'll get anything. I handed it over anyway of course. We all pull together around here.'

By now I was up at the till and paying for my shopping while Tabetha started to turn to leave.

'Shame. Well I hope they catch him soon,' she said as she headed out the door. After picking up my shopping, I followed quickly behind. As I left, I could see at least five people had followed in after me and were beginning to head towards the tills. The woman was right, it was a busy time of day.

We walked in silence a little down the road and around the corner into a residential street.

'Okay, you'll have to humour me, what was that all about?' I asked.

'Locals only gossip with other locals. If I'd gone in as a total stranger and asked outright if they had CCTV of the murderer, do you think they'd have told me?'

I hadn't thought about it, but as usual she was right.

'As it happens, they're not much help, but at least we've explored that avenue,' she said as we walked further along the road.

'Except I suppose we now know this was a very busy time locally,' I replied, thinking about what I'd heard. 'So, we've either got a very stupid murderer, or a very brave one. Or perhaps very clever. It's hard to pick out one random person from lots of people coming and going.' As I finished speaking, Tabetha looked at me and smiled.

'Yes, very good, very good,' she said. Then her face changed to super serious.

'Digestives, that's what you picked out, really?' she said, retrieving the pack of biscuits tucked into the top hood of the buggy. 'You could have bought anything, custard creams, ginger nuts. But no, you went with digestives, the blandest of all the biscuits.'

She handed them back and I tucked them under the buggy with a smile. I could feel she was pleased with how I'd helped, and it felt good to be useful.

As we walked back around the corner, Tabetha headed for the crossing and I followed, assuming we'd be going back to the crime scene. But on the other side of the road she quickly turned right and began to walk along the pavement past the centre itself.

We stopped outside the next building, a low-rise block of flats, probably ex-council. Some looked smart, others needed a good clean up.

'Let's see what other locals are saying,' she said, as we headed inside a small atrium. The first thing I spotted was a large buggy parked up, with worn wheels and the story of many children's sticky hands etched into every fold of material.

We crossed to the door opposite and Tabetha ushered me to stay back as she knocked on the door of flat A. No one answered. She crossed back over towards the buggy and knocked on Flat B. No one again, but we could hear a noise from inside, so she knocked once more.

A youngish woman opened the door a crack and looked out. Her hair was lank, pulled back into a pony tail out of her eyes. Her black vest had white marks of formula dripped down the front, with the straps of a greying bra visible underneath. I could hear a baby screaming from behind her. Judging by her clothes the woman was probably only in her early twenties, but her face looked older. It was a total assumption, but she looked like she was probably doing it alone, like so many women.

'Give me a break,' she said to Tabetha with a look of despair in her red eyes.

'Excuse me?' said Tabetha in response, now with her voice in a higher, posher register than before. 'I'm so sorry to bother you, I'm just popping into some local residences to ask some questions on behalf of the Council. We can offer ten pounds of Tesco vouchers if you can give us just five minutes of your time.'

The woman opened the door a little more and plastered a smile on her face.

'I'm sorry, it's just since the baby, the door never stops. Just this week it's been some stupid breastfeeding counsellor, the health visitors, even the social, it's never-ending, I just want to be left alone you know, but they keep coming.' She tried to laugh a little, but it obviously wasn't funny.

The baby screamed again, and she stepped back and reappeared with it in her arms. It immediately settled. The tiny baby was wrapped in the cleanest white blanket I'd ever seen. No matter how hard she was finding it, this mum was still getting something right.

'I'll keep this short; I promise. I've got one of my own, it's so hard isn't it?' Tabetha said, pulling a notebook and pen out of her bag with a smile.

'Oh, have you? I didn't realise how hard it would be, and all these people who are meant to help. They pretend they are your friend, can't do enough for you when they're here, take away all sorts of questions to sort for you, and you never hear from them again.'

Tabetha gave an understanding nod, then quickly changed the conversation. 'Okay, question one, how would you rate the community centre from one to five, one being very bad and five being excellent?' asked Tabetha.

'Oh, I don't know, three?' said the woman with a shrug.

'And how regularly do you use the centre: daily, weekly, monthly, rarely, never?' asked Tabetha.

'Weekly at the moment. I've been told to go to that new mum class thing. God, it's terrible though, the woman at reception's been killed there, just this week,' said the woman, gently bouncing her baby back and forth over her shoulder.

I could see Tabetha visibly relax as the topic naturally came up.

'I know, I just heard. She'd worked there for a while apparently. I guess you must have met her?' said Tabetha, moving into gossip mode.

'A few times, yeah, she was always there. Real hard worker she was. I saw that husband a few times too. Grumpy bastard. He used to hang around sometimes in the sofa bit in reception.

Used to make her get him cups of tea and biscuits and things. He had an evil look about him now I think about it. One of the other girls said he'd been in prison before apparently, drugs maybe, something like that. Nothing major, but still.'

'Oh really?' said Tabetha.

'It never ends well with men like that – he got her in the end, didn't he?' She looked sad.

'I heard something over the road about a strange letter he'd written or something, did you hear about that?' asked Tabetha.

'A strange letter?' Well he didn't seem like a big letter writer,' she laughed. 'It's the council's fault really of course. Oh, sorry.' She smiled apologetically.

'No, it's alright, I'm bought in from an agency for this, so no offence taken. What do you mean anyway?' asked Tabetha.

'Well, people are saying she should never have been locking up by herself. Men are just looking for an opportunity like that aren't they?'

'So, you saw him there last night, did you?' asked Tabetha.

'Well, no, but he'd hardly make a big show of going in if he was planning to kill her now, would he? And you can always come in from the back. Then no one would know.' The baby stirred in her arms and started to mew.

'Look, sorry, but are we done?' she asked.

'Yes, you're busy, of course. Thanks a lot.' Tabetha started to turn to go, but the lady put out her hand.

'Oh yes, the voucher...' She reached into her bag.

'Oh god, I'm so sorry I don't think they're in here.' She made a show of looking through her bag again.

The woman's face fell, she had probably already spent that tenner in her mind.

'Look, I shouldn't do this, but this is totally my fault. If you won't mention it to the council, then I won't!' Tabetha pulled out her wallet and handed her a ten-pound note. 'I'll just take back a token for myself when I'm back in the office.'

The woman looked delighted.

'Thanks, bye.' She quickly pushed the door shut, perhaps in case she was asked to hand the money back, and we headed back out the front doors of the block. Nellie was just waking for her next feed, pushing her around all day had kept her asleep most of the time. Probably she'd be up even more tonight to make up for it, but I didn't care right now, this was too interesting to interrupt.

'Ten pounds for that?' I asked.

'Well you never know what's going to be useful and what's not. There might be something there that we don't even know is information right now.'

I raised my eyebrows at her, 'I said might be!' she responded with a smile.

She looked at her watch. 'It's nearly seven o'clock, where has the time gone?'

'Oh god, Dan!' I said, reaching into the buggy bag. I pulled out my phone, which I'd put on silent that morning when I got to the coffee shop. Seven missed calls, and two texts. He must have been chasing me since he'd got in from work. We had a bit of a routine set up for when he got in. It consisted of me trying to pass over Nellie as quickly as possible hoping she'd stay quietly with him for more than thirty seconds. The idea being I could enjoy life's little luxuries, like have a leisurely wee by myself, before beginning an evening of cluster feeding.

I was just considering whether I should text or call to apologise, and what I'd say to explain myself, when I was suddenly starving hungry. I grabbed the biscuits and was opening the pack when I heard Tabetha say in her casual voice.

'Toby, good to see you again. How are you?'

I looked up to see Toby, Tabetha's maternity cover, walking towards us. His pursed lips said he looked shocked to see us there outside the centre and I could feel Tabetha bristle and pull herself upright as she spotted him. Then almost immediately her body dropped again into a relaxed stance. I'd seen it all day today, the way she could change her demeanour depending on who she was talking to and why, it was one of those 'soft skills' people talk about, and she was a master.

I tried to do the same and act 'normal'.

Toby slowed as he walked the last few paces towards us to give himself more time. He took a bit of a breath as if deciding what to do.

'Heading to the centre for a class? I think they've closed the whole lot I'm afraid.' He'd obviously decided to give her a way out. We all knew what was going on, but he looked like he didn't want to get into anything difficult. He probably had enough to worry about today.

'Mmm hmmm.' Tabetha made a little confirmation noise but looked away.

'How are you finding the team – giving you all the help you need I hope?' asked Tabetha changing the subject while she busied herself looking under the buggy for an imaginary something.

'They're great,' he said with enthusiasm. 'I know they are just waiting for you to get back. But no, they're great,' he said again. It all felt a bit awkward, like he was spending time with her ex-partner and wanted to be complimentary but not seem smug.

'And how are you finding maternity? You know I've got one on the way, don't you?' He asked with a nod towards the babies.

I saw Tabetha flinch and knew just what she was thinking. His career would hardly miss a beat when his baby arrived.

'No, I didn't, congratulations. When's it due?' she asked politely.

'October, so not long now. Marcia is working really hard at getting everything ready. She says she's 'nesting'. So, it's home from the office and straight onto painting the nursery, or baby proofing the kitchen or whatever. We're the last ones in our group though, so we had to give in sooner or later. And suddenly it was sooner...' he sort of laughed as he finished.

He looked at his watch. 'Talking of which I better run, we are wrapping up the details on site with the team now before I get back to the station. Have a fun evening.' He smiled and walked briskly away with a small wave in our direction.

'What a condescending bastard,' Tabetha said quietly, once he'd walked out of ear shot and towards the centre. It was now buzzing with police activity as two more cars pulled up outside and officers started to get out. I was a little surprised at Tabetha's tone, he'd seemed polite enough to me, considering we were clearly snooping around his case.

'*Have a fun evening*?' said Tabetha shaking her head. 'As if all I'm doing is sitting around drinking wine with my feet up while he's doing the real work. I expect once he sees what it does to *Marcia*,' she said the name with a strange squeaky accent, 'then he'll realise what a fucking nightmare it can be.' She looked at me pointedly.

'I mean, *have a fun evening*, did you hear that?"' she said again. It was the first time I'd really seen her lose her cool, but something about Toby obviously rubbed her up the wrong way.

'I don't think there was anything meant by it,' I said. She looked at me a little cross for just a moment.

'Okay, so he's nice and reasonable and polite,' she said, irritated. 'I hate him'.

'Come on, have a biscuit,' I said laughing, and starting to hand her the digestives, when for a second time a voice surprised us from behind: 'Oh, what a coincidence.'

CHAPTER EIGHT

I turned around to find Mike, the sandy-haired officer we'd bumped into earlier, looking at us. He was eating a grab bag of Doritos and was probably heading back over from the shops.

'Nothing's changed from this morning I'm afraid. I'm just heading over from the wrap up,' he said, as he licked his nacho fingers. It was clear he'd guessed she was up to something. He knew her too well.

'Oh?' she replied, trying not to sound too interested.

'Look, if it was me leading on this, and I'm not, Toby is... but if I was, then I'd probably be heading over to talk to the key witness. You know, the last person to see her alive?'

'Oh yes. That's Norman someone isn't it?' said Tabetha, playing along.

'Norman Brown, that's right. And if I did want to speak to him – which I don't, and neither do you – I'd want to head over there quick. He's just being dropped back off, and I wouldn't be surprised if he was lining up some local radio interview for this afternoon. He's a bit of a pain to say the least.'

'Interesting,' said Tabetha and her eyes flitted to me.

'1a, The Ridings, head down there, turn right, can't miss it.' Mike pointed with his elbow down a road a few buildings ahead of us, shook his head, jammed another Dorito into his mouth and headed off.

'Thanks Mike, I owe you one,' she called after him.

I could feel my phone vibrating in my pocket as Tabetha looked at me with those eager eyes, ready to move on.

'There's a bus stop just by the flats on our way back towards yours, we might as well stop off on the way, right?' she said, already starting to push the buggy in the direction Mike had pointed. Without looking at the messages, I sent Dan a white lie:

> So sorry. Mum thing over ran.
> Just getting bus now.

I tried not to feel guilty as I followed Tabetha. It was funny, I didn't want to be a single mum, of course. But the more time I spent with her it almost seemed appealing. She could do what she liked, deal with the baby as she liked, go where she liked, and when. And once she got home, it would just be her and Luca.

I watched Tabetha power walk ahead while I trotted along trying to keep up. We followed

Mike's instructions and ended up at a neat little row of tiny, mock-Georgian houses, and I mean very mock. Each one had some pretentious little pillars at the door and arched windows, but all the dimensions were too small and the materials too cheap.

I looked up the road and could see a bus stop with my local bus on the sign, so Tabetha hadn't been bluffing, we could easily get home from here at least.

She was about to head up the path ahead of me with Luca when she suddenly looked down at the buggy. We probably wouldn't get away with taking the babies in this time. She turned back towards me and I could see Luca was stirring.

'Why don't I take both of them and sit up at the bus stop. You'll never get much out of him with me hanging around.' I gave her a way out without her having to ask for help. She seemed like someone who wasn't great at that.

'You could be right, thanks.' She rushed back, handed over the buggy and marched off up the drive. I now had two buggies with me and immediately understood why people with twins had those tanks. I edged Nellie ahead of me and tentatively pulled Luca behind, inching crablike the few metres to the bus stop.

Finally I sat down, my arms on fire with the effort, and almost immediately both babies began to scream. Luckily no one was at the stop, but I grabbed Nellie quickly all the same and bunged her on the boob to calm her down. That always did the trick. But there was nothing I could really do for Luca, except bob around in front of the buggy from my seat. This didn't distract him for long and I tried to recall some nursery rhymes, but nothing came to me. I started singing what I thought began 'Five little speckled hens sat on a speckled...' then realised I had no idea what they were sitting on that could be speckled and perhaps they weren't hens in any case.

Now that would be a really useful thing to teach in NCT, nursery rhymes. I landed on Disney musical numbers instead and started on Frozen, followed by The Little Mermaid, both with my own take on the words, but at least I knew the tunes. I was just starting on a semi-confident *A Whole New World* when Tabetha finally came out. I'd let one bus pass as I'd waited, but as she headed towards us another came up the road and she put out a hand to catch the driver's attention as she sped up to a skip.

As the bus pulled in, I hastily put Nellie back into the buggy and then clumsily pulled her up into the bus with a clatter. I found a spot to stand, while Tabetha took a seat in a spare two behind me. She took out Luca and began a feed as the movement and white noise of the bus quietened Nellie in her buggy, and we were able to speak.

'Well, he is quite a charmer,' she began with an

eye roll. We had about fifteen minutes until our stop, so she recounted the meeting pretty much in real time.

He was a greasy looking man, who smelt too strongly of cheap aftershave. He had let her in no questions asked. Mike was right, he seemed to be getting some enjoyment from all the attention and was very happy to recount his 'fascinating' take on the events to anyone who'd listen.

He was one of those finickity sorts, who thought detail and specifics were a sign of intelligence. He'd been in the centre at 5.48pm precisely. He knew it was that time, and not 'about 5.45' as the police kept saying, because he left his house at 5.40pm every other weekday evening to go through the centre and the walk took eight minutes.

He always said hello to the lady at reception and passed the time of day. He thought she seemed a lonely type, so he always made sure he took the time to share a story or two with her from his week. Funny things were always happening to him, he said. Tabetha rolled her eyes again at this point. I could already picture what sort of a man he was. Living alone, careful routine, visiting his aunt was the highlight of his week. But, of course, he was also fascinating and entertaining... weren't they all.

On the night in question; and this was when he really leant in to talk about all the juicy information he had to share, he had gone in as usual at 5.48pm. The lady in question was at the reception, starting to get things ready for locking up. Despite needing to pop in and out from the back as they chatted, she looked very pleased to see him, but then they had struck up quite a rapport over the years (eye roll number three from Tabetha).

Had she seemed her normal self? Tabetha had asked. He was quite sure nothing was amiss. He relayed his weekend plans to Mrs Nolan, including finding out that a Waitrose was opening two stops down. She was shocked but seemed very grateful he'd let her know, as this was apparently her favourite shop for groceries. Although he acknowledged that with hindsight this had a bittersweet edge as she would never get to see said Waitrose launch now.

Tabetha had to nudge the story along, and after a few more distractions, managed to ascertain that Mrs Nolan had seemed herself throughout. She had behaved as normal, and after around six to seven minutes of conversation, Norman had headed out the back of the centre as always to get to the estate behind. Here he stopped at the chemist he visited every Monday just before 6pm to pick up his favourite breakfast health bar he then ate throughout the week. From there, he circled around the back of the centre and took the longer route back home to stretch his legs, as was his usual routine.

He seemed very pleased with his evidence, although to my ears there was absolutely nothing of use.

'So, sounds like she was fine, nothing out of the ordinary,' I said.

'Well, perhaps, perhaps not,' said Tabetha. 'He didn't strike me as having the most acute emotional intelligence. Perhaps he'd have noticed if she was crying, or told him she was upset or scared, but would he have noticed something subtler? I'm not sure. What if she was distracted maybe, or a bit quieter than usual? Probably would have passed him by.'

'Okay, good point. A useless meeting then.'

Tabetha swapped Luca to the other side and reached into her pocket to pull out a yellow Post-it note with some tiny, precise words written on it in fountain pen.

'I wouldn't say it was completely useless.' She handed me the paper.

The words said 'Clive Cooper, 0786 566787'

'Who's Clive?'

'Well Norman might have been the last to see her alive, but it was Clive who was the last person in the centre that night. Norman met him at the police station and got chatting. Turns out Clive is a plumber, and Norman might be getting in touch with some odd jobs for his aunt.'

Tabetha reached out to press the 'Stop' button on the pole next to her seat for me. I struggled off the bus and I could see the blanket squirming in my buggy as I glanced back up at

Tabetha who still had a few stops to go.

'I'll text you where to meet tomorrow,' she called after me, a definite statement rather than a question. I didn't even stop to think before nodding and turning towards my road.

I only lived a few minutes away, and though I knew I should rush back to Dan, it was still warm and I couldn't resist strolling slowly home with the buggy as the light dimmed towards dusk and that pinkish shade rolled over us across the sky. Couples walked past me arm in arm and small groups chatted and laughed as they weaved their way together in the other direction, heading into town for dinners and drinks. I didn't feel envious of them today. It was good to take a moment to think about everything that had happened, just me.

First thing this morning, I had been going to meet some mums for coffee. Not that I really felt like one myself yet. And this morning I had been a bored mum if I was honest. I'd maybe go so far as to say an unhappy mum. But this afternoon I had been Emily again, and not just normal old Emily. Detective Emily, Super Emily.

Tabetha had listened to me, we had spoken not once, but multiple times about things other than the colour of poo or bedtime routines, or how exhausted we were. It felt amazing.

Not for the first time, I wondered if I had really been ready for a baby, or whether I was one of those women who never really would be.

I looked into the buggy and saw two small eyes looking back up at me. I paused to push the blanket down to give Nellie some air and for just a split second a smile glanced across her face. Her first smile. It was there just briefly, but I was almost certain it was a real smile. It wasn't just on her lips, but in her eyes too.

Finally, finally I felt a real surge of something as I looked in at her. The surge I'd expected when she was born. She had seemed a stranger since she'd arrived, but in that one look suddenly she seemed familiar. Maybe she had my smile, or Dan's, or my mum's. I leant in and said in that baby voice we all do, 'Well done, Nellie, well done, lovely smile'. And she did it again, a longer smile this time, and it was definitely there. She looked into my eyes and really smiled.

It was as if I saw her for the first time.

I wanted to grab her out of the buggy there and then, but I was just around the corner from the house, so I carried on, rushing a little and looking down as much as I could to continue to coo and chat to her.

When I got to my front door I knocked as loudly as possible and very quickly Dan opened up as I unclipped the baby and pulled her out of the buggy. I was about to shout out 'she smiled', when I saw Dan's face.

'Where the hell have you been?' he took Nellie off me immediately, probably anticipating I wanted a break.

'I did text.' I said, defensive immediately. 'I was just with the mums. Things over ran okay?' I wasn't sure why I was acting cross.

He wasn't buying it.

'I was calling, and texting, and nothing. I was worried. Then that one message, that was it. And where were you coming back from that took so long, huh?'

I didn't say anything. He was right, and I knew it.

'She's not just your baby you know.' He tried again. And again, I didn't say a thing. I just stared at him.

'Where have you been? Anything could have happened,' he asked. I'd rarely seen him so angry.

I looked at him and mumbled something about mum friends again. He shook his head.

'It's nearly nine o'clock Em ...' His voice drifted off as he headed back to the living room.

I took my phone out of my pocket and checked the time, he was right, 8.52pm.

I could hear him already starting to undress Nellie in the next room to change her ready for bed. As I peeped in through the door, I could see the baby grow laid out neatly on the floor with a nappy, wipes and some cream next to it, I wondered how long they'd been waiting to be used.

He was holding the used nappy he'd just removed, bobbing it up and down in the air as if weighing it. He said a quiet 'phew' to Nellie, as I realised how full it looked. I hadn't changed her since this morning.

He leaned over her and kissed her tiny nose, smiling. 'I've missed you today little one,' he said quietly. Then I saw him jolt backwards.

'Emily!' He looked up and turned towards me at the door.

'She just smiled, she just smiled! I'm sure of it!' I rushed over and knelt next to him.

'I leant over her and smiled, and she smiled back!' His eyes were alight.

'Really?' I asked quietly, still testing the water.

'Look,' he leant over her and said again, 'I've missed you today little one,' then leant back up with a smile. Nothing.

'Or maybe it was the kiss?' He leant over and very gently kissed her nose again.

He sat back up and Nellie shared a little dopey smile.

'See! Did you see that?' He looked at me amazed.

'I did, that was a definite smile!' I smiled back at him and our little baby.

'Her first smile!' He lifted her up high in the air and brought her down for a cuddle.

Then she weed all over him.

CHAPTER NINE

For the first time in months we had sex after putting Nellie to bed that night. I'm not sure what it was, maybe arguing had reminded us who we were again, outside of being a new mum and dad. Or maybe it had been seeing that little smile as she looked up at us. Suddenly everything had seemed just a little bit more worth it.

People had said that before. That once they can react things get easier. But I hadn't really understood what that meant until we saw that little smile, and her eyes really connecting with ours. And not just because I was filling her up with milk.

The next morning the air was clearer. But not completely clear. I knew I still owed Dan more of an explanation, but for some reason I wasn't quite ready to share exactly what was going on. It felt like something that belonged to me. Nothing to do with Dan or Nellie or being a mum.

I changed Nellie and lay her on the baby mat, kicking her feet in the air and blankly moving her gaze from one hanging animal to another.

Once she was settled, I went back into the kitchen where Dan was standing at the counter eating some toast and scrolling through the news on his phone.

'I want to apologise properly for yesterday,' I said.

'You said sorry last night,' he replied without looking up from his phone.

'I know, but I really mean it. I'd be furious if you just disappeared for hours on end with Nellie.' I hadn't really thought about it that way until the words came tumbling out.

'But yesterday I had some time to myself, and I guess I got carried away. The time disappeared, and I was...' I was saying a lot of words without really explaining much.

But Dan looked up at me with a gentle smile.

'Look, you don't have to tell me everything you do. You are still you and I am still me. We're two grownups, you know. Obviously if you were off with some bloke...' He smiled a bit to show it was a joke but looking me in the eye he seemed like he wanted some reassurance.

I immediately shook my head and said, 'No, no, of course that wasn't it.'

'Well then just don't disappear with our baby again, okay? Or text me before you do!' He hugged me close.

'I will, I promise.' I said, hugging him back. Dan was great. He was almost always great. So why wasn't I just telling him what I was up to?

'I'm off – have a lovely day, ladies.' He kissed me on the head, and then Nellie, grabbed his things and was gone for the day.

Usually at this point I'd be sitting with the baby looking at the door and only thinking about the ten long hours stretching out before me. But today I had a smile on my face. I couldn't wait for the day to begin.

I busied myself for the next hour tidying up a little, singing silly songs I made up as I moved around the house, taking Nellie into each room and placing her with a toy on the floor. The moving around actually seemed to keep her more content than usual, and when she did have a little moan, I didn't feel quite so resentful, or full of panic. Scooping her up in my arms, I danced her around the kitchen and caught one more of those amazing little smiles.

Then my phone beeped, and my heart skipped a beat.

> Will walk by yours and pick you up on the way to the witness. See you in about 20 mins, T.

Just enough time for a quiet feed and to settle Nellie in the buggy for her first major sleep of the day, perfect for interviewing a witness.

We arrived at Clive's about 9.30am. His house stood on the corner of a cul-de-sac of ex local authority houses, large pebble-dashed boxes with new double glazing, all very spick and span.

Our tactic was for me to have Luca attached to my front in the carrier with Nellie in the buggy so that Tabetha could go in more easily this time around.

I lurked just around the corner outside the neighbour's end wall. She walked straight up to the front door and rang the bell.

'What?' I heard a great booming voice as he answered.

'Just here to ask a few additional questions and check some details Mr Cooper,' she said, obviously not rattled. 'Can I come in?' she asked.

I could see her start to step forward, as she had at Mrs Nolan's nephew's house, but it didn't work with Clive.

'No, you cannot come in,' he boomed again and stepped out of the door forcing her a metre or so back down the front path.

I now had a great side-on view of the pair and could easily listen in from my tucked away spot. Although I could have heard his booming voice from two streets away.

He was one of those men who based his whole persona on his gender. From his deep, gruff voice, to his stonewash jeans – too tight around the crotch – to his builder's boots and dark stubbled face. The white T-shirt stretched across his front was probably intended to highlight his six pack, and maybe it had twenty years ago. Now it only served to showcase a rounded, middle-age spread. The hideous animal garden ornaments lining the pathway and a glimpse of a red rose feature wall in the front room hinted that in reality it was his wife who ruled the roost.

'Okay, no problem. I'll keep it short,' she said, trying to appease him. But as he puffed up his chest, I could see he wasn't going to fall for her charms today.

'You got to the centre just after 6pm, is that right?' she asked, her voice sweet.

'Look, I'll tell you lot once more okay, but that's it,' he said, folding his arms across his broad chest. 'I was only going through that bloody centre to get to The Crown round the back. I don't always, 'cause it's usually closed at six, but it looked like the front was still open, and it saves me a few minutes. Wish I bloody hadn't now though,' he said gruffly.

'I went in, the place seemed deserted and the back door was already shut so I went straight back out the way I came, that's it. You must have some CCTV or whatever? Not that I'm going to do your bloody job for you,' he leant in a little too close towards her.

I'd managed to stumble into The Crown by accident once on a walk with Dan when we first moved to the area. It was as local as they come. No women, except behind the bar, the sort of place old men go to for dinner every night because their wife left them twenty years ago and they never bothered to work out how to turn the oven on.

'That's very useful information, Clive, thank you,' she smiled sweetly at him again. 'So just to confirm, there was nothing in there that looked out of the ordinary?' asked Tabetha.

'Listen love, I walked in and walked out. There was the computer thing that's there for checking in, a packet of fags and some baby book or something on the side. There's always buggies going in and out of there, bloody screaming babies.' I was glad we'd not taken the kids over to him now.

'And then I just left, alright, straight back out again.' I could see his face redden and his mouth become pursed. He wasn't just angry, but defensive too.

'How did you know it was a baby book?' asked Tabetha, sounding interested now.

'It had a baby on it,' replied Clive, deadpan.

Tabetha smiled. 'Did you touch it?'

'No!' he said quickly and loudly.

'And no one else was coming in or out, or hanging around outside?' she asked.

'Look, I didn't see anything,' he sounded exasperated. 'You can't put anything on me, okay? I went in, looked behind the desk, no one there, left. Like I said, there must be some CCTV or something?' he replied.

'Okay, that's great, thanks for your time,' said Tabetha, almost breezily.

She picked me up as she turned the corner and pushed Nellie as I continued to carry Luca. We started to walk slowly back into St Anne's; it was only a couple of miles and the sun was out.

Tabetha was very quiet, so eventually I kicked off the conversation.

'Well? What did you think of him?' I asked.

'I don't know. You?' she seemed confused, or more likely frustrated.

I shook my head. 'I believed him, personally.' We continued walking quietly.

'I would have thought by this point we'd have at least one big clue to go on. It feels like this is episode two and we should have a big new piece of evidence appear,' I said, as we started to walk again.

'Well there is that baby book,' said Tabetha.

I laughed. 'Exactly. If that's our main clue, we're screwed.' But when I looked at her, I could see she was serious.

'You don't really think the book's a clue, do you?' I asked.

'Well the fingerprints would suggest it is,' she replied.

'What? There were prints on it?' I asked, shocked.

'Rumour has it, no,' she said, 'no fingerprints at all.'

'What do you mean, someone had cleaned it?' I asked.

'Exactly. And who would deliberately leave a book at the scene of a crime, carefully wiped clean of all prints? An innocent man would leave prints, a guilty one would not.' Tabetha reached into her pocket and pulled out her phone, she began to fiddle around with it as we continued walking. Eventually she handed it over, open on one of the images of the crime scene we'd looked at back at the station.

Now I was looking for it, I could immediately see the book placed at one end of the main reception counter. I recognised the cover as a Mum's Diary. Not so much a book as a thick, magazine-style glossy. They were given away free to all pregnant women. Mine was still sitting on my bedside table at home. I'd checked the development section every week while I was pregnant. It pretended to be the diary of a real pregnant woman, and gave information and tips, like how large your baby might be now, what had developed, how you might be feeling. Then some good pointers for the first few weeks of being a mum.

'So, we'll need to work out who it belonged to, I suppose?' I asked, handing back the phone.

'Ideally. But I'm not that hopeful. All pregnant women in the UK are given one, and you could probably pick them up in most maternity wards or doctors' offices too, if you were looking out for one. But it is odd. It must mean something.' She looked closely at the photo again.

'Someone has gone to some trouble here to create a story – the letter, the location, the book. I don't quite understand it yet. These touches though, they suggest some sort of creative flair to me. Someone's gaining some joy from the theatrics, I reckon.' She shook her head.

'They are deliberately giving us some information, but not quite enough. Leading us somewhere...' She really did sound like a TV detective now. I could see her get a buzz off it.

'I mean, what do you think?' but she didn't give me time to respond. 'Is he, or she, anti-women? Anti-babies?' she asked.

'Or she?' I was surprised she'd said that. Even though we'd established back with Mike that a woman could have dealt the fatal blow, it felt like we'd still been speaking as if we were looking for a man for some reason. She didn't respond, but kept on talking.

'And why warn us first?' More questions. My mind was swimming.

'Is it about power? Because right now they've got all the power and we're just followers. Maybe that's it, the killing is irrelevant, it's the power over the police that's important. Maybe in their day-to-day lives they are powerless...' She spoke with conviction, but it was starting to wind me up. It seemed like we were going off the point a bit.

'It feels like we need to go back to the clues and the witnesses, rather than making any assumptions,' I said, thinking back to my favourite shows. 'So who are the suspects so far?' I asked, trying to get us back on track.

'You're right, let's make a list of all the suspects in the story,' she said faux-seriously. 'The husband, the nephew, the two witnesses,' she counted them off on her fingers. 'Well, based on that list and everything we've seen, I'm going to guess it was Clive, with a garden ornament, in the centre.' Her voice sped up and her tone tightened.

'That's the means, but what about the motive, you're thinking?' she continued, dripping with sarcasm. 'Well, the way he tilted his head to the left when he spoke suggests some sort of issue with female role models, possibly based on the relationship he had with his mother. Finally, poor Mrs Nolan didn't open the back door at the centre, and he lost it. It was the last straw. Right, grab the handcuffs Emily, let's get him.' She shook her head, as she put her phone away and started to walk more quickly, pulling away ahead of me.

I stopped in shock watching her.

She paused a few metres ahead, then spoke without looking back at me.

'Oh, come on Emily. I'm only kidding.' She took a deep breath and then turned around fully.

'Sorry. It's just at this stage I really still have no idea.'

I walked forward and caught up with her.

'I'm not Miss bloody Marple,' she said quietly.

'Okay, point taken,' I said. We walked quietly for a minute or so before I couldn't stand the silence. 'So, what do we do now?' I asked.

'Well we don't know who, how or why... so pretty typical of most real-world investigations at this point I'm afraid,' she replied. We stood quietly swapping over the baby carrier from me to her, holding Luca's head carefully to keep him sleeping.

'Well there must be something we've missed that'll lead us to the killer,' I suggested, trying to stay positive.

'Emily, we aren't actually in one of your TV shows you know. Let's get back to reality, shall we?'

She had shut me down. And for the first time I wondered why I was here.

'I know you were probably hoping we were going to find a load of prints, maybe the outline of a size ten boot on the entrance mat, or a drop of blood in the sink, just perfect for a DNA test.' The sarcasm wasn't quite the Tabetha I'd become used to.

'I'm not looking for anything. I'm just helping out, that's all. Carrying your baby, asking questions, trying to be useful. But if I'm not helping, you just say, and I'll happily go home and put my feet back up.' I was lying of course.

She stopped and looked at me, her face tight.

'I'm sorry, I'm just frustrated that's all. I've been waiting for a case like this for years, this is a career changer, potentially. And I'm on bloody maternity leave.' She spat the last couple of words loudly and Luca stirred on her front, right on cue. She quickly corrected herself.

'You know it's not even that. It's just the first forty-eight hours are so important. It feels like we're nowhere and I'm angry. It's not him... or you.'

I put on my project manager game face.

'Look, at the very least we have some interesting questions. Why Mrs Nolan? Why Newton Hill? Why a letter to you? And why a baby book? That's got to count for something,' I said.

We walked in silence again for a few long minutes more, the odd gurgling noise coming from one or other of the babies to remind us they were there. Tabetha's phone chirruped, and she looked, then put it quickly back in her pocket without sharing the message.

As she took a breath to speak, I readied myself for the next instruction, back to the centre? Off to interview a long distance relative?

'I've got a few jobs to do today, why don't we wrap it up for now and get some thinking space on it?' It was one of her rhetorical questions and she had already started to pull away ahead of me as we got to the corner. 'I can see my bus up there, I'm going to grab it, okay? I'll call you.' She skipped quickly ahead, put out her hand to the bus heading towards us and jumped on.

I stood almost in disbelief as the bus crawled past, and I could see Tabetha busying herself with getting settled down with the baby, not even a look back out the window towards me.

What had just happened? I headed to the opposite stop for my own bus home and thought through the morning. I hadn't meant to upset Tabetha, but it seemed that's what I'd done. Although I felt like, just for a second, a look had passed her face when she read that message on her phone. Had she received some sort of information from Mike, or even another message from the killer?

The thought of being cut out of the investigation filled me with dread. Finally, I had something back in my life, that felt like mine. Something that could really challenge me, something that didn't smell of Napisan and baby sick – and I could feel tears stinging my eyes when I realised that it might be over.

I took a deep breath and tried to pull myself together. Of course she'd call tomorrow I thought. We'd laugh about this and get back on the case. It was stupid to second-guess things. Dan often told me I overthought stuff.

If only he was right.

CHAPTER TEN

The following day dragged on, but I didn't leave the house. Between feeds, changes and naps (and with one eye on my mobile) I carefully fitted in the steps to cooking a Bolognese for the freezer at my mum's insistence. Why is it that you have a baby and suddenly batch cooking is a thing? I overcooked the whole bloody thing in the end anyway, and after rescuing a few bits for my own lunch the rest was straight into the bin.

The weekend came and, although it was nice to have Dan with me and Nellie, I still wasn't used to the fact that weekends were no longer my own time. It felt like more of the same old crap from the week, but the shops were busier. Nellie couldn't really do anything yet, so no bike rides or soft-play cafes.

She was still feeding every three hours in the night and, to top it off, I felt like I was in *Groundhog Day* with her most recent phase of waking me up every morning at 4.27am precisely.

My new morning routine was slowly walking her up and down the hall to try to get her back to sleep, with her screaming out if I so much as paused to scratch my nose.

The paranoia about how annoying the noise must be for our neighbours kept me going even as my eyes drooped, or frustration and tiredness spiked tears, and in the end I always gave up.

As Dan was working, it felt like I should be the one to get up early, even though I didn't manage to nap in the day either. I didn't argue, as it made sense rationally, but once it got to the weekend that felt even more unfair.

On a Saturday and Sunday, we'd now made an agreement that after she finally quietened, I'd go back to bed for an hour or so. Despite my crippling tiredness, I didn't want to waste this precious time sleeping and I pulled the covers tight over my head and tried to think about all the things I loved: dinner out, a large glass of ice cold white, a trip to the cinema... one day, one day...

On the Sunday, my parents popped round to see Nellie and I tried my best to show things were great. Why is it so hard to tell your parents you aren't doing well, or is it just me? My folks are extremely positive all the time. This has loads of benefits, but also means that they don't really handle negativity. It's almost like they just don't hear it.

On one particularly bad day of constant feeding early on, I'd shared with mum that things weren't as I'd expected. She nodded and then simply said, 'It'll settle down.' Then without missing a beat went into her favourite subject of how easy I was as a baby: 'You were just like Nellie, such a happy *easy* baby. You're so lucky Em, enjoy it, *please*.' Which meant, 'pull yourself together'. Then it was back to popping the kettle on and singing nursery rhymes until she left saying, 'It's so great to see you doing so well'. It was like the conversation hadn't happened.

My Dad followed her lead, but added in an extra verse of 'we're so proud of you', as he hugged me goodbye to make sure I didn't burst the bubble and reveal that my life wasn't perfect after all.

So now I just took a deep breath when they arrived and plastered on a smile. I knew they judged people on how happy they were, how clean the house was, whether they had nice food in for visitors, so that's what I delivered, and they left happy.

Monday came around again and I did everything I could not to think about Tabetha and the investigation. I kicked off the day with the inspiring task of going through mine and Dan's socks and throwing out any with holes, while Nellie lay in the washing basket looking at various bits and pieces that I hung over the sides for her. It felt like we'd been up for hours, but by the time I headed back downstairs to put on a coffee my phone told me it was still only 9.00am.

The elation I'd felt when Nellie had smiled had already started to wane, and the feeling that I wasn't cut out for motherhood was returning with each painful hour and minute that ticked by.

I quickly broke, and before I'd even finished my breakfast, fired off a message.

> Any info? I'm free this morning if you want to meet up.

I tried to sound casual, as if I sometimes had plans.

It was a relief when my phone buzzed with a response, until I read the contents.

> Sorry, visiting a friend in London with Luca, out of town the whole day. Coffee soon though, T

My heart sank.

By 10.30am I was going stir crazy, so I wrapped Nellie up in her cute, yellow summer blanket and put her in the buggy for a walk into town. I breathed in the clear morning air as we walked and wondered yet again why I was finding this so hard. Shouldn't I be enjoying it?

I turned right, away from the river, and crossed the road towards the shops. As I headed towards Boots I glanced absentmindedly into the Costa. That was where it had begun, just days ago, with that call to Tabetha. I paused as I remembered the thrill I'd felt as we'd headed to the police station and how it seemed like an age had passed.

As I looked in, considering whether Nellie would stay asleep long enough for me to have a coffee today, I saw a familiar face in the back corner. I felt a little sick as I recognised Tabetha's dark bob. She was sipping from a large coffee cup and nodding seriously as a woman, a bit older than me and very glam, sat opposite. They were talking intently, leaning towards one another.

I didn't recognise the other woman at all. I supposed she could have been a relative, but from the way they were talking, she didn't look it. Maybe they were colleagues? I noticed Luca was over the woman's shoulder and she rocked him a little as she spoke, stopping briefly to offer a tender kiss for his little cheek. She smiled warmly and leant in close with a laugh reacting to something Tabetha had said. They definitely seemed like friends, good friends.

Her clothes looked expensive, a crisp white shirt with a soft, neat, red cashmere jumper slipped on over the top. She didn't look like she'd grabbed them unironed from the washing basket that morning like me. She probably wasn't a mum, I thought, as I watched.

Then Tabetha took out her phone, opened something up and showed it to the other woman, who looked closely then nodded and spoke seriously. It could have been me sitting there as we'd been chatting just days before. Was that the photo of the crime scene she'd shown me? They looked at it closely again and discussed whatever was on the screen. I stood watching for a few seconds, but didn't risk any longer, as the embarrassment of being seen was too much to contemplate.

I felt so stupid that I'd been waiting for her to call and she'd obviously felt she had to make excuses not to meet up with me.

I turned away quickly and walked briskly to a little independent coffee shop outside the mall along the scruffier part of the old high street. I sat down with a coffee as Nellie stirred, but thankfully she went back to sleep.

Since Nellie had arrived, I'd felt removed from people around me. Even sitting now with a coffee, surrounded by people chattering and getting on with their day, I felt like I was in a bubble of my own. Soon I felt tears start to roll down my cheeks, and I looked down so as not to catch anyone's eye. I couldn't remember ever crying so much as I had in the weeks since the baby arrived.

A hand rested on my shoulder and I looked up in surprise to find a man looking down at me. 'Oh, sorry, I didn't mean to startle you,' he said. It took me a second to realise it was Toby, from Tabetha's work, who I'd met a couple of days before. He wasn't in a suit today, and he looked younger in his jeans and a plain black, round-necked T-shirt. I hastily wiped my eyes and plastered a smile on my face.

'Sorry, I was in my own world,' I tried to laugh

a little. He had a coffee in his hand and as the cafe was packed, I felt I had to offer the spare chair at my table. 'You can sit down if you like', I said, indicating the chair, and he took it.

'It's busier than normal today, isn't it?' he said. 'I dread to think how much I've spent here over the last few months. The guys at the counter have my Flat White ready before I walk through the door these days!' I didn't say anything in response, I wasn't sure how my voice would sound if I spoke, but I tried a little nod.

'It's my way of clearing my head coming here. Every day, 11am if I can. I'm not sure I've spotted you here before though?'

'No... I uh... I haven't been in here before, it's just today I couldn't...' I didn't really know what to say.

'Are you okay? Has something happened?' His square jaw tightened, and his eyes narrowed as he leant forward, then glanced around us as if he might see the reason for my upset sitting at the next table.

'I'm fine, honestly, just one of those days!' He smiled a reassuring smile and I could feel that he was just the sort of police officer you'd want to turn up if you were in trouble.

'Are you expecting someone?' he asked.

'No,' I replied quickly and looked into the pram, just so I could look away from him. But I couldn't stop the tears flowing again, this time in embarrassing suppressed sobs. He immediately moved his chair closer and put an arm around me saying quietly, 'It's okay, it'll be okay, whatever it is Emily. It is Emily isn't it?' and I nodded.

We spent the next forty-five minutes talking. I told him how it had felt when Nellie had arrived, how much harder it was than I had expected and how alone I felt. I told him about how I'd not really thought everything through before we got pregnant. I'd just thought it was the inevitable next step, and suddenly, when the baby arrived, I had realised how much was going to change. Talking to an almost stranger it was suddenly so easy to say it out loud. I couldn't bear to talk to Dan like this. It wasn't his fault. It simply boiled down to the fact that I was worried I'd done the wrong thing, and there was no going back.

Then there was the Tabetha thing. Feeling like my friends, not just her but all of them, had disappeared when I needed them. I didn't mention her by name, I knew it would be strange for him. If he guessed, he was kind enough to pretend he didn't.

Toby hardly spoke, just listened and nodded. Probably another police trait. The more I spoke, the clearer it became. Yes, I was upset with Tabetha for ditching me, but I couldn't expect her and the case to keep me going. It was the distraction from everything that had been so appealing, and the reminder that I had uses other than feeding a baby.

Finally, I took a breath, wiped my eyes on the hard coffee-shop napkin Toby had grabbed for me and smiled at him.

'God, I'm so sorry. I don't know what happened there.' I laughed a little and he returned the smile.

'It's okay. I can't imagine what it'll be like for us when the baby arrives. The baby isn't even here yet, but things are already changing.' I was surprised to hear that from a man for some reason.

'Marcia has always been so sure about babies, and although I know it'll be bloody hard for her, at least she seems sure that this is something she needs.' He looked down at his coffee, his grey eyes seemed darker now. 'I've just never felt that it was a definite. I was shocked when she first said she was pregnant. It's not always been plain sailing with me and her. But the baby, it's changed everything. That doesn't mean I know how it'll work, or what the future holds though.' He looked a little lost now. 'I've always loved my freedom. I'm guessing that's out the window!'

I thought about my work, my girls' nights out, how I'd been feeling guilty about missing that. But maybe I wasn't the only one.

On cue to break the tension Nellie woke with a squeak. I lifted her out of the buggy and jiggled her about in the way she liked, and which sometimes stopped that cry from kicking off so quickly. Toby put his hands out to take her and put her over his shoulder gently. She rested her body on his and tried to look up at him with her still wobbly little head. The cloud that had come over him had lifted and his eyes crinkled into a smile.

'Look, however you are feeling, and however long it takes to get really into the swing of things, the important thing is it isn't getting in the way of you being a good mum, you know?' he said.

'I see a lot of mums in my line of work, often just girls really. They're drug addicts, party girls, or under the thumb of some awful bloke, and I look at their kids…' he shook his head. 'I mean you wonder how they are going to make it.'

He held Nellie up and away from him to look her in the eye as she gurgled. 'She's so clearly a content, healthy, beautiful baby. It looks to me like you are doing everything right.' I could see his face light up; she must have given a little smile. 'She's just lovely, really,' he smiled back at Nellie and gave her a quick cuddle before handing her back. I was a little reluctant to take her, as it was so lovely to see her from afar for a minute, see her as her own little being.

'Thank you,' I said quietly, finally taking Nellie back and giving her a squeeze myself.

'Look, I'm no expert, but you just keep doing what you are doing. And don't worry if you have the odd bad day or even if you spend the next eighteen years not being sure if this was the right decision. You are doing the right thing by her and that's the most important thing.'

Hearing that, I could feel tears sting my eyes again. It was as if someone had pinpointed exactly what my main fear was. That my uncertainnness would impact on Nellie. But he was right, she was content and healthy, surely that's what I needed to focus on.

'You are going to be a great Dad,' I said to him. He laughed and said, 'God, I hope you're right.' He glugged back the last mouthfuls of coffee and jumped up looking at his watch.

'I better run. It was really nice to bump into you.'

'You too. Thanks for listening. It's just an intense time isn't it? The baby and then the murder too. It's just… intense, that's all I can say.' I looked up at him as he nodded.

'You know what,' he said, taking his business card out of his pocket, along with a pen.

'We have a support team,' he said, flipping the card onto the blank side. He leant on the table to write a number on it. 'If you want to talk to anyone about Mrs Nolan's death, how it's left you feeling, you can call them. Anytime.' He handed me the card and gave my shoulder a light squeeze before turning to walk away. It was nice to make contact.

As he walked away, I felt embarrassed about what had just happened. But he'd shared too, and it was a relief to hear someone else feeling similar about this massive decision that can't be taken back. Perhaps, it was harder for men feeling like this to share, as people defaulted to checking in on the mums.

I doubted Dan had thought in this much depth about becoming a dad though. In fact I wasn't sure he thought in this much depth about anything. It was hard to imagine having this sort of conversation with him the way we were right now. There was something about talking to Toby that had made it come easy. It did feel like a weight had slightly lifted.

I looked behind me to watch him walk away. He stood out amongst the passers-by, tall and broad, with his salt and pepper hair. As he was about to turn a corner he glanced up and back to me. His face looked deep in thought, but it quickly turned to a smile as he saw me watching him and we caught eyes. He nodded a final goodbye and turned the corner.

I finished my coffee then lay Nellie back in her buggy to kick about as we headed home. Maybe it was a good idea to have a break from the distraction Tabetha offered, just to think about being a mum and what that meant.

CHAPTER ELEVEN

I spent the rest of the week keeping busy. It helped to create more of a daily routine. It wasn't just important for Nellie, but for me as well, maybe even more so.

I stretched out everything as long as possible, breakfast might take an hour if I made each item individually and cleaned up carefully after. A stroll into town could take double time if I walked up and down residential streets on the way. Then we'd do as many jobs as possible out and about before walking slowly home to wait for Dan.

But there was one glorious hour before bed. In the dark of the room, with Nellie asleep in the cot next to us, when I could look through my feeds and scroll through the news in complete silence. Before it was time to head into a broken night and then get up to do it all over again.

At noon on Wednesday I headed to the NCT meet up. But Tabetha didn't join us. I put on my mum face and chatted with the rest of the girls while bouncing Nellie on my knee. But I was disappointed.

I nodded and smiled in the right places as Fay explained why there was a wet patch on her top where she'd wedged a pack of frozen peas into her bra to soothe her mastitis.

Priya was already thinking about nurseries and had set up a spreadsheet for her reviews. An actual spreadsheet.

Everyone had their worries and issues and it was reassuring. But, on the other hand, they all felt fixable.

As the weekend came, I planned all sorts of things to do as a family. Walks by the river, lazy pub lunch over Nellie's nap, even an hour to pop out to get my hair done while Dan took her for a coffee. Sunday night came, and Dan snuggled up to me on the sofa while Nellie was sitting in her bouncy chair for a few minutes, distracted.

'I really think things are getting easier,' he said as he nuzzled my neck, 'and it was so nice to have Nellie by myself for a while, we need to keep doing that.'

I wanted to agree, to snuggle up back and hold on to my new family filled with love and contentment. But I just couldn't.

'Thank you for taking her,' I said, almost absent-mindedly to fill the silence.

'No problem, I want to do everything I can to help you out.' He kissed me on the head like a kid. The idea that he was helping *me* out with our baby put my teeth on edge.

He sighed happily as he lay back down. For him, Sunday night meant one more evening before heading back into his adult life for the week. For me, all I could see was five more baby-days stretching out ahead.

As Wednesday rolled around again, I wasn't in the mood to meet up with the other mums. It was hard even to get up and out of bed, and for the first time since the baby arrived, I struggled to get us out the door. Everything seemed difficult, from picking out clothes, to getting Nellie to latch or finding all the bits and pieces I needed to take with us.

I tried to think back to what Toby had said about doing the right thing by Nellie. When the panic set in again, I counted what was going right as a mantra. 'She's healthy. She's content. She's dressed. She's changed.'

I was nearly fifteen minutes late once I finally got into town and headed up towards the Costa. I took a deep breath to try to build up my energy to chat. As I looked into the coffee shop, I could see the ladies already there. Jack was being held on the table in front of the mums, several hands propping him up, while Fay talked seriously as she ran her finger up and down one of his podgy little arms. She looked like she was showing the other girls something. Some dry skin? The mums nodded as if offering solutions.

I could see Tabetha wasn't there yet again. Before I knew it, I had turned back around and was walking quickly away.

I found a bench back out in the main square and almost collapsed down onto it. My heart was racing, and my head felt cloudy.

I took out my phone and, before I could think clearly, punched in a text:

> I need to talk to someone, are you free?
> I'm in the main square now, Emily

I sat for maybe ten minutes, wondering if I'd get a response, before I felt a familiar hand on my shoulder. I looked up as if from a daze and saw Toby looking down at me. I still had his card in my hand. The one he'd used to note the help line on the back.

'That wasn't quite what I meant about calling for support,' he said with a faint smile. 'You okay?'

'I'm sorry,' I said. I should have felt embarrassed but just seeing a kind face made me feel calmer.

'Well, you messaged at the right time,' he said, holding up his cup. It wasn't far past 11am and he must have been over at the coffee place again.

'Come on, I've got time for a quick walk,' he said, and put out a hand to help me up. I got up to follow him with the pram down towards the river. We walked quietly, before I felt like I should explain myself.

'The other day when we met, I really felt like

you got it. And what you said, about just being a good mum. It's helped,' I told him. 'But I'm still feeling very, I don't know, alone I guess,' I said.

'I'm sorry to hear that,' he said, as he led me towards a low wall looking out towards the river and we sat down. It was quiet and those tiny summer flies darted across the water.

'What about your friends and family, is there anyone who can support you?' he asked as he sipped his coffee.

'I just feel like they'll, judge me...' my voice cracked, and I couldn't carry on. I looked at him, practically a stranger and suddenly realised how mad this was. 'I'm so sorry I messaged; I shouldn't have. It's this weird time, I'm not myself,' I said and started to get up.

'No, sit down.' He spoke with authority and I did as I was told. 'Look, I thought a lot about our conversation too. It took me by surprise.' His voice softened again. 'It was the first time I really talked about the baby coming. And about whether we were doing the right thing. It's terrifying wondering if you will be up to the job. I think we *both* needed to talk.' He looked at me a little sheepish.

'Sometimes you find yourself somewhere in life, right?' he said, 'and it's a fork in the path moment. You have to decide, will you commit and move forward, or will you walk away? You know, I'm usually a walk away person. It's me, my job, my life that I'm focused on.' I nodded, it rang bells. 'But when you take that other path, those first few steps are hard, because... because, you can't go back. But if you go forward you know the risk of messing up again, well...' He looked over the river as he spoke, with his coffee cup clutched in both hands.

After a second he looked towards me and leant in. 'Does that makes any sense?' he asked quietly. His eyes searched mine.

I nodded again, silently. It did.

We sat quietly just looking at each other for a moment. For some reason it wasn't uncomfortable. He leant forward towards me until our foreheads were almost touching and I could feel his breath on my lips. It felt like we were in our own bubble.

'I have to get back to the office,' he said quietly after a moment. His voice was soft. I nodded and he moved forward to hug me goodbye, and somehow in that movement our lips met. Was it deliberate? It didn't matter, because for a moment we kissed, and I didn't pull away.

I hadn't kissed another man in nearly a decade, and it felt electric. Just for those few seconds.

And it was just a few seconds, before I did pull back. He looked as shocked as I was.

'I'm so sorry, I don't know what happened,' he said and leant back away from me sharply.

'It's okay, I know, it's okay,' I said quickly as his head collapsed into his hands. 'I know it was nothing, honestly.' I tried to reassure him, and he looked up, relieved.

'Wow, you're right, this is a weird time...' he shook his head and almost managed a smile. 'Let's just forget it, agreed?' he asked, putting out his hand and I shook it.

'Agreed,' I said back.

'I better go.' He got up and started to turn, then he twisted back around to me and smiled weakly. 'It will be okay you know,' he said, before hurriedly walking away.

I sat in silence for another ten minutes or so just thinking about what had happened. It had been a long time since I'd done anything really, really impulsive. I felt guilty, but it felt good too. Then a message came through.

> Heading home early, will pick up some lunch for us! Tell Nellie I'm on my way,
> Dx

I rubbed my hands over my face as if to wash away what had happened. Dan didn't need to know, no one did. It really was nothing. And as I got up, I mentally packed the whole thing away in another box with the lid shut. I was gathering lots of those now.

CHAPTER TWELVE

The next day I stuck to my routine as if everything was normal. If I carried on as before, just kept on going, maybe it would be.

By Friday morning I woke with an ache in my chest. It was now over two weeks since I'd last seen Tabetha and I'd had no word at all.

After breakfast I changed Nellie and quietly sang out my mantras to her as she gurgled on the mat in front of me – 'She's healthy. She's content. She's dressed. She's changed' – preparing for another day. Then the doorbell rang. No one ever just stopped by, I only seemed to answer the door to the Tesco delivery driver these days, so I hastily picked up Nellie, and rushed to answer it.

Tabetha was standing in the doorway, Luca attached to her front. She looked jittery, nervous even, as I pulled the door wide. 'Phew, you're here,' she said. Before I could decide if I even wanted to let her in, she stepped forward, one foot across the divide. I obliged without thinking, pulling the door further back to let her enter.

Suddenly my time-filling cleaning that morning seemed worth it. It might not be immaculate, but the house was fairly tidy, the washing machine was whirring in the background and I'd just taken a stinking bag of nappies out to the bin. The thought of Tabetha knowing how hard I was finding things, particularly since she'd disappeared, was painful.

I wanted to tell her to go, or at least ask her for an explanation as to where she'd disappeared to all this time. Maybe even get an apology from her. But her entrance made it seem ridiculous to bring it up. I wasn't thirteen anymore, and she wasn't my BFF. Even if I had wanted to question her a little, she didn't give me a chance to speak before thrusting a piece of paper at me, and I took the bait.

As I put Nellie into the bouncer, Tabetha stalked around the room, buzzing with energy.

Once baby-free, I looked at the paper closely. Before I even read the words, it was immediately obvious what it was. That hyper-normal paper and hyper-normal, round writing was easy to recognise.

Hi Ms Tate,

Well who'd have guessed it, I won the first round. Don't worry you'll have another chance. I'm just getting started.

Next to Clays Green on the 21st.

I can't wait, what fun we're having!

Your friend,
Mr Clever.

I looked up at Tabetha in shock and she nodded while dropping down into an armchair.

'We need coffee.'

I followed the instruction and switched on the kettle, reaching for the posh coffee reserved for guests. As the water boiled, I read the note again.

'Wait, the 21st? That's yesterday. When did you get this?' I asked.

'I know. I've only just got back to the house,' she answered and my ears pricked up. 'I spent a few nights at my sister's house,' she spoke just a little too quick.

'Oh?' I responded, trying to sound casual.

'Yeah. But I did tell the guys at the station I'd be staying away. It's been weeks since any contact, and they'd ruled out any possible link between the letter and Mrs Nolan. So, what am I meant to do, sit at home just in case?' she asked, her tone more than a little defensive.

'Oh, I didn't mean it was your fault,' I jumped in. Her being here now, the relief at seeing her, at sharing the next clue in the mystery, had eased my anger already. I may not have been totally back on side, but I knew I didn't want to fall out again, not now she was back.

'So, are they taking it seriously now?' I asked.

'Well I've made it very clear that they need to. They are still not officially linking the letter to the Newton Hill death, but I just know they are connected.' She was clearly frustrated.

'I was thinking about what you said, about looking back at the clues, that there must be something we were missing.' She got up then and walked over to the buggy to grab a clear plastic wallet with something inside from her nappy bag.

She pushed some books aside on the coffee table and put on some latex gloves. Then she carefully pulled out the contents and laid it on the table. It was the Mum's Diary.

'Where did you get that from?' I asked, shocked.

'It seems they'll let you change a baby anywhere these days,' she answered, not looking up. 'In fact, I might start to take him around even when I go back to work,' she finished.

I went around to join her at her side of the table, and we knelt to get close to the book.

We looked at the cover first, nothing out of the ordinary. Then she carefully lifted it up and flicked through the pages with her fingers, but nothing fell out.

She lay the book back down and the pages fluttered closed again.

'Wait a second,' I started to reach for the book, 'can I?' She handed me some more gloves from her pocket, which I put on before picking up the book again.

I flicked through the pages more slowly this time and was sure that it was naturally staying open just a little longer at one particular place.

'It was open on the counter wasn't it?' I asked, flicking the pages again.

'That's right, face down,' said Tabetha.

I laid the book down where it stayed open the briefest moment longer, picking it back up to see which spread was showing.

I could feel now that the spine had been broken a little from being open to that particular spot. The pages looked normal enough at first glance, then I realised one word had been carefully underlined in black pen. Easily missed.

What is the naughty step? it said.

'*Naughty*, now that's familiar!' said Tabetha, pulling out a copy of the first letter from a file in her bag. She laid it down next to the open book and pointed to the final sign-off, 'Mr Naughty'.

'If only they'd let us look at the scene straight off. I knew something had been missed!' she said, banging the table.

The noise was immediately followed by a squeak from the bouncer's direction. We both froze and looked at one another. A second squeak sounded, and I knew I couldn't ignore it this time. I quietly started to sing *Rockabye Baby* under my breath as I crept over. Nellie's eyes were droopy and flickering, and it looked like she'd half woken with the bang. I tried not to catch her eye. That was always a sure-fire way to wake her right up. I stepped behind her and started to push the bouncer gently from behind. She quietened down and I hummed the lullaby quieter and quieter down to silence.

'I need to call work now to let them know I've found the link,' whispered Tabetha.

She picked up the phone and paced across the room to the furthest corner.

'Hi. Is, is, Toby there?' she stuttered urgently. 'It's important, I need to speak to him now.' Her voice rose.

'They're all up there? Okay, can you let him know I'm certain now Mrs Nolan's death was connected to my letter, and they need to keep looking at Clays Green until they find something. Got that?' She put down the phone and started to gather her things together again.

'He's already put some extra bodies up at Clays Green to look around. It's a small area though, so if there's anything there, they'll find it. That is if they are looking properly.' It sounded like she'd lost some faith now.

'Do you know what?' she spun quickly back around to me, 'I need to get up there and make sure they take this one seriously myself. Forty-five minutes' walk from here do you think?' she asked. I hadn't even had time to pour the coffee, but I nodded and was almost immediately grabbing my baby bag and chucking some extra wipes in the top. I picked up Nellie carefully and gave her a gentle squeeze before popping her in the buggy and grabbing the keys.

'It could be a bluff though, couldn't it?' I asked as I slammed the door behind us.

'God, I hope so,' said Tabetha as she strode ahead as fast as possible, Luca strapped to her front again.

We walked towards the river, and it was then pretty much a straight line through the centre of town, out the back and up a steep hill past a large secondary school and some residential roads, then across a busy roundabout before we could see the green ahead of us.

We didn't talk much on the way, mainly just hypothesising whether we'd find anything, and if there wasn't a murder, why the letters had really been sent.

Once we got to the green, we chose to take the right-hand side towards the estate, and as I looked back over to my left, I could see officers talking to people at three or four separate houses.

I was just about to ask Tabetha whether it was normal for them to do door to doors like this, when I felt her hand reach for my arm as she stopped stock still. She was looking to our right down a street of family houses. Around half-way down several police cars were parked, and I became aware of the sound of people talking in raised voices. We turned down the road and, as we walked slowly towards the noise, Tabetha stopped again.

'There,' she said, and I looked more closely at what we were faced with. Several police officers were talking to a small group. They looked like a mix of neighbours, some in couples, a few individuals. And then one young female officer holding onto an older woman, maybe fifty years old, who looked to be sobbing. A witness? The woman eventually looked up, white as a sheet, and I recognised her face. It was the mother of Shelley, the young girl from our NCT group. She had come to pretty much every meeting, showing more interest in the process than her daughter had. But then Shelley had seemed so young. If anyone appeared to be unready for motherhood it had been her.

'It can't be Shelley though, can it?' I spoke without thinking, aiming the question straight out into the air.

We should probably have turned around at that point. Not only had Tabetha received the notes, but we knew the first location and now the second victim it seemed.

Something drew us forward, and as we moved closer a dark car pulled up on the opposite side of the road. Toby got out, smart in a grey suit. My heart leapt into my mouth and I looked away hoping he wouldn't spot us.

We were almost at the house by now though, and there was no missing us. He came straight over and I was sure he looked to me first as he said, 'I'm so sorry ladies.' For a second, I thought he was going to give us a hug. Then he seemed to remember his role and pulled up to his full height, looking directly at Tabetha.

'It is Shelley then?' she asked him bluntly before he could speak again.

'Yes. Shelley Carter,' he said. I realised I hadn't even known her second name.

'I asked her mother if there was any connection to your name and she recognised it immediately.' He shook his head in confusion. 'I told Derek we should take those letters more seriously.'

Derek must have been the name of the tall, statesman-like Chief Superintendent I'd met back at the station when this had all started.

I still wasn't able to say a word.

'Anyone you're focusing on right now?' asked Tabetha, slipping back into work mode yet again.

'You know I can't answer that,' said Toby.

'But you've let Mrs Nolan's husband go now, right?' she pushed.

'We'll have to. He's been locked up since the original arrest, so the most water-tight alibi you could ask for,' he confirmed.

'Good. At least that's one lead closed down, and we can finally start to look for who's really responsible for this mess,' she said.

'I know you are angry that we've lost time, I am too, but...' Toby tried to win her over, but Tabetha interrupted.

'Look, whatever's happened, this is where we are now, and we need to make these next forty-eight hours count. We can't let him get away again, right?' said Tabetha, trying to pull us all together. She didn't mention the book, there wasn't much point now, but I realised she'd probably get in a heap of trouble for removing it.

'I'm sorry, but you need to keep your distance more than ever now,' explained Toby. Tabetha leant forward to argue, but he cut in. 'Both of you,' he looked back at me too. 'If anything, we could be questioning you two at some point. I can't afford for any of the waters to be muddied. I'm sorry,' he apologised again. Tabetha huffed.

'I'll keep you in the loop when I can, okay?' he said in hushed tones, before turning to move away from us. 'I'll be in touch.'

I nodded silently as he headed towards the house with a deep breath.

While we'd been speaking, Shelley's mum had been led back inside and the small group of neighbours had dispersed. It was quiet now. We were standing in the eerie silence after a storm.

We turned around and walked back towards the green. As we did, I could see some activity in the far corner by a small church. Some officers were cordoning off an area and a white tent had been erected since we'd walked past before. It was just jutting out from a darker wooded space, behind a smart wooden bench. The sort of quiet place I'd go to think or meet a friend. I felt a bit sick.

'That's it, isn't it?' I could feel tears stinging my eyes as we carried on walking and could only think of the baby who must be somewhere right now, without his mum. He was probably back at the house we'd just left. Was Shelley's mum giving him a bottle and trying to hide her tears?

Tabetha swiftly led me the way we'd come; away from the cordon and back down the hill. Around halfway back to St Anne's we passed a small cafe and went in, grabbing a table. I sat down silently and before I knew it Tabetha was back with a large tea for me, loaded with sugar.

My hands were shaking. I held one up in front of me in surprise and then looked up at Tabetha.

'You're in shock. Just take a minute and drink some tea, it'll help.' I suppose she was more used to these things. But then I saw her rip the ends off three more sachets of sugar and pour them into her own drink. Maybe it was different when you knew the victim.

'What the hell is going on?' I asked as Tabetha's phone buzzed.

She was silent, scrolling through a message with interest. I saw her close her eyes for a little longer than a normal, blink hard, and then look again shaking her head a little.

'What is it?' I asked.

'Back of the head, again,' she leant in, 'could be any large heavy object from the look of this. They'll still be searching the surrounding area for it, but if there's nothing close by, I'm guessing the murderer took it with them. Which suggests they brought it with them too. Pre-planned.' She leant further into her phone and used her fingers to zoom in on something. Now I was sure she was looking at crime scene photos. This time I didn't want to see them.

'That baby book again; a Mum's Diary next to her,' she shook her head. 'Okay, that's it, the calling card. I'll check in with the team, but I'm betting there will be a word underlined and I could have a good guess which one. I'm afraid they really might be 'Mr Clever' with this murder,' she said, and I remembered back to the sign off on the second note.

'If only I'd seen the letter earlier, we could have been ready. Maybe we'd even have realised Shelley could be a target.'

I watched her as she looked down, shaking her head. Was that really sadness in her narrowed eyes? I couldn't read her today. We sat in silence for a moment. This was the time she needed reassurance from me, so why wasn't I speaking up?

'It was the police who told you to keep your distance,' I said, finally. 'I'm not sure they took the first letter seriously at all. If it's anyone's fault it's theirs.' I wasn't sure there was really conviction in my voice though. Something was making me wonder now if there was more that we, or maybe she, could have done.

We sat quietly again. Then Tabetha gave herself a little shake and looked at me, eyes fixed.

'Right, here's the big question for today. In some way I'm connected, and for my own sanity I need to know why. We did NCT with Shelley, but I really didn't know her at all. I think we need to speak to someone who can shed some light on who she was and why she's been targeted.' She started to get up, then looked back at me.

'Are you up to this. I understand if you aren't. I can call you guys a cab home?' She sounded sincere, but I knew I couldn't duck out now.

'I'm fine, I just can't stop thinking about that poor baby.' I gulped the last of the sweet tea with a wince and got up. As I checked on Nellie and got ready to leave, Tabetha was back on the phone. By the time we had stepped out into the street, she knew where to go to find some people who'd known Shelley: the pub just a few streets away, where she used to work.

The Anchor was a typical local spot. It had been modernised enough to draw in the younger crowds on one side, but on the other was still clinging onto that old British pub look, not charming, but familiar. Dark-patterned carpet, thick wooden tables, cushioned chairs which probably stank of beer if you got too close.

We headed into the more modern side, where there was a pile of kids' books and a box of mismatched building blocks by some sofas in the corner.

Nellie was stirring, and I took her over for a feed while Tabetha went to ask if she could speak to someone. The landlady headed out from the back and Tabetha brought her over in my direction. She was right, no one really suspected someone with a baby in tow. They barely glanced my way.

The woman looked like a typical landlady. Probably in her fifties, pale and a bit greasy. She didn't look like she'd been outside in weeks. She wasn't someone I would usually approach for a chat, but as she walked over, I could see the concern on her face. We were in a fairly small community and news that someone had been murdered had, unsurprisingly, spread quickly. Tabetha leant in and said something I couldn't hear, but I could see the lady's face crumple as she leant back out.

'Poor, poor Shelley.'

Tabetha helped her take a seat on a bar stool just behind her.

'Had you seen her recently?' asked Tabetha.

The woman half shook her head, then distractedly said, 'Look I'll have to get Carly. They were mates. I don't want her hearing about this through the old gossips around here.' Tabetha nodded, and the lady headed around to the other side of the bar.

Just a few minutes later she came back with a girl, probably nineteen or twenty, in tight black ripped jeans and a striped black-and-white crop top. Her hair was loose around her shoulders and she had a velvet choker around her neck. She was dressed as if it was 1994 and she was coming to my thirteenth birthday disco. I hadn't realised the nineties really had a style until it had re-appeared on the high street.

'Shelley's been killed?' said Carly. There was shock in her voice and her face read sadness, but her eyes looked a little excited too.

Tabetha nodded. 'I'm afraid it looks that way. We don't have much information right now, so this is just a time to find out as much about Shelley as we can. To get a full picture of her as a person before we continue investigations.'

It sounded like a very long-winded way of saying we were being nosey.

'When did you both last see Shelley?' she continued.

'God, she came in yesterday didn't she Val?' said Carly to the landlady. 'I can't believe it, she was looking great, and Alfie's just the cutest.'

Hearing the baby's name made my stomach drop.

'And how did she seem?' asked Tabetha.

'Fine, more than fine. She hadn't been in since she gave up work when she was, what, seven months pregnant?' She looked to Val.

'She couldn't hack being on her feet all evening, so she just gave it up. I think her mum probably wanted to get her out of here too. She could be a bit stuck up, you know?' said Carly.

'Oi,' jumped in Val, 'She's protective is all. I'd be the same if I was Shelley's mum, poor girl.'

'What do you mean?' asked Tabetha.

'Well, she was very sweet, but easily led. She had got in with a bad crowd or something before. Her mum's a friend of a friend, and I gave her the bar job as a favour. She was looking for something to keep her busy.'

'When was this?' asked Tabetha.

'Maybe eighteen months ago. She'd got into drugs as well, just some weed I think.' Val lowered her voice and Carly nodded enthusiastically. This was probably the most exciting thing that had happened around there in a while.

'She was meant to be in college, but her mum pulled her out to get her away from some boy she'd met there, was that it, Carly?' She looked to Carly who was still nodding, though less enthusiastically.

'Her mum even sent her to some summer camp or something,' Val went on. 'It sounded a bit like a rehab thing, with talks from ex druggies and the police and stuff – basically trying to scare kids into giving it all up before it got proper out of hand.'

'And then she came to work here?' asked Tabetha. Val nodded. 'And how's she been?'

'Fine. She wasn't the best barmaid, but she was good enough. Very quiet, pretty little thing. She seemed so young to me, but she was reliable.

'Then after a few months it turned out she'd got herself pregnant. The whole thing, the job and the camp, seemed like it had just been for show. Her mum went mad. She warned the boy off herself this time and kept a very close eye on Shelley. She'd drop her off here and pick her up, didn't she Carly?'

'Yeah, it used to drive Shell up the wall,' Carly nodded.

'So yesterday, she seemed well you said?' Tabetha looked back to Carly.

'Yeah, better than I expected. She was dreading having this baby, but it was so cute, and she was showing it off and everything...' Her voice trailed off.

'Yeah,' Val took up the thought, 'she looked very well. Quite dressed up too. She seemed... happy.'

We all went silent.

'God it's awful,' said Val eventually and she gave Carly a hug as the younger woman began to cry.

'I'm so sorry,' said Tabetha, wrapping things up. 'Thank you for speaking with us. I expect we'll need to speak to you again, but that's all for now. It might be me, or some of my colleagues, I hope that's okay,' said Tabetha, prepping them for the real police to come by. Val nodded.

Tabetha looked my way to indicate she'd be heading out. I finished up as quickly as possible and followed her out of the door. We stood for a minute at the front of the pub and I was just starting to say how sad it was that Shelley sounded so well that day, when someone appeared next to us. It was Carly, and she had dried her eyes rather quickly.

'Sorry, I just, I thought I'd try to catch you.' She looked behind her as if to check no one else had followed her.

'Look, it's common knowledge that Shelley never stopped seeing Tom, not really. Tom's her boyfriend. I just thought it might be important.' She leant in as if she was telling on a friend at school.

'Oh, okay, I see,' said Tabetha. 'Do you know him well?'

'Not really, I met him a couple of times at the pub and I haven't seen him in ages, but Shelley still spoke about him.

'She didn't want Val to know, as she knows Shelley's mum. They hated him.' She left a dramatic pause.

'Shelley always said he was a bit misunderstood. But I'm pretty sure he was dealing around here, and he never really had a proper job as far as I could tell. She really loved him though. She used to cry about him all the time.' She rolled her eyes and I was pretty sure they hadn't been such great friends after all. It was probably just the boys, clothes and gossip that kept them talking. Although, come to think of it, what else is there at nineteen?

'So, Shelley never broke it off at all?' asked Tabetha.

'I think she did when she first left college. Her mum kept her on a tight leash for months and then she got pregnant anyway!' she said it with a bit of a laugh. 'I don't know how he felt about the baby, I barely saw him the whole pregnancy. But he did turn up to check on her a couple of times before her mum picked her up at the end of her shift. Then I didn't see Shelley after the baby arrived really. Until yesterday, when she popped in. She seemed so happy when she came by.'

'Well, thanks for filling us in,' said Tabetha about to turn away.

'Was she off to meet up with him maybe?' I asked. It took Tabetha by surprise, but it felt like this girl knew more to me.

'Look he was a bit dodgy, but he wasn't a murderer if that's what you're getting at.' Carly paused, 'Was he? Oh my god, was it him? Should I have said something to Val about them still meeting up?' She looked more upset now that she thought she might get in trouble herself.

'Please don't worry. We are just doing early investigations, really. We've got a long way to go yet.' Tabetha stepped back in and gave her a bit of a pat.

'But, do you think they may have been meeting though?' I asked again gently. This time she responded.

'Maybe. She did look a bit dressed up and I kind of thought she was happy because they'd made back up for good.' She looked more thoughtful now, like the reality was setting in and the initial excitement was passing.

'That's really useful Carly, thanks so much for catching us.' I was pleased Tabetha had said 'us', not just 'me'.

'I don't suppose you know where we can find him?' Tabetha was speaking more softly now, moving into her best-friend mode, but I could hear the urgency. This was maybe the biggest lead yet.

'No, sorry. Her mum would know because she used to go around to his and drag Shelley home sometimes.'

Tabetha looked at me and I knew where our next stop would be.

It was time to face Shelley's mum.

CHAPTER THIRTEEN

We walked back up towards Shelley's road, where the police were swarming around. It looked like they were still doing door-to-doors, and a police car was now parked right outside the house. Our visit wasn't going to happen today.

We began to turn back, and I averted my eyes as we saw the police tent on the park again, where another was being erected a few metres away, like the beginnings of a summer camp from hell. I tried to think of something to say, but I felt empty. Tabetha filled the silence.

'Sounds like Tom is probably our best bet, but how would he fit with Mrs Nolan? I'll see if I can get any background.' I could see a woman heading towards us as we walked back down the hill again. She was looking right at me, as if she was thinking of saying something.

She looked in her mid-thirties, but I had the feeling she was probably younger. The only way to describe her was tough. Not scary, but a bit rough around the edges. Not someone you'd want to get in a fight with. She had on a long black faded cotton top over some black cropped leggings with lace bottoms and a pair of battered trainers. She wasn't quite a Jeremy Kyle guest, but maybe Judge Rinder.

I caught her eyes and could see she'd been crying. She was looking at me with some recognition and as I looked closer, I realised she did look a bit familiar.

'Are you a mate of Shelley's?' she asked directly as we were about to pass.

'Um, sort of, we were in her NCT class together,' I responded.

'Thought I'd seen you before, I came to one of them classes with Shell.' Her voice cracked as she said her name again.

'Oh yes, of course.' I tried to look like I'd recognised her, but if she hadn't said anything, I'm not sure I'd have been able to place her. I really hadn't paid much attention to Shelley, something that felt awful now. She seemed so different from me, so I just sort of blanked her out.

'I'm Kat, Shelley's sister.' Her voice cracked again as she said 'sister'.

'So you've heard about...' Her voice trailed off and she blinked hard.

'Yes, I'm so, so sorry.' I thought about stepping forward to hug her, but she didn't look like a hugger. Now I looked harder she did look similar to Shelley, but she was much more substantial, less fragile or vulnerable. I guessed she was the older sister; she had probably had to look out for Shelley a lot.

'How are you doing?' I immediately realised what a stupid question that was and before she could answer, I jumped in with a second go, 'Is there anything we can do?'

'The bloody police are still in with mum. I've had to take the kids over my mates for a bit, keep them out the way, you know?'

Tabetha stayed quiet. Kat was directing the conversation my way.

'I dunno what I'm meant to do now. What do I do?' she asked, more to herself than to me, I think. I stepped forward now and gave her the hug I'd been unsure about.

'I can't imagine how you're feeling,' I said as I held her.

She pulled away and I could see her physically shake herself trying to regain her composure.

'Sorry,' she said using both hands to wipe her face.

'There's no need to be sorry. It's just awful,' I said.

'What psycho would do this? Who would even want to...?' Her voice trailed off again and I could see her look over to the police tent.

'I'm Tabetha, I was in the same group with Shelley too.' Tabetha brought herself into the conversation. 'I'm so sorry. She was such a sweet girl.' I doubted Tabetha really had an opinion on her, but what do you say when someone's died. 'And she was going to bring up her baby all by herself, wasn't she? Well apart from you and your mum. I guess Tom will have to get more involved now?' Tabetha shook her head sadly.

'She told you about Tom then, did she?' asked Kat, looking surprised.

'Well not masses, but she mentioned they were sort of seeing each other again, that's right isn't it?' I could tell that while I'd been trying to think how best to comfort Kat, Tabetha had been thinking about getting the next piece of information she needed.

'They were always on and off, you know? Mum couldn't stand him, so Shell kept the whole thing secret. She was a right drama queen though, she loved it. Mind you, I don't think he knew what to do once she was pregnant. My mum warned him off again, but that hadn't stopped him before.

'He wanted to support the baby though. Had to respect him for that. I doubt mum'll want him anywhere near Alfie now. Ever.'

'Poor guy.' Tabetha shook her head again. 'Do you have an address for him, perhaps we could send a card or something to say how sorry we are?'

Kat didn't respond and when I looked back to her face, I could see she wasn't listening anymore. She was looking up the hill behind us intently.

'You can tell him yourself,' she said, 'he's just up there.' We looked behind us and a young man with a heavy black coat on was walking, head down, hood up towards us. As he looked up, I recognised him from all those weeks ago in the pub with Tabetha after class. He had a bunch of white flowers in his hand and I could see even from several meters away that his face was screwed up into a tight, worried knot.

'Tom!' Kat called out, 'Tom!' He looked in our direction just before he was about to turn down Shelley's road. He paused for a moment, obviously trying to decide whether to come down to join us or carry straight on. Neither were great options.

Eventually he walked towards us. He pulled his hood back and I could see him more clearly now. His dark hair was closely cropped, his face unshaven and a tattoo crept up his neck. I supposed he was good-looking, in a brooding way that young girls seemed to like, whatever the era.

'What the hell?' he asked Kat when he reached us, ignoring Tabetha and me completely.

'I know, I know. Have the police been round yours?' she asked.

'Yeah, first place they knocked. They think it's me, I can tell they think it's me, but it ain't, okay? I'm not lying.' He was obviously panicking.

'I'm so sorry Tom,' said Tabetha stepping forward. 'We were friends with Shelley from NCT, her baby class - I don't know if she spoke about it?'

Tom shook his head distractedly.

'It's such a shock, I can't imagine how you're feeling,' continued Tabetha, 'I know how close you guys were.'

'Is that what Shell was saying? It's not been like that since the baby come. That's what I told the police didn't I? I've not even seen her in the last couple of weeks, not properly.'

'Oh right, I didn't know. It's been hard with the new baby around?' Tabetha phrased it as a question, so he had to respond.

'Look, I know what everyone thinks of me, right. Like I'm a bad influence. Not just since the baby, from day one. Even when we first met and we was mad for each other, you know? Everyone wanted me out of the way. But like I told the police, she wasn't always whiter than white either.'

'Hey,' said Kat, stepping forward.

'I'm sorry, but you know it too – I always reckoned she was sleeping around. Maybe one guy, maybe all over the place, I don't know, but I know it was happening before and it was happening again. Ever since that baby arrived, she's been weird too. She started ignoring my messages, and she'd come off Facebook. Something was going on and she didn't want me to know.'

He sounded like a petulant teenager.

'You better shut your face,' said Kat in a quiet

and controlled voice, 'that was all a load of rubbish. She told you at the time and she'd say it again now... if she was still alive. But she isn't, so I'll have to do it for her.' She stepped forward again and I could feel the anger boiling.

At this point I pretty much wanted to hit the guy myself. Shelley was bringing up her baby alone, for God's sake, surely that gives anyone the excuse to be a little quiet on social media.

To his credit, Tom took a step back and held his hands up.

'I'm sorry. It's not the time I know. It's just the police... I can see it coming. They've got it in for me. They'd be quite happy for me to be put away for something, they don't care what.' He looked down at the floor and I could see from his jaw that he was grinding his teeth.

'Whatever happened, Shelley meant a lot to me, you know that.' He looked back up to meet Kat's gaze as he struggled to look her straight in the eye.

I listened closely to his tone. He seemed genuine. I thought back to the argument I'd witnessed back in the pub all those months ago though. The two of them obviously had some friction. What might he do in a moment of rage?

Kat looked at him, searching his face even. It seemed like she believed him, as she took a deep breath before responding, 'I know she did. I know.' She stepped forward and gave him a brief hug to make peace. It felt like she didn't have the fight today, and who could blame her?

'Just don't talk crap like that in front of me again, okay? Or my mum. If you ever want to see Alfie again, no rumours, no pointing fingers. She's gone now. There's no point.' She looked down to the ground as he nodded and glanced over towards the park.

'Come on, I better get back to mum.' Kat walked on past us and back towards her mum's house, with Tom following silently behind.

'God, that was intense,' I said as soon as they were out of earshot, before we finally continued back down the hill and away from this total nightmare.

We didn't speak much after Tom and Kat headed off. I gave Tabetha a tight hug as I left, but she only half-reciprocated. I could feel the tension in her body.

It felt like she was looking at this first as a mother, then as someone who knew Shelley, and finally as a detective. It must have been hard to feel all three responses at once.

I had mixed feelings about going back to my own home, but I was drained, and it was time to step back out of this detective fantasy gone sour.

I walked slowly back to mine while Tabetha took the bus back to hers. I was pleased to be alone, there was nothing to say really. Nellie looked up at me and waved her arms in that shaky, uncontrolled way all babies do. Occasionally she looked intently at one hand or the other, as if they'd appeared out of nowhere.

Babies really are amazing. It was strange though, sometimes it was like I had forgotten she was there and then she reappeared again. I couldn't really put it in to words. It was almost like she wasn't quite real yet for me. Was that normal? I don't know.

I thought of how Shelley's colleagues had spoken about her as a mum. She'd been showing off Alfie, proud of what she'd achieved and what she had to look forward to. It was like the baby would be the making of her, she'd gained a new purpose. Almost the mirror opposite of how I felt.

Maybe the difference was I'd already had a purpose, it had been my work. I hadn't really appreciated it at the time of course. But I hadn't yet accepted Nellie as my new purpose, and I wasn't even sure I wanted to.

I sat by the river at the end of the road and took Nellie out for a cuddle. She was soft and warm, and her skin was like spider's webs, hardly there at all. I gave her a feed and watched as her tiny eyes drooped closed. I had a brief surge of love for her. It had been one of those days when they were few and far between, but when it came it was still powerful.

I could feel the tears start again and I tried to hold them back so that they didn't fall onto Nellie. It didn't seem right for a pure baby like her to see adult tears let alone feel them. The back of my throat stung as I pushed my tongue up to stop crying. I listened to the quiet sounds of Nellie feeding and looked out into the river. It was still warm and bright, a perfect late summer's day. A boat of rowers went past, out-of-puff and pulling hard on the oars. They looked like friends, not sports people, a bit out of shape but still training together for the fun of it.

I approached my front door with a heavy heart. I mean that I actually felt heavier inside. It was harder to walk and to breathe and my brain was foggy with guilt. Twenty-four hours earlier I had been hoping for Tabetha to get back in touch and now I felt sick about it.

I put the key quietly in the door, pretending to myself it was to keep Nellie asleep in the buggy, not to avoid Dan. It didn't matter anyway as he appeared immediately with a big smile on his face, 'Ah, my girls are home!' He was eating a slice of bread without anything on it as he came over, which meant he had only just got in and was starving.

'Well hand her over. How has she been?' he said, taking the buggy after stuffing the last bit of bread into his mouth. He parked it up and looked inside.

'Ah, she's sleeping!' he said, then reached in to take her out anyway. He carefully placed her over his shoulder and quietly cuddled her little form and kissed her cheek. He sighed happily.

He didn't seem to notice I was still standing

in the doorway as he started to walk around the dining room humming a little tune. Then he looked back up and clocked me.

'You alright?' he said almost with a laugh.

'No, I'm not,' I answered quietly. 'Do you remember Shelley from NCT?' I asked.

'Yeah - that young one with her mum. I didn't think you'd kept in touch with her?' he asked casually, still oblivious to the bomb about to drop.

'She's dead,' I said, as I walked past him and into the kitchen. I grabbed a large glass and poured a big, strong squash. I was suddenly horribly thirsty and hot.

'She's what? What did you say? She's dead?' He followed me, urgent and confused.

'She's been killed, and Tabetha has been getting these letters, and it sounds like it's all connected, but we don't know how. And that poor little boy.' I put the glass down and lent over the sink not sure if I was going to be sick.

Dan laid the buggy back flat and put Nellie quickly but carefully inside before coming over to me.

'Right, you need to sit down and tell me what's happened, okay?' he said, leading me over to the sofa.

I turned to him and started to bawl on his shoulder. We sat for a while as I cried, and then for a little longer in silence. He could tell I needed a moment and showed more restraint than I would in the same situation. Finally, he pulled away and held me softly by my shoulders, 'Tell me what's happened, from the beginning.'

I must have talked non-stop for nearly an hour. I started from when Tabetha had received the first letter at the NCT meet-up and all the way through to leaving Kat and Tom to head home. I didn't get into all my stupid relationship stuff that had happened too; I wasn't ready for that and it seemed so trivial now, but I covered the murders start to finish.

He didn't say a word as I spoke, just nodded when needed, raised his eyebrows or shook his head in shock. And it was shocking, the whole thing.

When I got to the end, I looked at him and said, 'What do you think, it's crazy isn't it?'

'It is crazy, it's...' he shook his head again as his voice trailed off. 'Was there a reason you didn't tell me about what was going on?' he looked at me with his eyes dark. He didn't seem angry, just a bit sad.

'I don't know,' I said and looked away. I felt bad, but also embarrassed as I couldn't really explain it myself.

'It was all a bit exciting at first and something just for me I suppose, that was all.' I looked back up at him. 'But it's not exciting right now, that poor girl and her poor little boy.' I gulped back more tears.

'It's okay, it's okay,' said Dan giving me another hug. 'To be honest this explains things for me. You've seemed so distant, but I get it now.' He squeezed me and then pulled away to look me in the eye. This was typical Dan, maybe typical man, he was always happy to find a simple solution.

'So, what do we need to do now?' he asked, moving the conversation on, which I was more than happy to do.

'I guess we should send some flowers to her family and find out about the funeral,' I said, trying to think clearly.

'I meant about us. Are we potential targets?' asked Dan.

I hadn't even thought of that. Not for a second. But he was right. Were we targets now?

'Oh god, I don't know.' I was trying not to panic, but it was hard to control.

'You know what? There is no point thinking about it tonight. It sounds like if anything is going to happen, Tabetha will be the first to know.' He could obviously see I was panicked and wanted to roll back that thought.

'Look, don't take this the wrong way, but you look terrible. You've had a massive shock. You need to get some sleep, clear your head and then we can talk about it again in the morning and put a plan of action in place, okay?' he hugged me close again and stroked my hair as I heard Nellie start to squeal from her buggy.

'Have you fed her recently?' he asked, and I

nodded. 'Great - I'll sort her, you go to bed, okay?' I didn't usually like it when Dan got all bossy with me. But tonight, I needed it, and he was right. I really did just want to collapse into bed.

I pulled off my clothes quickly and crawled under the covers. Pulling them over my head to keep out the noise of Nellie quietly crying as Dan tried to put her down. I closed my eyes tight. My mind swam, and I thought for a second how I would never fall asleep, then suddenly I did.

It was pitch black when I next woke, and Dan was asleep next to me. I'd lost the whole evening. I could hear Nellie moaning through the monitor. I sat up quickly and took a gulp of air. It was a warm night. I could feel my heart pumping and the hair at the nape of my neck was damp with sweat. I'd been having a nightmare. I couldn't quite remember it, like a word on the tip of my tongue.

I blinked hard and lay back down as I listened to Nellie settling. I had been trying to leave her to 'self soothe', whatever that meant, and on the very odd occasion it did work.

I reached into my mind to try to find the dream and caught some glimpses. Walking across the park pushing the pram on a warm summer's day. Footsteps running. Evening in the park now. Dark and cold. Somebody singing, then someone coming from behind. I didn't want to remember the rest.

I picked up my phone, it was 12.45am, but this wouldn't wait. I messaged Tabetha:

> Are we in danger? Should we talk to the police again?

I put my phone back down on my bedside table and lay back onto my pillow, not expecting a response. In seconds the phone bleeped, Tabetha was awake too.

> Don't worry. Called Toby. He's organising a meeting with us all tomorrow. Get some sleep, T

I lay back down and closed my eyes, now I could sleep again. Then Nellie screamed out angrily.

Self-soothing, my arse.

❖ ❖ ❖

Natalie looked at the paper. It was front page of course, and there was that familiar face looking out at her, holding Alfie, smiling.

In the photo, Shelley looked happy, clean, bright – like she had everything to live for.

She hadn't looked like that the last time Natalie had laid eyes on her...

She opened the calendar in her phone, pulled up the details for yesterday's appointment and hastily deleted the meeting.

She couldn't get back out of bed. She'd made it to the local shop but that was probably it for today. It was difficult to understand how she felt. Confused. Angry. Sick.

She pulled the duvet over her head and closed her eyes tight shut.

CHAPTER FOURTEEN

The next day was Saturday and despite my early night, I still felt that sick sort of tired where your head is foggy, and your limbs feel like sodden towels. I closed my eyes tight, then opened them as I sat bolt upright as if powering myself to get back up to start another day.

I could see my WhatsApp NCT group flashing as people had heard about Shelley's death. Tabetha had messaged first thing.

> Meetup Hyde Park Community Hall 10am.
> Police coming to brief us on Shelley and answer any questions. RSVP.

I responded straight away to say I'd be there.

The hall was cold, dank and dreary. Despite windows along each side, it was dark and shadowed. A large, old and worn poster proudly stated it could be booked for birthday parties or weddings, but I couldn't imagine any amount of organza and bunting could brighten it up.

Dan held the door as I wheeled in the buggy, I was glad he was there with me today. Sometimes it was better not to go it alone. The room was already busy as we entered. Priya and Anil were both there with Shay, chatting intensely with Tabetha. Fay had come alone and was talking with Derek, the Chief Superintendent, by a kettle where some tea and a large multipack of the cheapest-looking biscuits were laid out. The ones that taste like ninety percent sugar.

Nellie had woken up, and I took her out of her buggy and started a feed, Dan's arm protectively over the back of my chair. Tabetha came to the front of the room looking at her watch. I tried to catch her eye, but she didn't look my way.

'Hi everyone, thanks for coming. I know this is very different to our usual meet up, and it's a worrying time for us all.' Tabetha spoke in that professional detective tone she had when we'd been to the station. The room vibrated with murmurs and she let the noise settle before speaking again. 'I've asked along colleagues from St Anne's police today to talk us through what's happened and what is going to happen next. They can also answer any questions you may have.' She indicated for Toby to come to the front. As usual, I felt a twinge of embarrassment seeing him. He didn't look my way, but I still felt a little awkward with Dan's arm around me.

As he began to speak, a clatter came from the back and he paused as Nina pushed her ginormous tank of a buggy in through the doors. She bent down to shush into the hood where screaming could be heard. Behind her was her harassed-looking husband.

'Sorry, sorry, sorry – she had an enormous poo just before we meant to leave,' said Nina with an apologetic grimace at Toby.

'No problem at all, please, take a seat.' He pointed to some spare seats left in the three short rows in front of him.

Nina and Alek clattered through the room and spoke in low unintelligible Bulgarian as they lifted their giant, well-fed baby out of the buggy and sat down. The baby finally stopped screaming as Nina bunged her on the boob and I could see her sigh, relieved to have settled her.

Toby started again. 'First off, I just wanted to say how very sorry we are for your loss. Shelley's death has come as a complete shock to the whole community and you must be feeling this very hard. I know this is an extremely sad time for you all.' He paused as we all looked down in sombre acknowledgment. 'Secondly I want to reassure you that we have our best guys working on this flat-out to find out who was responsible and why.

'We are following a range of leads and we also have more officers walking the local area to ensure the safety of everyone in St Anne's and beyond.' He spoke confidently and clearly. I guess part of the job is being able to simply reassure people.

Derek stepped forward next. He spoke with that deep, comforting avuncular way he had, like you could trust him with anything. You would never guess he'd already overlooked several major clues during the investigation. He was reassuring and confident and it made me squirm. I saw him quite differently from that first meeting now.

He gave a whistle-stop tour of where things had got to. There had been two deaths so far and they were being investigated as connected. He described how the police had received some warning of the murders connecting the two but mentioned nothing of Tabetha's involvement. I wasn't sure if that was at her request, but I was relieved for her. The way the room felt, buzzing with tension and fear, you wouldn't want to be on the receiving end of the questioning right now.

Derek spoke very practically, with dates, names and locations at the forefront. I think he was trying not to fuel any panic in the room, but that was going to be hard.

Then his expression changed, and he said with more concern in his voice, 'We have some reason to believe that there may be a connection to motherhood, and local mothers in particular.' He must have been referencing the Mum's Diary baby guides, which we now knew were being used as a sort of calling card. As well as the motherhood connection between Mama Nolan, Shelley and of course Tabetha who had received the notes.

Murmuring rippled around the room.

'What are you saying - we could be targets, we could be in danger?' asked Priya, straight to the point as ever.

'We have absolutely no indication that anyone in this room is a target. However, we would be foolish to ignore the fact that you are uniquely linked to both of the victims. There is the potential that these incidents are the beginnings of a series of crimes.'

'Well that sounds pretty dangerous to me,' continued Priya looking around the room for support. Her husband put a hand out to calm her, but she batted it away and continued.

'So, what do we do? Are you going to do anything to protect us?' she asked.

'As we said, there are more officers on the beat than ever, and we are working round the clock to catch whoever is responsible. We are also confident that we will receive a warning before he tries anything again. This is his pattern and experience tells me he'll stick to it,' he said with confidence.

'In the meantime, please continue to practise the usual precautions. Lock your doors, avoid anyone acting suspiciously and call us if you have any concerns. Anything at all. But, as we aren't going to go public with the full details right now, please practise discretion.

'That brings me to the other reason we wanted to gather you, to warn you that local media are probably going to show a lot of interest in this. Please, please do not engage with them. We want to be careful how much we share and how much may be picked up by whoever is involved in these crimes.' It hadn't even crossed my mind that the press might be interested in this, it made sense though. Young mother, local angle, no suspects, it was probably what editors prayed for.

'We don't want any information to either fuel the person responsible or push them further to ground. But there's also a balance, as sharing some information may well draw out people who know things; people who might otherwise not come forward,' he explained.

'With that in mind, we would also like a quick chat with each of you today. These will not be formal interviews, but a chance for you to flag any concerns or thoughts you have on this matter with us now. Before we do that though, any final questions?' he asked, with a look that suggested he hoped there wouldn't be any.

The room hummed, and questions continued for thirty minutes. What was in the warnings? How was Shelley killed? Did they have any suspects yet?

Mostly he answered that they couldn't comment, and I realised just how much more information I had simply from being involved through Tabetha. I could feel the frustration in the room, and I was pleased when they broke us into our couples for a chat each with an officer.

Our interviewer was a young man who looked like he could have been on work experience. His uniform looked a little too big and he struggled to keep eye contact with us, as if he wasn't used to speaking to real grown-ups. But then it was a small local force and they probably had to put everyone available on the case.

There wasn't much Dan and I could offer. We hadn't known the first victim at all, and we'd barely known Shelley. It was hard to answer some questions where my answer might drop Tabetha in it with her work, but luckily sexism made it much easier for me to stay quiet as our male officer tended to direct the questions more at Dan than me. I nodded or fussed with Nellie whenever it seemed I might drift into a question I didn't want to answer.

The truth of it was I had met a few potential suspects, maybe even the killer. There were the two witnesses from Mrs Nolan's murder, her husband, and even Tom, Shelley's boyfriend. But I assumed all of them were on their radar.

After the meeting ended, Toby headed my way and I could feel my body tense. There was just a flicker of embarrassment behind his eyes, he almost looked a little shy. But after a quick check behind him that Dan was over with the dads, his face softened and he spoke quietly and quickly. 'Are you okay?' he asked. I nodded and we exchanged a half smile. The bustle of the room disappeared as we chatted quickly about the case and the hope it would be wrapped up soon. Nothing about what had happened before, that was closed now for both of us.

'Can I just check in on a few things, officer?" came Priya's voice to break the moment as she marched our way, with her baby over her shoulder. He took a deep breath and raised his eyes to the ceiling, before turning away from me to her. Half his job must be reassuring people.

As he headed over to Priya I looked around for Tabetha to see if we could have a bit of a debrief before we got back on with our own investigations.

But she was gone.

I didn't hang around to discuss everything with the other girls, I just wanted to head straight home and wait for Tabetha to call, which I was sure she would.

But she didn't. That day, or the next day, and I realised that disappearing was obviously her thing.

The next two weeks I tried to get back into my routine that had worked before, but this time around I couldn't even take that on. As the days passed, it was a push just to get out of bed when Dan left for work.

Luckily Nellie was starting to take more of an

interest in things around her, and I continued to spend a lot of the day moving her between various locations as she wriggled around and looked about above her or held a kitchen implement from the box of random objects I'd put together. It was like running a tiny little baby amusement park.

Dan suggested I met up with my old gang, but I felt so out of the loop it seemed pointless. I didn't know what they were doing, they didn't know what I was doing, why bother? I avoided the flashing numbers on my Facebook and WhatsApp messages.

But I was following social media, in fact, more than ever. Watching as my old friends posted party pics and soppy kisses at drunken weddings, or the NCT ladies put up idyllic-looking days out with the babies, strolling around gardens in the sunshine, smiling, laughing, looking lovingly at one another. Others had titles such as #datenight, with couples leaning in to shot at a smart restaurant table clinking champagne flutes.

I made sure I got some of my own too. Me and Dan with a glass of wine on the sofa "Finally she's asleep! #Shhhh!", a selfie with Nellie in the garden "Happy days!", Nellie grimacing in a polka dot baby grow, "I've got a present for you mummy! #nappydays". What a total fraud.

I followed anything to do with the case, and it was really picking up interest. The photos of Shelley the press had collected from friends and school from when she was younger fascinated me. Some showed her with over-straightened highlights and school skirt rolled up as far as possible without flashing her knickers. Then there were the photos with friends at the summer camp, all looking a bit sulky with way too much eyeliner and enormous overdrawn eyebrows, undertaking wholesome activities like kayaking and abseiling. Finally, there were the more recent images of her, probably the ones her family had hoped would be used, looking smart and happy, holding Alfie proudly, like a real young mum.

The press loved the idea of this 'bad girl done good' story line. Becoming a mum seemed to have cleansed her of her past identity. If she'd died a couple of years ago, it wouldn't have been half as interesting. Now she was a local young mum who'd turned her life around, cut down in her prime.

The more recent pictures were often shared by locals talking about how lovely she was, how smart and beautiful. I doubted they'd ever met her.

Then they started covering the motherhood angle with more fervour. Two murders had been connected, and although no mention of Tabetha's letters yet, they had picked up on the baby book calling card.

Yes, Mama Nolan had no children of her own,

but she was a well-known mother figure and supporter of all the mummy groups coming in and out of her centre. And Shelley was the young mum with everything to live for.

Then about a week in, carefully chosen photos of Tom looking like a total thug, face grimaced and eyes shadowed began to be sprinkled across the articles.

He didn't do any interviews and was probably being advised to keep a low profile. But his lack of comment and the sinister photos of him coming in and out of various pubs and grubby looking flats painted a picture of someone you could imagine getting a bit too physical with his girlfriend. Theories of him being jealous of the attention Alfie was getting from Shelley were shared by 'anonymous friends' and stories of his anger at her friendship with other men swirled around too.

I still had mixed feelings about him since our meeting, but he was probably the front runner as far as I could tell. Why he'd want to attack Mrs Nolan though, made no sense at all, and why the letters to Tabetha? I wished I could speak with her and find out what she thought.

A second week began and still no Tabetha. I kept pushing on. Tidy the house, change the baby, feed the baby, try to sleep, tidy the house, change the baby, feed the baby, try to sleep...

Dan was heading into work early again and often home late, so I didn't even have to try to hide from him, it was easy just to avoid any real conversations. He grabbed Nellie when he could and was happy just to have some food bunged down in front of him with a peck on the cheek. As far as he was concerned, we were just busy young parents. He didn't have the time or the headspace to think about things in too much depth, let alone discuss them with me. And that suited me.

As the nights began to draw in, the leaves turned from green to yellow to brown and cute woollen hats appeared in the shop, I realised all of a sudden that Nellie wasn't such a tiny little thing anymore. She was three months old now, and I couldn't believe it.

Just seventeen years and nine months to go.

CHAPTER FIFTEEN

It was Wednesday again, and I'd decided to skip the mum meetup for another week. I was sitting in my usual spot in front of the telly with Nellie out of sight but safe on the playmat, when there was a knock at the door which made me jump.

Immediately I was brought back to the last time I had an unexpected visitor and Tabetha had appeared back into my life.

I stood up quickly and checked in the mirror above the fireplace. I hadn't looked in it today, maybe not yesterday either, or the day before. It was quite a shock when I saw myself. My hair looked lank, my jaw line was dotted with spots and my face looked sort of puffy. Even my eyes looked strange. A bit grey, or maybe just sad. I wasn't sure. I quickly tucked my hair behind my ears to neaten up a little and went to the door.

I plastered on a smile and opened up apprehensively. But it wasn't Tabetha standing there. I took a quick intake of breath as Toby came into view, eyes down at his phone to compose a message. He looked up with a nervous smile, which changed to that look of concern I'd seen before. It obviously wasn't just in my head that I was looking terrible.

'Hi. You okay?' he asked.

'Yeah, yeah,' I tried to sound casual, 'just knackered, baby's been up all night... again!' I said with a little laugh. 'Thank god she's cute!' I followed up with a forced smile.

'Sorry to drop by unannounced like this. Do you mind if we have a chat?' he asked, his eyes half lowered, testing the water. I paused for a second, and he looked up and inside the door, as if hankering after an invite.

'Of course,' I said honestly, it actually was good to see someone. I led him into the kitchen, hastily clearing away some empty mugs and picking up a sponge to wipe down the side, as he took a seat at the breakfast bar.

'Cuppa?' I said getting down the teabags and he nodded.

'Sorry I'm such a state,' I said, as I caught a fuzzy reflection in the chrome kettle. 'I wasn't expecting visitors. Sometimes it's just nice to sit in with Nellie and have some one-to-one time at home, you know?' And suddenly I remembered I'd left Nellie back in the other room. Casually I walked past Toby back to the front room and grabbed her from the floor, rocking her like a good mum as I walked back into the kitchen.

He reached out to take her for a cuddle while I finished making the tea and I handed her over gladly.

'Any new leads in the case? Is that why you are here?' I asked.

'No, quite the opposite I'm afraid. Nothing. If anything, I feel like we are further from the solution than ever.' His voice sounded defeated, but he put on a smile for Nellie as he lifted her in the air.

'Oh no. I was hoping things had gone a bit quiet, you know with Tabetha, because stuff was kicking off, not slowing down.' I dropped her name in quickly to see if he knew anything about her whereabouts.

'Ah, so you haven't been in touch with her either then?' he asked.

'No, not in a couple of weeks. But then it can be like that when you are a mum, time just disappears!' I laughed as I lied.

'I'm going to put my cards on the table Emily. I'm stuck, and I need some fresh eyes. Tabetha wanted to be involved first off, and clearly there's some link with her, or NCT, or someone she knows. I don't know. But I think we pushed her away too quickly, too early.' He shook his head as he tipped Nellie over his shoulder.

'I was hoping to maybe get her back on side.'

'I don't know, she was pretty frustrated about being side-lined,' I replied. I'd been theorising that was one of the reasons she'd stepped away from me and the case.

'I said that to Derek. I have a feeling me crawling back now might just rile her more. But there's something we are missing, and my feeling is Tabetha holds the key, even if she doesn't know it.'

'So, what's your plan?' I asked.

'Well I thought you might have an idea of how to approach this, you guys are such good friends?' I turned away to pour the kettle and rolled my eyes to myself. I had thought so too, not long ago.

I don't know if it was having someone new round for the first time in a while, or the positive energy Toby just seemed to give off, but suddenly I found myself offering to help.

'Look, why don't I pop round there and see what's what?' I said, and his eyes lit up.

'That would be amazing! If you could just put the idea out there, maybe say we'd bumped into each other? And don't be afraid to use some flattery! Honestly, at this point I'll do anything to find a fresh lead,' he said.

I nodded as if this was an easy ask. The thought of seeing her filled me with a mix of dread and excitement. Maybe this was what I needed?

Then I realised I didn't even know where she lived.

'This is going to sound crazy, but I've never actually been to hers - you know, we're more ladies that lunch! Do you have her address?' I tried to make light of it.

He passed Nellie back to me and took out a notepad, copied out an address on a new page and ripped it out.

'I really appreciate this, Emily, if you just smooth the way a bit that would be so useful.'

And with that he picked up his tea and we moved on, chatting more about parenthood and what Toby had in store. Although it was hard to take my mind off of what I'd just agreed to, and when I pushed the door closed a few minutes later, my heart was beating hard in my chest.

I jumped straight into the shower, put on a bit of makeup and a favourite dress to give me some strength. I checked myself over in the mirror and decided I looked almost normal and would pass in the real world.

Only an hour or so after Toby had left, I was standing across the road from Tabetha's address. It was a smart street, really smart now I looked around. Her house looked Victorian or Edwardian, double-fronted red brick with large sash windows. The door had beautiful stained glass in an organic pattern and original green and blue tiles around the entrance. It was beautifully looked after. I'd imagined her in a modern flat or maybe a quirky cottage, this seemed much more traditional, and almost grand.

I wondered if she would be as nervous about seeing me if things were the other way around.

Or maybe she had no idea how I was feeling. Maybe our friendship just wasn't a big deal to her, and I had simply dropped off the radar like some people do now and then.

Then another solution occurred to me. Perhaps something else was going on. She was ill or something awful had happened, like a family member had passed away suddenly and she'd had to drop everything. I began to feel a bit guilty for how I'd been feeling. What if I'd made it all about me, when it wasn't?

I lingered across the road, plucking up the courage to cross over and beginning to think through what tone I should use to say 'hi' and what expression to take when she came to the door. Concern was probably the safest way to go.

I was just about to cross over when the front door opened. Two people stepped out onto the tiled pathway into the sun and I got my first glimpse of Tabetha. She didn't look ill, or sad, she was smiling broadly, laughing even. She looked more relaxed than I'd ever seen her, with velvety looking moccasins on her feet and her hair pulled back with an Alice band. She looked softer than usual as she leant against the door frame, holding Luca tenderly in her arms. She said a few words. It seemed like she was seeing off the other person. I looked to see who she was talking to and immediately recognised the woman from Costa all those weeks ago. I could see her more clearly from this angle.

Today she was more smartly dressed in a dark blue trouser suit with a shirt lined with thin pink stripes. I could tell she was a little older than I'd previously thought, maybe late forties, early fifties. She laughed back at Tabetha, and carefully took Luca in her arms giving him a big kiss and a cuddle as if to say goodbye. She reached back inside the door and pulled out a medium sized travel case on wheels and something small, probably keys, from the table by the door.

She indicated into the road and I could see a car waiting with someone inside. The engine started up as she waved. It looked like a cab waiting to pick her up.

She pantomimed a sad face to the baby and handed him back to Tabetha then leaned in, hugged her and kissed her full on the lips. Not a quick friend peck, or a European-style double-cheek kiss. But a loving, caring kiss of a partner saying goodbye.

I can't explain it, but I felt tears sting my eyes. I tried to turn away but as they both turned towards the taxi for her to leave, I saw Tabetha clock me and there was no escaping.

She looked a bit embarrassed, then pulled herself together and beckoned me over.

I delayed a bit by checking for something imaginary in the baby bag to make sure the other woman had gone and then crossed the road, trying to smile, but probably showing more of a grimace.

'What are you doing here?' she asked smiling, as if nothing had happened.

'I've come to speak to you about the case, see if you had any new ideas.' My voice sounded strange.

'Ah, okay. Come in.' She continued to smile and led me inside, but I knew her, she'd have picked up on every tiny crack as I spoke.

'Do you want a coffee, or a tea?' she asked as we came inside, and she popped Luca onto an expensive-looking play mat with various lights and sounds and crinkly toys. He ignored them all and just lay there kicking his legs in the same way he would have done on a five-pound mat from Wilko.

'Coffee please,' I said on autopilot as I parked up the buggy in a quiet corner and looked around. The place was immaculate, and full of expensive things. On the walls were original pieces of abstract art and black and white photos of New York and Paris. I had to admit it all looked a little pretentious, which wasn't how I thought of Tabetha. I continued through the living room to a large kitchen with gleaming white cupboards and dark granite surfaces. She put some capsules in a black, shiny coffee machine on the side and it started to whir.

I looked around the room and could see a large canvas print of Tabetha with the woman from outside, treated with an Instagram-ready retro filter. Tabetha looked a little younger and fresher. It was a great selfie, with a temple or something in the background, sunlight streaming across their beaming faces. It wasn't a recent photo. I stood in front of it for a second and when I turned, I realised Tabetha was watching me.

'Thailand, on honeymoon.' She said it confidently but there was something a little brittle in the tone.

I looked again at the picture then back to her and realised I really didn't know her at all. We weren't friends, not really. I was suddenly furious.

'So, I'm confused,' I said, as an invitation for her to explain what was going on.

'Look, you were the one who assumed I was a single mum,' she said, as if that explained everything.

'Excuse me?' My voice rose.

'I'm a very private person. I don't have to tell every Tom, Dick and Harry everything about myself the first time we meet.' Her expression had changed, and she was looking at me with daggers, as if *I'd* done something wrong.

'Oh, okay. It's just I thought we were friends?' I asked. She shrugged.

'I told you about my life,' I said, 'you've met my husband, you've been to my house, you've... I've been honest with you,' I continued.

She shook her head and looked away. She didn't even look like the Tabetha I knew.

'I don't get it.' I tried again.

'I don't have to explain myself to you, or anyone.' She took the two coffees out of the machine and brought one over for me.

'No, I realise that. You don't *have* to do anything,' I said. We sat in silence in a bit of a stand-off. I considered whether to just walk out, but I didn't even have the strength for that. Then she looked up and I thought she was going to apologise or explain at least.

'Look, you can't come here talking about being honest when you have been lying to me for weeks.' She looked not just defensive now, but angry.

'Excuse me?' I asked, shocked.

She sighed. 'I didn't want to do this Emily, it's not my place to question what you do. But you've arrived here basically interrogating me and I can't just be attacked and not say anything.' She looked at me almost pitying.

'I haven't come here to interrogate you at all. In fact, I came here for someone else. Toby asked me and stupidly I thought it might be a good idea.' Now Tabetha was rolling her eyes at me and gave a chuckle.

'What?' I asked.

'Of course, he is involved. That's what I'm talking about. You. And Toby.' She looked me in the eye as if it was my turn to speak. I just looked back open mouthed. Eventually she spoke again.

'I get it, it's obvious things aren't right with

you and Dan, but Toby? Do you know what a difficult position that has put me in. I've had to step away from you, do you understand?' she asked.

'Tabetha, I have no idea what you are talking about,' I said. She rolled her eyes again.

'I've seen you together, in town,' she said pointedly.

'In that cafe? I bumped into him for God's sake, he was consoling me after I'd seen you out with her,' I indicated the giant canvas on the wall. 'I really needed someone,' I spat, 'and you had said you were out of town, remember? We were just talking,' I explained, furious.

'No, not in a cafe. You were in that bit of park, tucked away behind the Old Town Hall by the river. I was late for our NCT catch up, and when I spotted you on my way, I was foolishly about to go over to you. And, well, you weren't just talking, let's put it that way.'

I was about to respond, but I couldn't. I had no idea anyone had been there.

'As I say, it's not for me to tell you what to do, but it makes everything very difficult, you know?' She spoke more calmly now. I didn't look up. I couldn't look her in the eye.

'That was the only time we met up alone, after the cafe I mean,' I said quietly into my coffee.

'That's what I'd hoped, so when Shelley was killed, I came back. I thought I'd give you the benefit of the doubt that it was a one off. Then at the briefing with the police, there you were again at the end, the two of you having a cosy little chat in the corner. I could see it was more than that,' she said.

'No, no, we were just talking, that was all. We both said straight off it was a mistake, a moment of madness. Not that it really was anything anyway.' I felt so stupid now. All this time she'd been thinking I'd been keeping some big thing from her, when it was nothing at all.

She put her hands up as if to say I didn't need to explain any more, but she didn't speak, and I felt I had to give more before we could move on.

'I was confused when you disappeared. I didn't get it, and then I bumped into him in that cafe and it turned out we both needed somebody to talk to. He just understood, and he listened,' I said.

'And then he left me his card when he went, and I didn't expect to use it. But you didn't reappear for days, then weeks, and... and... it was just nice to have a little bit of attention just for me.'

Tabetha let out a snort.

'It was, I didn't want anything more,' I said, although I couldn't be certain. 'Do you know how he's feeling about the new baby coming?' Tabetha shook her head a little. 'Well he's panicking. He feels like I do. That he's not cut out for it, like he might let everyone down.' I tried to explain myself.

'We were both feeling a bit lonely and...' I drifted off. 'We haven't met up since, until he stopped by this morning to ask me to come here. If you hadn't seen it, I don't think it would ever have come up again. And it shouldn't need to affect our friendship,' I said.

I looked up, but she didn't look ready to accept my sort of apology yet.

'People don't surprise me often, I told you that when we first met. But you have, and I don't know what to make of it.' Her head cocked to one side like it had that first time we'd really connected in the pub, when she'd told me I was interesting, and I'd thought we were going to be great friends.

'I'm sorry, it's hard to explain how it feels to be me to someone like you,' I said quietly, and could see from her expression that was not the right thing to say.

'Someone like me?' she asked, sounding a little offended.

'You have it all together don't you, nothing worries you. You don't care what people think. You aren't affected by anything. Everything comes easy to you.' Suddenly I could hear how childish it sounded, but it was how I felt. Then she laughed a little. I looked up, shocked.

'Please, please don't laugh at me,' I said, with tears in my eyes.

'Emily, it doesn't all come easy, and I do care

what people think. Why do you think I didn't tell you about Claire?' she asked.

'I don't know - because we aren't as close as I thought? You said it yourself.'

'It's not that. You had this picture of me, and I didn't want to wreck it. You seemed a bit in awe of me. I felt stupid I hadn't corrected you straight off, and maybe I liked you thinking I was some sort of super woman. The pregnancy, leaving work, then the baby, they all chipped away at me a bit.'

I'd been furious that she'd kept part of her life from me, but I'd done the same. Neither of us had wanted to upset the particular mum roles we'd chosen to play, or perhaps others had given to us. I thought back to the first conversation we'd had. She'd said everyone was like a playing card, just one in a pack. We'd obviously been trying to hide which card we'd been, which character we were playing. Maybe I hadn't spoken honestly, really honestly since back then before babies. That confidence to show my hand had gone. It was like the pack had been shuffled and I wasn't even sure what suit I was anymore.

'I hadn't realised how close we'd get,' she said apologetically. 'It wasn't part of my planning. But having someone I could rely on through all this has been important to me.' I was surprised by her honesty.

'Me too,' I said. 'Having a baby sounds like the most natural thing in the world, but it's been the hardest, loneliest thing I've ever done.'

For a second, I felt relief that she felt it too. Then I had a realisation. If even Tabetha didn't have it completely together, what hope was there for me?

She could see the fear in my eyes because she leant in and said, 'But we've done it, haven't we? And you are doing great.'

She sat back again with a half-smile of reassurance. I wanted to just say thanks and move on. Like I had to Toby, to Dan, to my mum, everyone who told me how well I was doing when I tried to explain how hard it all was.

But I had an overwhelming feeling that I couldn't do that anymore. Tears started silently rolling down my cheeks, great big embarrassing tears.

'Do you know what, I'm not doing great,' I said and couldn't help but laugh at how silly this seemed. Sitting in someone's house for the first time, someone it turned out I didn't know very well at all, and properly letting go.

'I'm tired, I'm so, so, so tired Tabetha. I can't even explain how tired.' I looked her in the eye.

'I know, it's hard, and when they go through those phases of not sleeping it can be torture,' Tabetha replied, with a nod of solidarity.

'No, it's not just that,' I said forcefully with a shake of my head. Now I'd started, I really wanted to explain it right. 'I mean that bit's awful, and it's not a phase with Nellie, she has never slept, never.' I looked up to Tabetha and really tried to get across with my eyes what I was trying to tell her. 'But that's not the worst part, it's more than just lack of sleep, it's...' I tried to think of the words and Tabetha gave a little nod to push me.

'It's just so absolutely sick-to-my-stomach exhausting trying to pretend to everybody twenty-four hours a day that I'm not utterly miserable. And I don't mean feeling a bit sad or angry or resentful, although I do feel all those things, but I mean waking up every day, realising where I am, and feeling a knot tighten in my stomach. A heavy, horrible, scratchy knot I want to reach inside and pull out with my bare hands.

'It's a feeling that makes it seem almost impossible some mornings that I'll be able to force myself out of bed to pick up my own child.' I looked at Tabetha and could imagine she must be disgusted with me, just like I was.

But she simply asked quietly, 'How long have you felt like this?'

'I don't know, on and off since about five minutes after I brought the baby home,' I said indicating Nellie with a laugh.

'That perfect little gorgeous baby who ninety percent of the time I just wish would go away and leave me alone,' I said and could see Tabetha did look shocked now.

'And that look is exactly why I haven't told anyone. Because I'm a horrible, ungrateful person and I hate myself for it. And I don't want anyone to know that I just want all this to stop, so I can go back to being me.'

'If I look shocked, that's because I am,' said Tabetha. 'But not because I'm judging you, just because you've hidden it so well. I had no idea you felt so strongly. I've been so focused on the case and then on this stupid thing with Toby.' She reached forward and took my hand.

'I kept hoping it's a phase,' I said, 'and I've kept on pushing through, forcing myself up, making myself go out, doing the stupid bloody mantras and I've had some moments of real joy and then it's just... gone again. Completely gone and I don't know how long I can carry on. I really don't.'

As the words left my mouth, I realised I meant it: something had to change.

'Look at me Emily,' said Tabetha, taking both my hands and looking me in the eye.

'You can carry on, you will carry on and we will all help you to.' She said it with that confidence I still loved. 'But first off. You need to lie down and sleep.' She took my hand and stood me up.

'Now?' I said, shocked, as I wiped my hot, tear-stained face.

'Yes, now.' Tabetha led me into a second smaller living room, a 'snug' I suppose you'd call it. A soft-looking velvety sofa was along one wall and she lay me down and covered me over with a blanket which had been neatly folded at one end. It smelt expensive and felt like heaven.

'I won't be able to sleep. I haven't been able to this past couple of weeks since it got really bad, even when Nellie finally does, I'm just awake, I can't explain it. I've been trying.' I protested even as I lay down. It was true, I really hadn't slept properly in weeks, my brain was whirring, it was like a constant flight or fight feeling.

But then, as Tabetha tucked the blanket around me, kissed me on the head and started to walk towards the door, my eyes did feel heavy and I could feel my mind clear just a little.

I had the deepest sleep. I don't remember dreaming at all.

When I opened my eyes again it was still silent. I looked at my watch and could see I'd been asleep for over two hours. Then I could hear the quiet murmur of people talking in another room. I got up and looked in the large mirror above the fireplace. Mascara tears ran beneath my eyes and smeared across my face. So much for putting make up on for the first time in weeks. I grabbed a baby wipe from the pack on the side and cleaned myself up as much as I could.

I quietly opened the door back into the hallway and worried for a second that Tabetha might have called Dan, and I wasn't quite ready to talk to him yet.

I headed towards the sound of talking, which was coming from the kitchen, and stood close to the door. I couldn't hear the exact words, but quickly recognised our health visitor's voice. I stood for a second to anticipate the conversation. What if they were discussing whether I was a fit mother? Or whether someone needed to step in and take Nellie?

But there was nothing I could plan for now. There was no use in hiding how I was feeling. I'd told someone and now I'd have to face the consequences. I opened the door to join them.

CHAPTER SIXTEEN

Tabetha left Tilly and me alone to talk. At one point she appeared silently with Nellie for her feed and took her away again as soon as I'd finished, presumably to lie side by side with Luca ignoring the fancy toys, and each other. I didn't hear a peep from Nellie, it was like she knew I needed some silence.

In the quiet, I talked for over an hour. Tilly just listened initially, and I told her how I'd been feeling - the sleeplessness, the fear, the numbness. How I'd tried to appear to have it under control, but I was so unhappy. How I'd hoped it would go, but it just seemed to be gradually getting worse, day by day.

I even told her how recently I couldn't see how it would end and that I'd started to think Nellie might even be better off without me. And that I was certain I would be happier without her too. Admitting this was the hardest part of all and tears came again.

She did a lot of nodding, and offered the same

reassurance as others had, that motherhood is hard, and I shouldn't be so rough on myself. For a second thought that maybe she wasn't going to understand either and that I should have kept quiet.

Then she said something new: 'Have you spoken with your GP about the possibility of post-natal depression?'

I was shocked, it hadn't crossed my mind. Obviously, I knew about it, but how I was feeling seemed not like an illness, but like a failing. A failing in me. Something to be accepted, not overcome or treated. I just looked at her open mouthed.

'What you've described sounds like depression to me Emily. And if it's impacting on your life, then you need some support to deal with it, and you need it fast. I'd like to get you an emergency doctor's appointment today if I can,' she said. 'Would that be okay with you?'

It all sounded so serious suddenly.

'What do you mean it's impacting on my life? It's the other way around isn't it – it's my life that's the problem? It's just motherhood, right?' I asked, it seemed crazy to think that a doctor could help sort out motherhood for me.

'Emily, you don't have to change you to become a mum. Look, I always think of the same simple questions to find out if something needs quick attention from me, or from a doctor. Number one; is how you are feeling affecting what you do day to day?' she asked pragmatically.

'Yes, yes,' I answered immediately. 'I don't really want to do anything to be honest. A while ago I could find distractions almost, but now... until today I have found it hard even to get off the sofa.'

'Okay, number two; is how you are feeling affecting your relationships with your family, with your friends?' I nodded, but this was a hard one. I knew that I'd lost touch with people, in fact I'd been ignoring some calls from my old friends, I just couldn't face seeing them. Wasn't that just part of having new responsibilities? And my relationship with Dan was always going to change, wasn't it? I'd been trying to accept this for weeks.

'Question three; how do you think you are bonding with Nellie?' she asked. I thought for a few moments before answering.

'I thought we were getting there. But recently she's felt more like a stranger than ever. And some days, in fact more and more days, I've started to just wish she would disappear.' I felt totally ashamed saying it. 'But then I'm frightened most in the world about that too.'

'Okay. And final question; do you feel like yourself at the moment?'

I thought of how I pictured myself before; confident, strong, bolshie even. Happy at the very least.

'No,' I murmured quietly, 'not even close.' I wasn't me right now.

'Things change when you have a baby, of course they do,' explained Tilly, 'but this isn't a choice between being miserable with a baby or finding happiness without her. You will be able to find the balance, but you may need some extra help to get there.'

She had hit the nail on the head completely. That was the choice I felt I had to make. If I couldn't find peace with Nellie then I'd either have to get on with it and live with how I was feeling or leave, one way or another. It seemed that simple. When had I decided those were the choices?

Suddenly it felt like maybe there was a secret option number three.

'But what if it's not depression, what if it's just me? What if I just don't have it in me to be a good mum?'

'You are a good mum Emily.' She seemed so sure. 'That door hasn't closed just because you've had a tough beginning. It's okay to need some help. If I'm right, then you've been ill, and like with any illness, you're going to need some time, and some treatment to get well again. It won't be tomorrow, but it will happen.'

She smiled at me almost like she was proud of me. She gave me a hug while I sat just thinking through everything she'd said. It was going to take a while to sink in that I could change how I was feeling.

Once Tilly left, Tabetha took me home and waited with me until Dan arrived. Usually I'd have told her to go while I waited, to not be so silly. But thinking about how I was feeling as an illness allowed me to accept the help for some reason. It wasn't just me being dramatic, or weak, I needed help. I NEEDED HELP. Having been scared to think it before, it was like I wanted to shout it out.

Tabetha quietly left when Dan arrived, and I sat with him into the night talking about how I'd been feeling. I even admitted to thinking we should break up, and that I'd been scared I didn't love him or Nellie anymore. I told him how I'd been resenting him and the freedom he still had. Some of it sounded like such contradictions. I wanted him to help, to take more of the responsibility. But I also wanted to be the best mum I could and to do it all myself. It wasn't easy to unpick. I just laid it all out.

He took a few moments to digest what I'd said and then looked at me closely before speaking.

'I'm so sorry I didn't see what was happening for you,' he looked down.

'I'm used to you being the strong one around here, knowing where everything lives, what we're having for dinner, when to send out the birthday presents. You are always the one out of us that's got everything under control,' he said.

'I know,' I replied. 'And I don't want to let you

down now. Do you think maybe you settled with me under false pretences?' I was trying to lighten the tone a little.

'Don't be ridiculous. You could never let me down! If anything, I'm the one who has let you down. I knew things weren't quite right, there was something I couldn't put my finger on. I should have asked more, pushed you more about it. Things are so busy, and I suppose it was just another thing on my list which I never got to,' he said.

I went to bed with a clearer head on things. Even just knowing the doctor's appointment was booked made me feel calmer.

Dan took time off the next morning and I took a long shower and did a final feed with Nellie, before he dropped me off for my appointment and they drove away to spend some time together.

When I'd spoken with Tilly, she had been sweet and soft, speaking carefully and calmly, like a teaching assistant trying to get a difficult child to listen. Dr Khan was the other end of the spectrum, but I liked it. She was a no-nonsense professional.

I gave her the twenty-minute version of how things had progressed. She nodded silently, made some notes and then simply said, 'I'm pretty comfortable to support a diagnosis of post-natal depression here. It's important we get that diagnosis on the record, so we can get the right treatment quickly.' She turned to make some final notes on the computer before turning back to me. It really was like being diagnosed with the flu, or warts (God forbid). She just listened carefully to the symptoms and made a decision. After all these weeks of worry, it was such a relief to move to the next stage.

I left with a booking to meet a psychiatrist in two days' time, a booklet with advice to keep moving to get my endorphins going, and to make sure I ate well. Along with a prescription for some mild anti-depressants which wouldn't mess with my breast milk.

I went home more hopeful than I'd been in months.

Dan took the rest of the week off and dropped me at my psychiatrist appointment a couple of days later.

My third specialist in as many days was Dr Shore. A little balding man with tiny round glasses and a bit of a goatee. He spoke fast and high, his pin-prick blue eyes sharp and focused.

His office was out the back of one of the larger doctors' surgeries in the area, with a broken blind lopsided at the window and a large pot plant in each corner. They were probably meant to brighten up the room and make patients feel calm originally, but now stood wilting, a little unloved.

'Lovely to meet you Emily, lovely to meet you,' he spoke quickly as he ushered me into the room.

'Let's get straight to it shall we? Tell me about how you have been feeling?' he said, taking a seat himself, putting his pen and paper down and pushing his glasses back up his nose.

I talked him through the whole sorry story, and I finished by telling him about how my conversation with Tilly had finally led me here.

'I just feel so embarrassed to be honest. I'm an intelligent, capable person, you know? I realise rationally that I should be happy right now, but I just can't seem to get out of this spiral,' I said.

He nodded. 'Tell me more about the "spiral" you mention'. The whole thing reminded me of the coaching course I'd taken at work. Using questions to help people to find their own solutions. Ridiculously frustrating when you are on the other end and just want an answer presented to you, but ultimately it did seem to work.

'Ummm, I suppose I mean that I've been going in a loop. Feeling dreadful, trying to pull myself together, then finding myself dropping even further than before. Round and round, and it gets worse each time. Any little setback hits me like a sledgehammer. Does that make sense?' I asked.

He nodded again. 'And is there anything in particular that triggers that drop that you describe, do you think?'

'It's hard to say. I guess when I get involved in something outside of motherhood is when I go up again, but only temporarily. Like a distraction. Ultimately, I do have to come back to earth and deal with being a mum, and that's the point I drop down. Is that typical? Do you hear that from other women?' I asked.

'Well, depression is different for everyone Emily. Some people have clear triggers, others find it harder to identify. But it sounds like there is a pattern here for you,' he said.

'We can explore this more next time, but I'd like you to think more about this pattern, and about how you can ensure that those ups that you describe can still be part of your life. To think about how you can find a balance that works for you.'

He looked up at the wall and I was shocked to find the first of my six sessions was already over, but it had been useful. Just to have an hour to think clearly about what was going on and why.

Perhaps it was the pills kicking in too, but I left feeling another little step up on the positivity scale.

As I waited for Dan to pick me up, I sat on a bench outside the surgery with the autumn sun bright on my face and I thought through all the advice. I closed my eyes in the warmth, listening to the leaves rustling in a large sycamore with its branches overhead, and the quiet chatter of people coming and going.

I closed my eyes to enjoy the calming warmth and could feel myself drifting off for just a second.

I was back in the psychiatrist's room. The letters from the murderer were laid out on the low table in between us, along with that Mum's Diary from the first murder scene. I was picking them up to read and inspect over and over again. The words drifted in front of my eyes.

I could hear Dr Shore's voice as I looked at the papers: 'Some people have clear triggers,' he was saying. 'But it sounds like there is a pattern here for you'. I looked up at him as he said it again: 'It sounds like there is a pattern here for you, Emily...' I was looking back at the papers again as I could hear him calling my name, 'Emily, Emily.'

I opened my eyes with a start and could see Dan had pulled up in a car in front of me and was calling out of the window.

'I'm on double yellows, can you jump in?' he asked.

I gradually started to sleep better. I did what Dr Shore had asked and realised that lack of sleep was a definite trigger, so Dan and I set up a strict programme of turn-taking throughout the night, especially now Nellie didn't need as many feeds.

It seems simple, but it helped. I needed my sleep. I really, really needed it.

Slowly, as the days passed, things changed. I looked for what helped me lift my mood a little each day, like cooking a healthy meal with my favourite music on, or sitting watching a film by myself while Dan took Nellie out for a walk, or picking up the phone to my mum for a chat about nothing. To begin with, I had to force myself to try to do things again, but every little uplift in mood helped me to do more. I created a new spiral, but back up, not down. Not that it would always go up, I knew that. But if I kept on going, picked myself up at every dip, I felt like I could get there and that was a big step.

Tabetha messaged me every few days just to check in, but I was pleased she kept her distance for a while. I could see that I'd placed a lot of pressure on our friendship and the distraction the case had given me.

Soon it was three weeks since I'd been at rock bottom at Tabetha's house and nearly six weeks since Shelley had been killed. I felt like so much had happened. I'd been obsessed with the case not that long ago, but in the last few weeks I'd had to focus in on me. No distractions.

As Dan started to return to work again, and I re-emerged, I knew I needed to speak to Tabetha, and find out if the case was any closer to being resolved. I felt like I'd solved one drama of my own, and now I needed to solve the other.

CHAPTER SEVENTEEN

I messaged Tabetha the next morning and she invited me over for a coffee before heading to the NCT Wednesday meet. Nellie had been up since 5am, which was pretty good going. Mornings were still the hardest. Not long ago I'd have been trying desperately to hold out at home to what I thought was a more reasonable hour. But now I just did what I felt I needed to, and Tabetha didn't question it when I arrived just before 8am.

Claire was getting ready to head out as I arrived, with a slice of toast in her hand. She gave me a one-armed hug and kiss as I came through the door as if we were old friends, keeping the sticky toast away from me with her other hand.

She must have known what had happened, but if she did, she didn't show it. She gave off an easy confidence, less tightly wound or serious than Tabetha, a little softer, and I could see it rubbed off on her too.

They touched one another often as they pottered around, passing Luca between them as they got Claire's things ready for another work trip. I sat at the breakfast bar watching them rush around, drinking another delicious coffee from their expensive machine. It was the sort of family feeling that I wanted, and that I was starting to think was in reach. Busy and noisy, but warm and loving too.

'What is it you do, Claire?' I asked, as she packed up a beautiful red leather satchel with papers.

'Oh, I'm a Chief Inspector,' she replied, sounding surprised that I didn't know.

'Well I'm not really practising any more, if you know what I mean,' she smiled. 'I'm a "consultant",' she said, using her fingers to denote the speech marks. 'It basically means I travel around telling people how to work better together. Or money for old rope as Tabby calls it.

'I'm also involved in the Women in Leadership Programme, you know, mentoring, keynote speeches, guest blogs. Which is hilarious really,' she said, laughing.

'Oh, I see,' I replied. That explained it. I remembered Tabetha saying she'd been mentored before she got her job. Inadvertently I looked over to where she was standing with a coffee in one hand while holding Luca over her shoulder with the other.

'I caught that look,' Tabetha said to me, 'yes, that's how we met. She took horrible advantage of me.' They both smiled as Claire came around to her, kissing her on the cheek, then one for Luca.

'If memory serves, I think it was the other way around.' She took a gulp of coffee and stood in the doorway into the hall.

'Do I look okay?' She asked standing back in some geometric-patterned cropped trousers, a white T-shirt and a brightly clashing Moroccan-patterned jacket. On me it would have looked crazy, on her it looked great.

We both nodded, and she gave a wave and headed out the door.

'She's wonderful,' I said to Tabetha when the door closed.

'Yeah, she is. But her work is all consuming sometimes. She's trying to stay home more, but she's dedicated to her job.

'I stayed over with my sister on and off not long ago, just so that I wasn't alone so much. I think that scared her. She's been staying back more.' I don't think she'd have shared that with me a month ago, but it felt like we were both trying to be more honest with one another. Hiding how hard motherhood could be didn't help anyone in the end.

Staying at her sister's house also explained her earlier disappearing act, and why she'd missed the second letter that she'd felt so guilty about.

'I'm not sure I would have done all this right

now if it had been just my choice,' she said, indicating Luca with a nod of her head. 'But she'll be fifty next year. Age isn't usually an issue between us, but there's no fighting your own body. It was getting to now-or-never time.'

'Are you pleased you did it though?' I asked, genuinely wanting to know. When we'd met, she seemed reluctant, much more so than me, and I could never quite tell if she thought she'd done the right thing.

'Yes, god yes. It's hard, but amazing.' We sat quietly while I thought about how I'd been feeling. Motherhood was so different for everybody. I'd been excited about motherhood, and on the outside, I'd seemed like I had everything all together, but I had really been struggling. Tabetha hadn't been sure, but it turned out she was loving it. I'd made a lot of assumptions about her.

She laid a sleeping Luca into a bouncy highchair and opened the bread bin, taking out a pack of croissants and putting them on a plate on the side.

A knock sounded from the door. 'Help yourself,' she said, as she left the kitchen to answer it.

I took a croissant and started eating absentmindedly as I thought about how relieved I was that I had come clean about everything. Tilly was right, it hadn't happened immediately, but I could feel things clearing.

I looked up as Tabetha came back into the room and could see something was up. She put a box on the side and picked out a letter from the top of a bundle in her hands. She laid it on the side in front of me and I recognised the writing on the envelope immediately.

Without saying anything she picked up her phone and made a call. Just a few minutes later and Toby was walking through her front door.

'Well this is going to complicate my plans for the day!' he smiled as he marched into the kitchen. 'I'm taking Marcia for another one of those scans,' he said, looking at his watch. 'She'll meet me here in half an hour, but we'll need to rush to make it,' he continued, sharing just the smallest glance in my direction, 'so she won't be able to stop in or anything I'm afraid.' He was reassuring me of course, as he had no idea Tabetha knew about the kiss.

He took a seat beside me and we all stared down at this new piece of evidence. Very quickly the kiss and our conversations, where I knew we had shared too much, seemed a world away.

'Right, open it up,' said Toby after he'd examined the envelope and we'd discussed for several minutes what could be inside.

She opened it carefully and laid it on the table to read.

Hi Ms Tate,

I'm disappointed. Seems like you don't have a clue!

Third time lucky? See you at Tatten Waters on the 4th of November.

Will you come along for the rides?
Your friend,

Little Miss Trouble.

That final line gave me the jitters immediately.

'Little Miss, Little Miss...' said Tabetha slowly.

'The 4th is this Saturday, right?' I asked, and Toby nodded. It was Wednesday, so just three days away.

'Little Miss Trouble, and Tatten Waters,' I said quietly, looking at the location again. It wasn't far from here, but in the other direction from Clays Green where Shelley had been killed. Something came back into my mind.

'A pattern,' I murmured without thinking. That was the phrase in my mind after my session with Mr Shore. 'There's always a pattern,' I clarified. 'Where are we up to, about episode three? The perfect time to spot the pattern,' I said.

Toby looked confused.

'Emily's been starring in her own detective drama, haven't you Emily?' said Tabetha.

'Hey, don't knock it, it's helped out so far,' I said.

'Oh, I'm not, don't worry!' she smiled and

reached out to get copies of the other two notes to lay out next to one another. Underneath she laid out copies of the two Mum's Diary spreads as well, and then beneath them pictures of each of the victims.

We all looked at the clues laid out in front of us. At the letters, the pages from the books and the photos.

'God, how didn't I see this before? Naughty, Clever, Trouble,' said Tabetha, 'with murders in Newton Hill, Clays Green and Tatten Water,' she continued.

'And victims Mama Nolan, and Shelley Carter,' finished Toby. 'So there's the pattern!'

'Oh my god, N-C-T,' I said, as the penny finally dropped. 'That's mad.' I shook my head in disbelief.

'Absolutely,' agreed Tabetha. 'But if these letters, this pattern, really is the key, then we can draw a pretty clear picture of the next target. Tatten Waters, November 4th, with a victim named T,' said Tabetha.

'That is absolutely psychotic, right?' I said, letting out a deep breath and looking between the two of them. Tabetha raised her eyebrows, but neither of them responded. It seemed so unbelievable.

Finally Toby spoke: 'As mad as it seems, someone out there is getting a kick out of this elaborate set up. Probably even having a good laugh at our expense. And there is no bloody way I'm going to let them hit that final target. No way in hell. So let's make sure we've done everything we can, right?' he looked between the two of us for agreement.

We both nodded, and he continued with renewed purpose. 'I think we can safely say women are the targets, given the victims so far. New mothers and those connected to mothers more specifically.'

'Mm hmm,' said Tabetha in agreement.

'And the first Little *Miss*,' she continued, 'a good reminder not to rule out a female killer?'

'Maybe, but let's keep an open mind for now,' clarified Toby. 'Either way, that's a lot to go on.' He sighed with relief. 'And at least, finally, we're getting somewhere,' he finished quietly.

They were both looking intently at the letters side by side and I thought how similar the two of them were. Ambitious, focused and assured. That was probably what had drawn me to both of them. I could also see myself standing like that with colleagues, poring over a new brief. Work could be a pain but when you were on your game it was the best feeling.

'Right, we'll need to get our guys all over the location on the 4th, we can't risk missing him again,' said Toby.

'November the 4th though, a busy day around here,' I said.

'What do you mean?' asked Tabetha.

'Well it's bonfire night weekend isn't it, and

there'll be the big fair up at Tatten Waters both days again I expect,' I answered.

'Come along for the *rides*. Of course,' she said. 'Well, we'll need to focus on the fair then.' She looked back at Toby who nodded and took out his phone to start making calls. Before he did, he looked at the two of us.

'Thanks for helping me on this one,' he smiled. 'You need someone to bounce ideas off. Derek is really experienced, but he doesn't really talk things through or give you the chance to try out new ideas. He's old school, you know?' He looked to Tabetha who nodded knowingly.

'Well, I mentioned we were speaking with you again. And now this new letter has come along, he'll understand you need to be kept in the loop at the very least,' said Toby. Tabetha gave him a look in response that said thanks without needing to say it out loud.

'Marcia's been worried about how the baby will affect her career and I've always reassured her that it doesn't need to make a difference, but this isn't filling me with confidence to be honest.' Toby shook his head as he went out to make some calls.

I hadn't even visited my work yet. I was feeling like it was probably time soon, but didn't want to rush it. It still felt like work was where I wanted to be viewed the same as I was before. Well maybe not quite the same. There were a few women at work where people would be shocked when they found out they had kids, and out would come those classic lines, like, 'if anything, she's *more* efficient since coming back' or, 'I really don't know how she does it all'. On the one hand it was patronising and sexist, on the other hand I'd sort of love to hear people say that about me. Just another one of my modern mum contradictions.

'Right, likely candidates,' said Toby, coming back into the room. 'We know Mrs Nolan's husband is out of the picture for Shelley as he was in the cells at the time, and besides, he's hardly the type to set up an elaborate serial killing spree. Unless he was working with someone else perhaps? Let's keep him on the list, but towards the bottom I think,' he said, while getting out a pad and pen to make notes.

'What about her nephew, Ben. Anything more on him?' asked Tabetha.

'Headed out of the country as soon as we'd let him after his aunt died, so nowhere near the place when Shelley was killed. Does that rule him out?' said Toby.

'I'd say so. Then there's Norman and Clive, the two men who last saw her alive,' followed up Tabetha.

'Well, Clive said he didn't see her when he stopped by, which could mean she was dead already, or could mean he killed her and is trying to cover his tracks,' said Toby.

'And if she was dead already,' continued Tabatha, 'then we shouldn't trust Norman that he had the conversation he relayed to us. It could have been him who killed her, and Clive is telling the truth. Have you found any connections from either of them to Shelley?'

'Nothing.' Toby shook his head. 'Plus it's hard to see what sort of grudge they had against Mrs Nolan herself. We considered an affair of course, but we've found nothing to back that up yet.'

'Shelley then,' cut in Tabetha, 'anything come out of the woodwork on her?'

'We've run background checks and done some digging on her work colleagues, her family. Nothing of interest. She had a volatile relationship with her mum and sister though. She was always teetering on the edge of trouble and they were hard on her, although with good reason probably. She ran away a couple of times when she was younger, and both police reports site arguments with her mum as the reason. But she came back of her own accord both times, so....' his voice drifted off as he looked back at his notes. They both looked a bit stuck.

'And what about a stranger, someone targeting at random, how likely is that?' I asked, trying to input something useful. 'Could there just be someone out there who hates mothers, or babies, or women? Like a Hannibal Lecter type, playing one big sick game?' I knew it sounded a bit simplistic, but it was hard to see how any of the suspects we had fitted the profile completely.

'That's the most frightening possibility of all,' Toby shuddered, 'because if that's the case, I don't think we stand a chance of identifying them before Saturday.'

We sat for a few moments, with Tabetha staring at the letter, while Toby scrolled through information on his iPad, looking for anything he'd missed.

'What about the boyfriend?' I asked. 'It's often the boyfriend, isn't it? Maybe Tom has a link to Mama Nolan that we just haven't found yet?'

'I like it,' Toby looked pleased with the suggestion and glanced over to Tabetha for confirmation.

Tabatha nodded and rose to her feet. 'If you have a feeling about it, let's go and speak to him again. If nothing else, it will get us moving.'

'And that's as good a reason as any,' said Toby, also standing and grabbing his bag.

With perfect timing, Luca called out through the monitor, and the high squeal woke Nellie who had been quietly napping in her buggy. Tabetha put her bag back down and frowned.

'Why don't we head to mine first?' I suggested. 'Dan is coming back at lunch to work from home and I'm sure he'll be okay to watch the babies for a couple of hours.' I didn't want to go into the details with Toby here, but Tabetha looked at me knowingly.

Dan had been getting back to work gradually after my big dip into the wonderful world of depression. He'd either help in the morning or come back earlier for the afternoon and at the very least I could take a nap or read a book in quiet while he spent some time with Nellie.

'Great,' Toby smiled. 'Why don't you take the kids over to your house together and I'll stop off at the office to check in. I'll pick you both up just after lunch?' As he spoke, the doorbell went and he looked down at his watch. 'Oh, shit,' he said under his breath, 'that'll be Marcia, I better run.' His voice sounded casual, but I knew he wouldn't want us to cross paths.

He headed quickly to the door. I'd really not thought about her at all. Was I some sort of other woman?

'Sorry,' said a small, high voice as the door opened, 'I didn't know if I should ring, or just wait, or...' he obviously didn't want us to spot one another, as he opened the door as little as possible. But I caught a glimpse as he stepped through.

I couldn't help but compare us just a little. She was small, with a neat rounded bump. Very pretty with delicate features. Her hair was pulled back tightly and she hadn't put on any make up that morning. In fact she looked knackered. She was probably at that point in the pregnancy when you just can't wait for it to all be over. I felt a little ball of guilt drop in my tummy.

'Let's just get going,' he said a little sharply, keen to get moving. As she turned to walk back down the path, he put a hand on her back to lead her away and then twisted back to us for a second, to call out, 'See you later', before he slammed the door.

I turned around and caught Tabetha's eye. Her eyebrows raised a little, she knew what I was thinking. 'Don't worry,' she picked up her coffee and took a sip, 'she'll be okay. God, she's got enough to worry about preparing for a baby. And with him out all hours on the case. She won't have a clue about what happened and she doesn't need to.'

I felt terrible.

'Refocus Emily!' Tabetha raised her voice and clapped her hands with a smile to snap me out of it. 'We've got a suspect to follow.' I could see the glee in her eyes. This was Tabetha in her element. And to be fair, I couldn't wait to get going either.

CHAPTER EIGHTEEN

Dan had looked terrified when I left him with the two babies. But they'd had a good roll around with Tabetha and me while we grabbed a sandwich for lunch, and were both full of milk, so I was hoping he'd mainly get their nap time. Although the thought of him having to deal with them both for a little bit didn't seem so bad anyway.

We parked up outside Tom's house and could see him pass across in the front window briefly as he got up and sat down again in front of a widescreen telly attached to the wall. It was like being on a proper stake out.

We started to talk through a game plan when Toby shushed us. 'Off he goes,' he said, and I craned my neck to look over from my seat in the back to see Tom leaving the front door, wearing a dark coat with the hood pulled close over his head.

We waited for him to get to the end of the street, then pulled out to follow quickly. At the corner we could see he'd walked about halfway down the next street and we followed again.

Tom walked briskly ahead, until he reached a bus stop. We carried on driving past, then pulled into the kerb further along the road. I watched from the back seat until Tom boarded the number forty. We waited until the bus passed then followed as it overtook us.

When he got off, around ten minutes later, we pulled in and then followed carefully on foot, holding back when needed for just a couple of minutes until he stopped outside a house I recognised. It was all as it looked before, neat and tidy with those strange garden ornaments lining the path.

Tom knocked on the door of Clive Cooper's house and went inside.

'Now this is interesting. What the hell is he doing here?' asked Toby.

We parked and waited in silence, but not for long. Within a couple of minutes, the door opened again, and Tom came bustling out, pulling his hood back up over his head and walking down the path at the same, brisk pace. Then Clive followed and called him back. We couldn't hear what they said to one another, but it looked intense and it ended with Clive pulling Tom close by the scruff of his hoodie and then pushing him away. I could just make out, 'now leave me alone' as he shouted to him down the path.

'Now we're getting somewhere,' Tabetha said,

as Tom reached the end of the garden and turned left down the street. He walked away from us, without looking back, straight along the road and back to the bus stop. 'He's heading home. Let's get there before him and go in for a chat. What do you think?' she asked.

'Yep, I'm on it now,' confirmed Toby and he pulled straight out, passed Tom and drove back to his house to await his return, parking discreetly behind another car across the street from his house.

It was about fifteen minutes before we saw him walking towards his house, head low. But as he got to his gate and we were about to step out, he carried on, straight past.

'Where's he going?' I asked.

'I think we'd better find out,' said Toby, getting out of the front of the car, and Tabetha and I got out too. We followed from a long way back as he turned right. I didn't know the area too well, but I did recognise the steep road we turned up, which headed back up to Clays Green. The same road where we had bumped into Kat and Tom all those weeks before.

We were just a few roads away from Shelley's house now, and it was a similar set of homes. Mostly ex council, mostly tidy and clear, with a few old-school houses with a half-broken chests of drawers or mouldy mattresses on the front lawns. Who is it that is constantly chucking out the mattresses that turn up in front gardens?

We continued to follow and finally, without a look behind him, he turned down a path towards one of the smarter roads of houses a few streets before Shelley's. He knocked, and from the opposite side of the road I could just make out Kat Carter, Shelley's sister, opening the door.

We pulled back and turned down a cul-de-sac to the left to get out of sight.

'So, he knows Clive, and now he's at Shelley's sisters'. What the hell is going on?' I was starting to feel completely confused.

'They could all be in it together?' posed Toby, 'but I can't for the life of me think why. Tabetha?' he looked over to her and she shook her head slowly.

'Whatever is going on, there's no way we can get him back into the station based on just this though. I wonder if we might have to casually drop by...' As she spoke, she looked around in my direction.

'What do you mean?' I asked.

'Well you seemed to have a good rapport with her when we met before, and she remembered you from NCT. How would you feel about being a kindly new mum checking in on how they are doing?' she asked.

I looked over to Toby, who nodded in agreement.

I was surprised, but pleased, that they asked me to do something useful. Finally, I could be of some practical help. They prepped me with some questions, but mainly we wanted to see how the two of them were together. And of course, if I could subtly find out why he'd been with Clive and how long they'd known each other then I'd be the hero of the hour.

We popped back to the small high street and hastily bought a bunch of flowers and a baby grow with a gift bag and I headed back to Kat's house, hoping Tom hadn't left yet.

I rang the bell and it took a minute or so for Kat to appear. As I expected, she looked very surprised to see me.

'Hi, it's Emily, from the NCT class, we've met before a couple of times,' I explained, hoping the heartbeat in my ears wasn't obvious to her.

'Yes, I remember. What are you doing here?' she asked, just a bit defensive.

Her face softened as I lifted the gift bag.

'I'm sorry to just appear unannounced. It's just I've not been able to get Alfie out of my head, and I was in the area, so I thought I'd drop these around. These are for you.' I lifted the flowers.

'Sorry if I sounded a bit, you know. Things are still...' she searched for the word, 'hard,' she finished, simply.

I nodded. Neither of us moved and I glanced into the house, hoping she'd invite me in. Now I could see down the hall into the back rooms, where Tom was sitting at a dining table with his head in his hands. She spotted that I'd seen him, which may have been why she decided to invite me in. There was no way she could hide him now.

'You remember Tom? He just stopped by too. Come in,' she said, moving aside and I walked through to the table where Tom was sitting.

He looked terrible. His dark, sallow eyes suggested he hadn't slept in days.

'How are you doing?' I asked softly. It's hard to know if the right tone is going to come out when you speak to someone grieving, and he did look like he was grieving. He made a noise but didn't really respond. He looked deep in thought.

Then, as Kat put on the kettle, he looked up at me sharply like a cat turning towards a mouse, about to pounce.

'Do you know anything about dreams?' he asked quietly, his eyes wide and focused. It wasn't what I'd expected.

'Um, not really. I mean, I have them though, a lot. Nightmares and things.'

'Yes,' he said, leaning in, 'Nightmares. I never used to get them.' His eyes were blazing then; he almost looked insane.

'Tom, don't get yourself all worked up again,' called Kat from across the room.

'I suppose I should expect it, what with everything that's happened. But this one has come back the same for weeks now and it's driving me mad.' He looked at me intently, like he was wishing me to ask him for more.

'What happens in it?' I obliged.

'I'm in the park, the one across the way, where,' he paused for a second, 'where they found her,' he finished.

'Yes,' I said, trying to spur him on. I'd dreamt of the park too.

'First off, I'm just looking for Shelley, we're meant to be meeting. We've had a fight or something and when I get there, I take out this box, a big heavy box. Like a jewellery box or something... you know?' he said, still looking me directly in the eye.

'And I'm searching in the park to find her, and then I see her across the grass sitting on a bench. She's not looking around for me though, she's just sitting, completely still.' I nodded to reassure him, and he looked down.

'Then the next thing, I'm not across the park anymore, I'm right behind her, and she doesn't know I'm there, and...' he looked back at me as I stood stock still.

'And I lift up the box above my head and... and before she can even look round, I smash it down and down and down. And then she's on the floor and I know she's dead.'

'Okay...' I said, trying to sound calm, but my heart was beating out of my chest; was this a confession?

'Only when I look down at her body. It's not Shelley there, it's Kat.' Now he turned away and looked to Kat, who was standing by the kettle still and silent. It didn't look like the first time she'd heard it.

'What does it mean?' he asked desperately, looking at each of us in turn. 'I can't keep going through it, I need to work out what it means.'

'Well it probably means you are completely messed up in your brain right now because your girlfriend's been murdered,' said Kat forcefully, clearly not wanting to tackle the possibilities. Her reaction sort of explained why he'd asked for my opinion too.

'Did I do it?' he said turning to me. 'I know I didn't, but why am I having that dream? I wake up and I just feel so, so guilty.' He hid his head back in his hands.

'Well you aren't, are you,' said Kat coming over and putting an arm awkwardly around his shoulders, 'so get that out of your head.'

'It's probably your mind playing tricks on you.' I tried to reassure him, because what else could I do. 'You could be feeling guilty because you wish you'd been there to save her,'

'And Kat's face?' he asked.

'Well, you've spent so much time with the family, things are just getting confused, that's all,' I tried to sound convincing.

It obviously worked, at least a little, because he nodded and wiped his face with the back of his hand and gave himself a little shake.

'Yes, yes... If I can just clear my head a bit, think about something else for just a day, an hour even, it'll help. I just can't stop...' his voice drifted off.

'You need to start moving on from this. Shelley would have wanted that,' said Kat.

I never really believed that sentiment. The last thing I'd be hoping when I die is that Dan would go and find some other woman straight away. Maybe a few years down the line, okay maybe five or six years. He doesn't have to be miserable, just quietly grieving for a good while (although at the funeral, at least, I do want misery; people should be wailing and throwing themselves on the coffin, I've fully briefed my friends on that).

We sipped our tea quietly for a minute or so.

'I did something a bit stupid today,' said Tom looking embarrassed.

'Right,' Kat sighed. He'd obviously decided to get a few things off his chest, and I'd walked straight into it.

'I found out the address of that guy who last saw the old woman alive, or not as it turns out. She wasn't there once he got to the centre. Well, so he says. She was probably dead already. That's what he reckons anyway.'

'Why did you do that?' asked Kat.

'I just wanted to take a good look at him and see if I recognised him, I wondered if maybe he was a local from Shelley's pub or something.'

'And did you recognise him?' I tried to keep my voice casual.

'No, nothing. He didn't look at all like someone Shelley would hang out with. He chucked me out once he realised who I was. I asked him if he wanted to do a bit of investigating with me, you know, find out who really did it. Clear our names. But he just told me to leave him alone,' he said.

'And he's right,' Kat said, eyebrows raised for intensity. 'Leave the police to sort this out, or not as the case may be. We need to focus on Alfie, right?'

A message tone sounded, and Tom looked down at his phone. 'Just be a sec,' he said, getting up and heading out of the room with it.

'Poor thing,' I shook my head. 'He's really struggling, isn't he? Have the police got anywhere with finding out who did it?'

'Look, I didn't want to say anything with Tom here, he's going crazy with this stuff. But I know who you are and your friend.' She looked at me pointedly.

'Um, I met Shelley at NCT,' I repeated, my voice sounding a little robotic.

'I know, but your mate is police, isn't she? I don't know why you're snooping about, but if you see her again, just tell her to drop it, okay?' Her lips pursed, and her eyes narrowed as she leant into me.

'Don't you want to know what happened?' I asked. She looked behind her to check Tom hadn't reappeared.

'Shelley was my blood; I'll always love her.

But Tom was right that day, she wasn't all whiter than white like everyone's saying now. She loved the drama, the attention, the blokes. She could be selfish and greedy. I can say the truth, because I'm family. But the main reason she was so much happier just before she died wasn't because she was so in love with Alfie, or such a great mum, or whatever. If anything, it was because she was getting a load more attention since the baby arrived, and not from Tom,' she said raising her eyebrows.

'What do you mean?'

'Look, I just want what's best for Alfie. I want everything to settle down. I want Tom to move on and be able to be the good dad I think he can be. Dragging up all sorts of stuff about Shell isn't going to help anyone. She's dead, isn't she? Nothing is going to bring her back.' As she finished, Tom re-entered the room and Kat gave me a look to close the conversation.

'Right, thanks so much for the tea, I better be heading off,' I said, standing up quickly.

'Me too,' said Tom, his dark eyes still filled with sadness.

'Actually, I had a few things I wanted to speak to you about Tom... about Alfie,' said Kat.

I saw a look pass between them, and I recognised it from myself not too long ago. A look which says you need someone even if you shouldn't, because you are hurting.

I got up and started for the door as Tom sat

back down.

'Well, thanks for the flowers.' Kat walked me to the door as she spoke. 'Say hello to your friend for me.'

I stepped outside, and she quickly closed the door hard behind me, with a simple, 'Bye.'

I looked through the mottled glass and I could see Kat returning quickly to Tom at the table.

Back at the car, Tabetha and Toby were talking as I approached, leaning in, their foreheads only inches apart. They stopped as they spotted me, and I got into the back. We drove ten minutes or so away and then parked up and I recounted what had happened.

Only at the end of the story did I hold back. I just said that there was a look that seemed loaded, a little more intimate than it should be.

'Okay,' Tabatha began, 'So the question is, is it a full-on relationship between them? If so, were they in a relationship when Shelley was around, and could that have been a motive for getting rid of her?'

'But even if they were, and it was a motive,' Toby raised an eyebrow as he spoke, 'why in the hell would they also kill Mrs Nolan? Then again, if the two of them were in it together, then Tom's alibi for the night Mrs Nolan dies is a moot point, as it could have been Kat. We've never asked for her alibi for that night, but it might be worth checking. And if there is a motive there too...'

Tabatha nodded. 'It's not perfect, but it's a

narrative to explore.'

Toby looked at the clock on the dashboard. 'Shit, I need to go back to the office for a meeting with Derek. He wants to see the new letter and catch up on leads.' He started the car to drop us back at my house.

We agreed to meet at mine in two days' time, when Toby would know if any progress had been made and how the police would be handling the day itself.

He left us as we went down the path, with a quick beep of the horn as he pulled away. It struck me as another easy way not to meet Dan, which was a relief. Tabetha and I went into the house to find Dan rocking a sleeping Nellie in his arms.

'Shhhhh!' he said as we bowled into the room talking about what had happened. 'Super Dad!' he said quietly with a smile. 'Look…' We followed his gaze to Luca, sleeping soundly in the bouncy chair as Dan proudly rocked it with his foot. 'No hands!'

CHAPTER NINETEEN

Toby and Tabetha arrived Friday morning after Dan had left for work. I put on coffee as Toby filled us in on the details.

The previous evening they had run a carefully controlled press conference to release just some information. Derek had decided to go public with the target date and the possible importance of the initial T. Also, that they anticipated an attack may happen in the area. But they didn't identify Tatten Waters as the location. The message was that they were confident of catching the culprit before any further attacks took place and they were actively following various lines of enquiry. Although in reality it sounded like they were still pretty much in the dark.

The hope was that releasing some of the next set of details would flush out people with information, or maybe even the murderer himself, who may get a kick out of the press coverage.

What they still hadn't said was who the letters had been sent to. They wanted to keep Tabetha out of it as much as possible. It was a relief.

Toby and Derek would be spending the day visiting each of the NCT families in turn, to let them know what information they had and that the risk had heightened since the new warning had been received.

As he left to start his visits, Toby dropped in casually that he'd also be looking out for any 'reactions' and I realised that not only were we all potential targets, but potential suspects too.

Now I thought about it, once Shelley had died, it made perfect sense to add the whole NCT group into the mix. Even me. If you read any modern crime novel, I'd be the perfect suspect. In fact, if I wasn't me, I'd have thought I did it. Did Toby? Or Tabetha? My paranoia was certainly on high alert.

After Toby left, Tabetha and I settled down with the babies to think through where we were and what we could do.

Before we got very far, my WhatsApp fired with a message from Priya from NCT.

> This is too much now, I'm panicking. Can we all meet? I don't trust the police to get this under control anymore (no offence Tabetha).

None of her usual winking faces or love hearts, but straight to the point. I could tell she was one message away from vigilante territory and said as much to Tabetha. Perhaps it was best to avoid them and keep on our own path of investigation?

'I don't know,' she said, much to my surprise. 'This could be the best next step. Let's get everyone round and, like Toby said, let's see how people are reacting.'

'Really?' I asked.

'Sometimes you need to make a bit of a stab in the dark to get a new lead or direction. We have Tom and Kat on the back burner. Let's see what the NCT side gives us. If nothing else, it may help us to think differently by talking it through with new people.'

On the day, Priya arrived first, flustered and flushed. She marched in and parked her baby in the car seat in the corner of the living room, while simultaneously handing over some still-warm fairy cakes in a plastic carrier, with a look towards the kitchen. As I left to find some plates, I could hear her berating Tabetha about the lack of progress from the police and asking who she could complain to.

Fay arrived next, with Tim, and Priya went straight over to them. 'You must be terrified Tim, aren't you? I thank god it wasn't a P they chose; I wouldn't be leaving the house!' she said, giving Fay a big hug.

'Well it sounds like it's surnames that are the problem, and women. I think I'll make it through the week.' He laughed a little as the women's eyes widened. 'I mean, not you guys though obviously!' He tried to take back the sentiment, but it was too late, and Fay burst into tears.

'Come on Fay, I didn't mean you, we'll be okay.' Tim reached for her shoulder, but she pushed off his hand and marched towards the sofas, as he followed like a naughty puppy.

Nina arrived next, late as ever, and was dabbing at her eyes as she entered. Alek was away making deliveries with work, so she was alone and panicking. She held Leah close, like a mother bear, which made me feel a little guilty that mine was spark out in the buggy and parked in the downstairs loo where I thought she would stay quiet the longest.

Priya stepped in, hugging her close and carefully leading her into the living room by the arm to sit down, fluffing cushions as she did.

'They've just told us to be careful, but what does that mean?' asked Nina, fighting tears, as she took a seat opposite Fay and Tim.

'They mean be sensible, keep together and have your phone on you,' said Tim, probably trying to be reassuring, but just upsetting her further.

Fay looked at her husband, her eyes like daggers. 'Shelley is dead, Tim. She's actually dead. I think we need to do a little more than keep our phones on, don't you?'

'Exactly!' said Priya, coming back into the

room. She took a gulp of tea and a mouth full of cake with a big nod, as if Fay had made some insightful new point about the case.

'I know,' said Tim, more carefully, 'I just mean, if we stick together then we'll be safe.'

'Tim's right, Fay,' Tabetha stepped in. 'The best thing to do is make sure we all stay with trusted people and keep our eyes open. There's not much more we, or the police, can do right now.'

'So the police are going to do nothing about it. Exactly as I thought.' Priya raised her hands in disgust. 'Well I don't know about everyone else, but I am not prepared to sit back and wait to see who gets it next.' She looked around the room for any show of solidarity.

'I agree,' nodded Fay, looking to Nina, who just whimpered a little.

'Is there any way we can get this guy before he gets us? Anything at all we can do to help?' Priya looked over to Tabetha.

'Well, the ideal would be identifying the killer before he's able to strike again. It may sound glib, but has anyone got any idea who may be involved? Anyone who has shown a particular interest in you, the group, or in Shelley? Anyone acting suspiciously or asking around about the case?'

There was silence for the first time since everyone had arrived.

'What about people who knew Shelley,' Priya

cut in. 'I don't want to be the one to say it, but if any of us hung out with the odd dodgy person, it'd be her, wouldn't it? She was sweet, but, well you know.' Priya's words revealed the assumptions that had led all of us to keep Shelley at arm's length.

Tabetha glanced my way, then spoke: 'I can assure you there has been and continues to be ongoing investigations into Shelley, her friends and family... but nothing conclusive.'

'Well what had she been doing that day, who had she seen?' asked Priya.

Tabetha took out her mobile and I could see her click on a document in an email from my seat next to her. I wondered how she had the information, then remembered Claire may well have been helping. In fact, when I thought Mike had been filling her in early in the case, it now crossed my mind that it could have been Claire all along.

'So her mum said,' she read out from her phone, '"Shelley had an awful night with Alfie and was very distant first thing. She had a baby appointment at her home in the morning which hadn't gone as she'd hoped, as Alfie wasn't putting on as much weight as they'd wanted. She brightened back up after lunch though and dressed in some of her favourite clothes then popped into work. Colleagues reported her positive and glowing,"' Tabetha looked at me as she recounted this part, reminding me we'd met her colleagues the day she'd been found. '"Then, early evening she headed out to pick up some milk and bread, just some basics for breakfast the next day, but she never returned." Her mum did report that in retrospect she had been a little more dressed up than usual.'

'That's it?' asked Nina, 'She just went out for milk and never came back?'

'Well I expect she hadn't really gone out for milk. She'd probably gone to meet someone, but who, we don't know.' Tabetha lowered her phone as she spoke.

This sharing of information felt provocative to me, and not the discreet Tabetha I knew. I wondered if she was trying to test them. If she was, it didn't work. Fay spoke first.

'Didn't she have a boyfriend? I'm sure she said she was seeing someone. Or they had just broken up or something?' she looked around at the other ladies.

'Tom?' nodded Tabetha. 'Yes, I know the police have been speaking to him. Does anyone know him?'

There were vacant looks all round. I doubted any of the ladies in the room spent much time in the area around Clays Green.

Priya, obviously not ready to give up yet, joined in: 'And is there anything that links Shelley with the death of the other woman, the old lady at the community centre?'

'Well there was the book,' said Tabetha.

'The book?'

'A baby book - well a Mum's Diary. We probably all had one.' Tabetha's eyes scanned the room.

'Weird,' Tim muttered, speaking for the first time since his telling off. 'Why would someone leave a book at the murders?'

'Seems like a bit of a calling card,' said Tabetha, 'with words underlined in each copy.'

'But warning letters, and calling cards... Why would a murderer bother with all that?' asked Fay.

I stepped in, pleased that my secret obsession with crime could be useful, and public, at last. 'Well, it's quite rare, but not unheard of. BTK, a serial killer in America in the seventies, used to leave letters and poems for the police. It was his downfall in the end. And then there was the Nightstalker in San Francisco in the eighties. He used to leave pentagrams in lipstick at every crime scene.'

'Wow, you know a lot about this sort of thing,' said Priya, her eyes wide.

'It's a bit of an interest of mine.' I glanced over at Tabetha. 'It's more well known in crime fiction though, think of the Jigsaw pieces in *Saw*, or the element symbols in *Angels and Demons*,' I explained.

Tabetha nodded, taking over. 'It can mean different things to different killers. It might be that they are trying to send a message to the police, or to someone they hold a grudge against. Or maybe to a person who receives the warnings.'

I tried not to catch her eye, as I was the only one in the room who knew it was her the killer had contacted.

She got up from her seat to stand at the front. She was there with her detective hat on now. 'What we do know, is it usually says more about the murderer than the victims. And in this instance, the initials, the targets and the books suggest motherhood is important to him for some reason,' she shared, 'And it might not even be a *him*. It usually is, in cases like this, but not always.'

As we all started to chatter about what this might mean, there was a knock at the door. I opened it to find Derek, the Chief Superintendent, on my doorstep, deep in conversation with Toby. They turned as I opened the door and Derek gave me what was probably meant to be a reassuring smile.

'Hi there Ms Elliot, can we come in? We want to give you an update on the case,' he said, already starting to enter.

It sounded like Toby hadn't told him how involved I already was.

'Of course, ummm,' I was starting to think how to explain the group he was about to find, when he looked into the room and then back to me and said, 'oh, I can see you have already heard the news.'

I stepped in ahead of him and tried to get into the room to give a warning.

'Hi guys, the police are here, so we can get more info, if we need it,' I said pointedly, seeing Priya roll her eyes and shake her head as soon as she spotted them.

Tabetha didn't look surprised. 'Great, come and join us. I was just explaining that the letters, and the information the murderer has given to us, probably means there's a bigger message hidden in there, but it's hard to know what it is right now.'

The two men came forward and joined her at the front.

'It sounds to me like they hate mothers, plain and simple,' said Priya, wasting no time. 'It's some god-awful man who can't bear women to be happy, successful mums. Bloody typical of this patriarchal society.' She looked round for support, gathering the feminist troops for a charge at Derek and Toby.

'Yes,' said Tabetha carefully, 'Or it could be a woman… maybe even a mother.'

'What?' gasped Priya.

'Well, the killer has been able to get hold of new mum books from somewhere. And it strikes me that it seems like Shelley was comfortable with whoever we are looking for. She seems to have met them willingly, she had no defensive wounds. Both her and Mrs Nolan were bludgeoned from behind, quick and hard. Mrs Nolan an older lady kneeling down, and Shelley a slight girl. Both easier targets for a female killer.

'And I've been thinking more about Mrs Nolan. The killer went in and out of the community centre with no eyebrows raised. What better cover than a buggy? I've found out firsthand that it can be a great way to get people's trust.' The room was silent, a couple of the mums shifted in their seats.

'I'm not saying it definitely is a woman, I'm just saying that we shouldn't rule it out here.'

'That's true, that's true,' agreed Toby, 'but I have to say, from the comparable profiles out there, I think your friend could be closer to it. We know it's more than likely a man is involved and we need to keep focus here,' he nodded in Priya's direction.

'Oh?' asked Tabetha, 'I think I've got a more intimate knowledge of the person responsible.' Her words were tightly clipped.

'What do you mean intimate?' asked Priya. I looked around the room and everyone looked equally confused. Tabetha didn't speak and eventually I felt I had to.

'Come on, they need all the information, it's everyone potentially in danger now,' I looked at Toby and Tabetha, willing them to tell the group more. It felt like a duty.

'Okay,' Tabetha looked to Toby who nodded. She scanned the room slowly, 'I was the one the letters were sent to, we still don't know why, but for some reason I seem to be connected.' The room was fizzing now.

'What? You should have told us immediately. Is there anything else you are hiding from us?' asked Priya, with the disapproving tone of a headmistress.

'The most recent one included a date: tomorrow. That's everything, and I'm sorry if it's worrying, but I do feel like everyone needs to know the full extent of the warning at this point.' Tabetha looked around at Derek who was stepping forward. Before he could speak, she quickly added, 'For the record, I don't know why I've been chosen, but I'd be stupid not to realise that this puts me in the frame as the final target.' I almost gasped. She'd given nothing away that she'd felt in personal danger. But the pattern placed her right in the firing line.

'I can't put my finger on it,' she continued, 'but I just feel, deep down, putting together everything I've seen and the tone of those letters, something is telling me not to rule out a woman.' She looked back to her colleagues again.

'Tabetha, this is neither the time, nor the place,' Derek said, a measured tension in his voice.

'Do you know what?' said Toby, stepping between the two, 'at least we are all on the same page now. Maybe not a bad thing. Whoever is behind this, man or woman, and whoever is the target, we need to make sure that final murder does not take place. We know the next important letter in the sequence is T, and we even know the date and location. That is a lot to go on.' He looked reassuringly around the room.

'Right, well then that's where we need to be. All of us together at Tatten Waters. We can all pitch in now,' said Priya.

'Hey, you guys can go,' Fay said, cradling little Jack in her arms, 'but me and Tim won't be anywhere near Tatten Waters this weekend, I can promise you that.'

'I get it,' Tim nodded, 'you're scared. But come on Fay, I want to catch whoever this bastard is! I say we all go, stay in pairs, and keep our eyes open. Surely the more bodies on the ground, the better.'

'But will we be safe putting ourselves in the firing line like that?' asked Anil, Priya's husband.

'Oh, for god's sake...' said Priya shaking her head.

'It's the big fair this weekend, there'll be thousands of people there,' shot back Anil.

'Well we can't just sit around waiting for someone else to sort it out! I won't have it on my conscience if something happens. We can all stay in pairs, like Tim said.'

Derek stepped in. 'I absolutely agree with your friend, and advise you all to stay away from the fair.'

'Oh, you do, do you,' Priya turned on him, 'And what sort of protection are you offering us if we stay at home, waiting like sitting ducks?'

'We have no reason to believe anyone of you is directly in danger, and we will be focused on Tatten…'

'So that means none,' said Priya looking at Derek. She turned back to her husband.

'What if something happened to Tabetha? Or what if she isn't the target and there is some other new mum out there, about to head to the fair, just like we might with Shay, and then never comes home, leaving another baby without a mum? How would you feel when we knew the risk and could have done something about it?' she added.

Anil didn't respond.

'Okay. That's settled. We're going.'

◆ ◆ ◆

Miss Natalie Clare Tovey tried to smile as the girl rubbed her damp hair with the towel and told her to relax while she waited for Sam to come over to do the cut.

She took a deep breath and tried her best, but it was hard.

She pressed her thumb to her phone, and it opened straight to the news. She'd been watching nonstop for anything about it recently, but then everyone local had.

'Police name Tatten Waters as potential new target for the Surrey Slayer,' flashed the headline.

Her stomach turned as she frantically flicked to the list in her notes.

There it was, 4th November: Tatten Waters.

'Right let's get going,' said Sam, making her jump. He sat on his swivel stool, pulled out a black comb from his pack of tools and looked into the mirror with a smile.

'Any plans for the rest of the weekend?' he asked starting to ruffle her hair with his free hand.

'No, nothing. Nothing at all,' she lied.

CHAPTER TWENTY

As people left in a buzz of excitement and fear, Dan took Nellie up for her bath. I was left tidying away the bits and pieces while Tabetha, Derek and Toby talked in the living room.

Derek began: 'I don't want to patronise you by saying you should not have shared that information without my explicit say-so. And if you really felt you were the main target, you should have spoken to me before today. And certainly not in front of a room of potential targets! And let's not beat around the bush here, potential *suspects*.'

'I know, I know. I didn't plan it this way,' said Tabetha.

'I'm not sure you are making the best decisions right now, Tabetha,' replied Derek, with a patronising stress on her first name.

This stopped me in my tracks. I couldn't imagine she was criticised very often. I stepped back from the sink where I was washing the extra mugs that wouldn't fit in the dishwasher and leant back just a little so that I could see along the hall and back into the front room.

'Look, you've just become a mother,' his voice softened, 'and you're probably very tired, not to mention full of hormones...' I could see Toby physically turn away from the conversation at this point, anticipating it wouldn't go down well.

Derek didn't look finished, but Tabetha cut in.

'I know what you are trying to say, but if you don't mind *me* saying, I have had a baby, not a lobotomy, sir.'

I could see her puff up a little to stand her ground. When he didn't respond, she took a step back. Whether she was regretting what she said or not I couldn't tell from her face.

Toby had taken a step even further away, busying himself with his phone.

Finally, Derek smiled and shook his head a little. 'Okay, okay, have it your way. But I think we can agree today was not your finest moment. Correct?'

'It won't happen again, sir.'

'Okay,' said Derek, closing the matter with a little swipe of his arm.

'DI Bolton,' he turned now to Toby, and away from Tabetha, cutting her out of the conversation once again, as he began to plan the following day.

Tabetha stood silently, but didn't leave the room. I wondered how often it was like this at work in that kind of environment. Was it because she was on leave? Because she was a mother? Or simply because she was a woman, that she seemed side-lined? I watched as Derek and Toby continued to talk about the profile, who they were looking for and who could be the next victim, not once glancing at Tabetha. She seemed smaller suddenly.

It was hard being a new mum. It was a vulnerable enough place without having to admit to everyone that you might be the target for some bloody serial killer.

Eventually I heard her walking Derek and Toby to the door. They called through to say thanks for the tea, with a little wave goodbye, as if I was their best friend's mum, cleaning up after a play date. Once the door closed, Tabetha came through to join me, carrying the last mugs from the room.

'Do I need to apologise to you too?' she said coming over to join me, 'I mean for not sharing that I've been thinking I'm the final target? I'm not sure I've got the energy.' But I could already see an apology in her eyes.

'Don't worry about it, I'm getting used to you keeping some things to yourself. Hey, I do it too. I'm just worried for you, that's all. You must be scared, right?'

'It's a theory that's been in the back of my mind, and then when we saw the NCT pattern I knew it was a real option, that I was the final piece for the puzzle. If I'd told them down the station, they'd have pushed me even further away. I don't think we can afford for them to shut me out again. I'm pleased it's out in the open, even if Derek is pissed off.' She sat at the breakfast bar.

I opened the fridge and took out a bottle of wine, raising my eyebrows at her. She was just about to speak when Dan came in the room. I turned to him to offer a glass, but he smiled weakly and shook his head.

'I don't know about you, but I'm knackered after all of that – it's a lot to take in.' He looked at Tabetha and she knew immediately what he was getting at. She stepped down from the stool quickly and started to gather her things.

'It'll be an early start tomorrow. Toby and I will come by here in the morning. I won't have Luca, so we can just shift your baby seat into the back, but it'll be a bit of a squeeze. It's not far down to Tatten Waters though.'

'God, what the hell are we doing?' I asked with a nervous laugh. I couldn't help it, but I felt excited. Finally, it felt like we were going to find out what was going on and who had been doing all this. The letters, the books, the killings.

'Are you up to it?' asked Tabetha seriously, looking me straight in the eye. 'And I don't mean because you are a mum. I mean because you haven't been well, and I don't want you to go back there again.'

'That's very sweet, but to be honest being back in the thick of things, getting back to normal a bit, is helping. I promise. I'm looking after myself though. I am!' I smiled reassuringly at her and she leant in and gave me a close hug. I knew that didn't come naturally to her, but we'd gone on quite a journey together. Not just with the case. And it really felt like it might be about to conclude.

'Try and get some rest, okay?' she said as I watched her head off down the pathway. I took a deep breath as I turned back into the house. Tomorrow was going to be massive.

As I walked back towards the kitchen to finish off, I spotted Dan sitting in the living room, deep in thought.

'You okay?' I asked, as I started to walk past.

'Come and sit down, Em,' he said without looking up.

I felt a sinking feeling as I went to join him and sat in the armchair across from him.

'You aren't seriously thinking of going tomorrow, are you?' he asked. I could see the tension in his jaw.

'What do you mean, of course I'm going. We're going,' I said without missing a beat. In the moment I couldn't really think what he meant.

'You think that taking our baby to the potential scene of a murder is a good idea? Not to mention putting yourself into a ridiculously stressful situation after the few months you've had and the time I've put in, that we've all put in, to getting you better again.'

'But I am getting better, that's the point. I can't be wrapped up in cotton wool forever.'

'You aren't better Em, you aren't. And it's not been close to forever.' He looked up finally and he had a look in his eyes like the smile you give to a child with chicken pox stuck in bed. I could feel my frustration grow. 'You might be getting there, but you are not back to normal,' he finished.

'Normal?' I asked.

'You know what I mean, back to how you were before Nellie, before all this, you are far from it,' he shook his head.

I took a big breath and looked straight into his eyes. 'You're right, it hasn't gone completely. But I'm having better days, better hours, than others. I can get out of bed, I can get through the day without crying, you know? They sound small, but those are big steps for me. I need to keep doing what I want to do when I feel strong enough to do it, and right now I do.' I just hoped I was making sense. Then I took another deep breath and tried to explain the bigger picture. I spoke slowly: 'I don't know if I'll ever be exactly what I was before, so please don't be waiting for that.'

Dan nodded and thought for a moment. 'I miss the old you, that's all.' I knew he was trying to give a compliment in a clumsy kind of way.

'What is it you miss?' I asked.

'Just you. Your voice, your touch, all those little cute things you used to do for us, as a couple, and for me I suppose. But it's not just that, it's how you are without me too. You have always been so confident, and so independent. I love that about you.'

'But that's exactly it... I'm not independent like I was. I literally have a dependent. We both do.'

'But we always used to say that we wouldn't change after she arrived, we'd carry on doing what we always had, right?' Even as he said it his voice sounded uncertain.

'Yeah, well, we were wrong, weren't we!' I couldn't help but laugh. 'Look, you've been great and understanding and supportive, helping me get back on track. But I don't want to pretend it was just a little blip. This isn't something I'm going to get over, because what's happened isn't going away.' I waved my hand around the room, littered with Nellie's toys, clothes and books. 'We'll have to get used to the fact that there is someone else in the house who we both love more than each other now.'

That was the only way I could describe it.

'Does that make sense?' I asked. He didn't respond, and I tried again.

'I didn't give birth to just a baby, it was a whole different life. Different food, different evenings, different TV channels, different weekends, different holidays, different sex life, different parties, different schedules, different future... and it's going to keep changing as Nellie changes.' It felt like a sudden turn-around, trying to explain things to him, but it was like I'd been going through hell to find my way into the new world, while he'd been blindly waiting to get back to the old one.

He looked down with hands dangling between his legs limply, like he'd given up in a fight. Maybe that was why it hadn't hit him so hard. Because he hadn't really accepted things had changed at all.

'I know it probably sounds stupid,' he looked back up again, 'but I genuinely hadn't thought beyond Nellie being a baby.'

'It's not stupid,' I smiled. 'I think that's what I've been trying to get my head around. But things aren't worse, they are just different. Completely different. And that's okay.' I went over to give him a hug. 'If you are waiting for me to get back to how I was before, and for our lives to resume, I just don't think that's going to happen,' I broke it to him carefully.

He leant his head against me as I stood awkwardly cradling him from the side. Then he looked up at me. 'I get it, you're different. But I have to say, that little speech sounded more like my Emily than any of our other recent conversations, about nap time, or the colour of different poos.' He smiled a little.

We stood in silence and I felt his body release a big sigh.

'Look, however you feel about going, Em, I still need to do what I feel is best for Nellie. Nothing you can say to me will persuade me that heading out with our baby to the scene of a crime is the right thing to do.'

When he put it like that, I could see what he meant.

'I'm not happy about you wanting to go, but I understand if you do,' he continued. 'But can we agree that Nellie is staying at home with me?'

I nodded slowly. Most importantly, it was safer for Nellie that way, but being alone would also make things easier for me.

As I started to get Nellie ready for bed, I thought back to when he'd talked about 'helping' me with the baby, and it had made me so cross. It all sort of made sense now, that he hadn't accepted that this was a joint endeavour, and neither had I. That was partly where the panic had come from. I'd always done my own things, and I'd treated Nellie the same. My thing. And just tried to get on with it alone. That wasn't fair on me, or Dan, or on Nellie.

Now I thought about it, before Nellie we'd really spent our time together just doing fun, loving, crazy things we enjoyed. We'd mostly shared the best of ourselves with each other. Parenting was making us see the worst of each other too. The tired, drained, selfish, envious, needy

parts of us... and it was a bit of a shock.
I messaged Tabetha before I went to bed.

> Just me tomorrow, Dan will keep Nellie at home to be on safe side.

She replied:

> Makes sense. You sure you want to be there?

I responded, immediately:

> Absolutely. Let's end this.

CHAPTER TWENTY-ONE

I didn't sleep much that night. My mind was racing, firstly with my conversation with Dan and then with what we might find at the fair; or more importantly, who.

Nellie had recently settled down a little at night into two feeds, but she was still up early. I'd probably had four broken hours of sleep, and although that was a regular occurrence, I still wasn't used to it. I lifted her quietly out of her cot and took her downstairs so as not to wake up Dan. We settled on the sofa under a blanket and I latched her on to feed. Her body felt warm against me and her hand rested on me like a puppy's paw. She fed with her eyes closed, on the edge of sleep.

It was still dark outside, and I could hear the wind in the large sycamore at the end of the garden and the regular click, click, click of a fence panel wobbling back and forth. I sat silently thinking through what might happen that day.

On the one hand I was prepared that nothing

at all would occur. Presumably the killer had seen that Tatten Waters had been leaked in the paper as a possible location and would know police would be streaming around the place.

On the other hand, from the boldness of the letters, the killer seemed so sure about what he was doing, so arrogant, that I didn't think he would want to give up on whatever this crazy plan was. Or she, I supposed.

What sort of person were we looking for? Perhaps a woman, maybe even a mother, if I followed Tabetha's train of thought... or a man if I sided with Toby's hunch. Whichever it was, there was one commonality: Tabetha.

This brought me on to my main question: How did Tabetha fit into all this, and was she really the next target?

Dan came down as Nellie was finishing off her feed and opening her eyes. She gave me that sweet goofy smile, and I tipped her over my shoulder and patted her back softly as he filled the kettle.

She was starting to feel much more substantial now, more like a human being and less like a little animal.

'Tea?' asked Dan as he took out some mugs.

'Yes please, but I'll make it,' I said, getting up and passing our little girl to him.

In my mind we needed to share the jobs both ways if we were going to naturally share in the future. Just a little thing, but making our tea was symbolic to me, that I was able to do things for myself and for the two of us, not just for Nellie. And, as he sniffed her little bottom, and got out the nappy mat, it felt like he was also trying.

We didn't talk about the night before, or even about what might happen at the fair. But rather than rushing for some precious time alone as soon as he took Nellie, I sat down on the sofa with my tea as he lay Nellie on the floor to do some kicking, and we talked about a project he'd started at work. It was nice. Boring, normal and nice.

Suddenly it was eight o'clock and I rushed up to the shower. I took the chance for my Sunday morning ritual, regular since Nellie was born, and pulled on my old jeans, a size fourteen that I'd always felt my best in. I pulled them up tentatively over my thighs and tried to close the button, they didn't quite go. I lay back on the bed and pulled each side closer and finally the button just made it into the hole, for the first time in a year. I stood up and wriggled the waistband a little higher onto the narrowest part of my waist. Not the same shape as it was, but still there, just. I looked in the mirror. There was a bit of a roll over the top, but not that bad. In fact, not bad at all. I pulled on one of my favourite old T-shirts, dazzling with neon stripes, and you could hardly see the added baby weight.

I pretty much skipped down the stairs, back to Dan and Nellie. I was having a good day. I grabbed a cereal breakfast bar as I said goodbye and Dan beckoned me over.

'Don't do anything stupid, okay? We need you.' His words were slow and deliberate. 'Promise?'

'Of course. I'll stick with Toby and Tabetha the whole time. What are you guys doing today?'

'I think we'll stay here and chill out, right Nellie?' He picked her up and she gurgled happily in return. Part of me wondered if I should just stay with them and chill out too, but a knock sounded at the door.

Tabetha was waiting as I opened it and she looked as excited as I'd felt skipping down the stairs. I shouted a goodbye and headed out. It was bright outside, with a fresh, autumn coldness in the air, which I always loved. The beautiful weather seemed surreal, given where we were going and what might happen.

'Dan okay?' asked Tabetha. Maybe she wondered if there was more to him staying at home than I'd suggested.

'He's fine, just being protective, that's all.'

'I get it,' she nodded. 'In our line of work, you get used to putting that danger to the back of your mind, but even for Claire this one feels a bit too close to home.'

'There's no way we could miss the final day of this,' I said with real confidence, and she nodded as we got into Toby's car.

We drove in silence, but I could feel the palpable excitement in the air.

From my spot in the back, I watched passers-by as we drove. The closer we got to the fair the more suspicious they seemed. A couple talking intently, then stopping to look behind them. Looking for a potential victim? No, just waiting for a friend to catch up.

A man outside a shop looking up and down the street. Waiting for a getaway car? Then he put a cigarette up to his mouth for one last drag before heading back into the cafe next door.

I wondered why people would even come to the area after the name had been shared on the news as a possible location. A date hadn't been given though. And then I remembered, after the London bombings, how quickly people returned to the affected areas.

Life had to go on.

If anything, there was a little tingle of excitement passing through those areas, particularly if you weren't local. There was something intriguing, fascinating about crimes and death. The nervous tension lingered in the air long after the events themselves.

'About five minutes away now guys,' said Toby.

As we inched closer, I thought right back to how this had begun. Chatting with Tabetha in Fay's living room. New mums and dads, all of us knackered, all of us unsure, but embarking on a new adventure.

When I'd got up that day, I'd not known what direction things were going to take for us. And not just with the murder. The last couple of months had taken me to a place I'd never expected. Everything had continued to look the same from the outside, but underneath my clothes there hadn't just been a broken body after the birth; there was more damage than that. I remembered, at one of our first NCT sessions, I'd said I was afraid of the pain of birth. Tilly had replied: 'Just remember, people do this every day. It's the most natural thing in the world.'

I'd really felt comforted by it then. But looking back that was a ridiculous thing to say. People die every day too, but we all accept that it is still hard when you have to deal with it yourself. Wouldn't it be better to plan for the pain (and not just physical pain), to acknowledge that it can be really hard, that things can go well or go wrong, that plans won't work out sometimes, that people around us will be affected?

Although, as I watched us pull up to the other ladies grouped by the fair entrance, I remembered that Tilly didn't have kids. This seemed to be the same with a lot of the people I met in the baby world, many who were most vocal about sharing their 'professional opinion'. It explained their optimism.

Priya and Anil where both in dark outfits, as

if they might be trying to blend in. It made me smile. They were holding hands tightly while Priya pointed at Fay, making some important point. Shay must have been with one of their millions of relatives, as they were babyless, with just a dark satchel across Priya. I imagined it was packed with emergency snacks, a notebook and pen, maybe even a walkie talkie and some pepper spray.

Nina and Alek looked much less sure of themselves. In fact, Nina didn't look like she wanted to be there at all. I had spotted frantic WhatsApp messaging last night though, with Fay and Priya rallying the troops and saying we had to all be there, so I guessed she'd felt like she couldn't pull out.

Alek was the one stepping up this time, nodding as Priya spoke, with his arm linked through Nina's. Nina herself was standing a little back, looking anxiously around while holding tight to the buggy with Leah inside. Toby parked the squad car half on the pavement (were police just allowed to park anywhere?) and I could hear Nina's baby screaming, as usual, as I opened the car door.

Fay and Tim walked up next, with Derek ahead of them, talking to a uniformed officer, who he patted on the back before the uniform headed off into the fair. There must have been police crawling all over the place since it opened.

As we got out, I realised that I was the only one without my partner there. But otherwise, this was the whole lot of us from our reunion when it had all begun with the first letter.

We stood together as Derek gave us a list of warnings. He didn't look happy we'd all arrived, but what could he do?

We were not to approach or follow anyone. We were to call Toby, Derek or simply 999 if we saw anything suspicious. Suspicious meant anyone who looked out of place, anyone who seemed to be behaving unusually, or anyone who approached us and tried to take us anywhere, even if they seemed genuine. At this I could see people straighten up a little. This wasn't a game.

He finished by reminding everyone that we were merely citizens today. Although his team would help to keep us safe if they needed to, we were not an active part of the investigation and had chosen to come against his advice. Maybe he thought we'd step back at the last second.

'We're not backing out now, Chief Superintendent,' said Priya looking around the group, most of whom looked just a little reluctant as they nodded in support.

'Fine, I don't like it, but fine. I want you back here at twelve noon, that's one hour and twenty, to check in. Right?' Everyone nodded again.

He turned, and Priya stepped in. 'We should split up in our couples okay?' She looked around the group. 'Me and Anil will go anti-clockwise around the edge. Nina and Alek, why don't you head into the centre and take the left side as we look at it. And maybe you guys can head in and to the right?' she said over to me and Tabetha. Toby stepped forward then too, he was going to stick tight to Tabetha today. 'I'll go with these guys. And remember, all of you, no one is to approach anyone, you understand?'

We did.

Toby, Tabetha and I walked into the throng. It was a typical local fair. Stalls with garlic, olives and peculiarly-flavoured sausages that looked like they shouldn't really be out all day in the sun, but people were still buying them. Tables covered in containers of sweets which people packed greedily into bags even though they never would in a shop outside of a fair. A few stalls had near-identical local chutneys and I wondered how people made these small businesses work.

Then away from the food stalls on our side were some rag-tag fairground rides. One took people high in the air then dropped them straight down. It looked particularly vomit-inducing. Kids went around in teacups, and the dodgems were full of dads trying to look like they were enjoying themselves with their screaming children. At least we weren't on the other side, where Nina and Alek were looking around local craft stalls and mediocre water-colour collections, avoiding the trestle tables with members of the council waiting to chat to people and hand out expensive-looking branded bags with flyers about local services.

We walked around the area once, which took a meagre ten minutes. Then we paused at a good spot by the teacups where screaming kids were queuing with tired looking parents. Toby got us all coffee from a stall selling overpriced donuts, which smelt delicious. Only my near-miss with my jeans kept me from indulging in those too.

We did another circuit around our section and made it back to the teacups where the queue had barely shifted since our last stop. It was going to be a long day. Being a police officer must mostly be extreme boredom punctuated by abject fear when something does eventually happen.

We set off again and I spotted someone to my left giving a wave. It was Nina and Alek on their own circuit with the buggy. I stopped and gave them a thumbs-up with a questioning raise of my eyebrows. Nina put out her hands with a shrug as if to say she had no idea if she'd seen anything useful or not. It was so hard in such a crowd to know what to look out for. I nodded back and waved again before starting off.

'You seen something?' asked Toby as I began walking again.

'No, nothing, just looking around. It's tricky to know what's important, isn't it?' I said.

'We'll know when we see it.' His confidence buoyed me.

'I need the loo,' called Tabetha back to us from where she walked slightly ahead. She pointed to a block of toilets with a fairly long queue outside. Toby took a walk around the block, checking for other entrances and exits, then came back to us and nodded.

'Okay Tabetha, we'll be over here,' he said looking around and indicating a quiet spot in front of a stall with handmade leather goods priced in the hundreds, where anyone who stopped seemed to very quickly move on.

We could see the queue from the spot he'd picked. Then he turned to me and I realised maybe he had let her go because he also wanted to talk in private. To me.

'How are you doing? You seem really... well.' He had that caring police officer look on his on his face again, like he was checking in with a victim.

The last time we'd really spoken I'd been so miserable. We'd only talked about the case since, but he must have had an inkling of what I'd been going through.

'I'm okay, I'm getting better. I've not been myself. I'm not sure you have either?' I asked, phrasing it as a question, though I'd already made my own conclusion.

'Yes, well I wanted to properly clear the air about that,' he looked a bit sad as he said it. 'I wanted to thank you actually. I was so frightened about the baby arriving. I didn't know what to expect, but I had a bit of a sense of doom about the whole thing.' He smiled at me, knowing that I'd get it. 'You opening up to me was a bit of a relief. Even you were finding it hard. But not giving up, you know? It gave me a bit more hope I guess, does that make sense?'

I was shocked to hear him say I'd given him hope, just like Tabetha had for me.

'Well,' I shrugged, 'I was getting through it, but only just. It should be me thanking you for listening, when you really didn't know me at all. I think we probably both needed someone completely outside of our own circles to talk to. I'm sure it wouldn't have happened otherwise.' I hoped he'd know I was referring to that kiss.

'It wasn't just that though Emily, not for me anyway.' He stepped a little closer and looked down at me from his six-foot height. 'I just wanted to let you know, because I suppose I don't want to make excuses for what happened. Because, if things were different, you know...' he sounded a bit nervous and I was shocked. I obviously didn't hide it on my face, as he grinned at me, his slightly-crooked smile making his eyes a little crinkled. I'd been feeling almost invisible recently. And that kiss, well I'd written it off as just a slip, one strange moment in time.

'But things aren't different and... and we've done the right thing,' he finished.

I really didn't know what to say. I nodded weakly as he looked towards the toilet block, where I could see Tabetha had now gone inside and wouldn't be able to spot us. He leant forward and gave me a close hug, his cheek pressed against mine.

I closed my eyes for just a second to enjoy the feeling of... well, just feeling things again. When I opened them, I could see two familiar people walking across the fairground in front of us, just a few metres away, looking around them as they did.

I pulled away from the hug and focused in on them. It was Shelley's sister Kat and she was walking through the fair with Tom.

'Look,' I said to Toby as I turned him towards the pair. 'What are they doing here?'

'Stay here and wait for Tabetha, I'll speak to them.' He pulled away and his face hardened back into detective mode. Toby moved at a slight jog into the crowd and caught up with them.

I watched for a minute or two as they talked. Kat gesticulated broadly. The fair was beginning to get much busier, as people arrived mid-morning with kids, looking to fill the day. I suddenly felt vulnerable. I kept losing sight of Toby talking to the two of them, as people passed between them and me.

Tabetha still hadn't come out. How long had it been? She must have been in there ten minutes or more.

I started towards the toilet block. It seemed crazy now that we'd let her go in by herself, and I didn't even apologise as I pushed through the queue to look inside.

'Tabetha, Tabetha?' I called in urgently, but no one called back. I waited a minute or so at the sinks, then began looking beneath the cubicle doors, each one in turn, but didn't recognise her shoes.

I left again and looked to where Toby had been standing with Kat and Tom, but he was definitely gone now. I had no idea what to do. I took out my phone and called each of their numbers in turn, but no one picked up. It was so noisy, with the bustle of the crowd and the music on the PA booming out, that I couldn't imagine anyone could hear a phone anyway.

I went back to the leather stall, as it was the last place we'd all been together. Turning in circles, I looked and looked at every face in turn, hundreds of them near and far, looking for someone I recognised. The rumbling noise and the smell of popcorn, hotdogs and donuts overwhelmed my senses as I started to panic.

Just as I was going to call for Derek, I looked way into the crowd towards the fairground rides, and there was Tabetha. She was standing perfectly still staring ahead of her. She had a strange look on her face, I could tell even from a distance. Focused.

I tried to follow her gaze but could only see floods of people walking past.

I looked around once more, but Toby wasn't in sight, long gone, probably looking for us. So, calling Tabetha again on my phone, I started towards her through the crowd. Finally I saw her look down into her bag and reach in to pick up the call.

She disappeared again in front of me as I heard her on the line: 'Yes? Yes?' I could hear the urgency in her voice.

'I'm coming towards you now, don't move,' I said as the line crackled. I could hear a response, but had no idea what she'd said, and even as she talked, I caught a glimpse of her moving farther away from me.

'Stop, wait!' I shouted into the phone.

'Find Toby,' I heard, then the line went dead.

I carried on in the direction she'd been walking, jostling through the crowd, looking left to right for Toby like I'd seen police officers do on the TV when they trailed a suspect.

As I moved forward, ever farther, I started to lose hope. The fair was so crowded by then that it was impossible to pick out one person, particularly when I had no idea which way to look.

I kept moving forward and before I knew it I was at the end of the park, at a perimeter hedge dividing it from a road. I looked through an open gate leading out of the park and then up and down the street, in case Tabetha had left ahead of me.

There were some smart-looking houses, a grotty-looking pub, and a tall old factory building. It was Victorian, maybe, with a decorative crown of metalwork along the top, before a final level jutted out above. It must have views all across the fair. Below it were large iron letters spelling out the word, 'Violet'. I could see it had been converted into offices, but they looked to be standing empty.

My gaze fell back down to the ground before landing on Tabetha at a large metal door. She was pulling hard at it and looked surprised to see it open. Then she went inside.

I looked behind me, hoping one more time to see someone else who might be able help – Toby, Derek, anyone – but there were just streams of strangers walking in the opposite direction, through to the fair.

I looked at the time. It was nearly 11.30. We'd been told to stay together, but I had been alone for maybe twenty minutes already. I could start to head back to the meeting point, but would anyone be there yet? And I couldn't just let Tabetha head in by herself, could I?

I tried Toby's number one more time as I crossed the road. Finally, I heard his voice.

'Where the hell are you?' he shouted over the noise of the crowds.

'I'm out the back of the fair... there's a tall old factory building... looks like it's office space now… it says 'Violet' on it. Tabetha went in. I'm going to follow her.' I tried to explain everything as quickly as possible.

'What? Don't go anywhere. Are you with anyone?' he shouted again.

'No,' I called back as I tried the door. It opened.

'Right, I'm back by that bloody bag stall. I've been going around the whole fair looking for you two. I'm coming now – you went out the back of the field?' he asked. He was breathing heavily.

'Yes, head behind the rides, to the far hedge, there's an open gate, I'm just across the road. Should I go in after her?' I called, still holding the door handle. I wanted to go in, to find Tabetha, to check she was alright. But my feet were lead on the ground. My heart pumped.

'No! Stay put. Do not follow her. Do you hear me? I'm on my way.' He hung up. What if she'd been lured in there by the killer? But even if she had, what could I do?

Finally I let go of the door and watched as it slowly swung closed. I looked behind me, willing Toby to appear.

I felt cold suddenly. My heart pumped in my ears. I pulled my arms around me and stood solid, still, watching the gate.

Then, there it was. An almighty thud sounded behind me. More of a slap, hard and horrific onto the ground.

I knew what it was before I even turned

around. I'd never heard it before of course, but there is something about a human body hitting the pavement from a great height that you just know. Something soft becoming hard with the speed and smacking the floor at full force.

I froze. It felt like minutes. Hours. An image flashed before my eyes, Sherlock falling down a roaring waterfall, Moriarty laughing from above. I knew I had to turn around.

The body was about ten metres behind me. I couldn't see any blood. In fact, it could have even been someone sleeping on the floor from this distance. Except for that awful sound still ringing in my ears under the hard beat of my heart drumming.

No one else was around. It was just me and the body. Slowly I took a few steps towards it, from here the main thing I could see was a mass of hair. It was clearly a woman. As I walked closer, I could see she was facing down onto the pavement. Closer still, I could see her legs were bent at strange angles and her body was motionless. From where I stood then, I could tell: she was definitely dead.

I paused again and took a deep breath before making it over the final few metres.

I looked down from above, considering whether I should touch anything, or turn her over, when I saw lying next to her a book that must have fallen with her. A Mum's Diary.

I started to reach down when a hand landed

on my shoulder.

'No,' I heard close to my ear as I turned around and found Tabetha standing behind me. I grabbed her fast and close. She was here.

'Don't touch anything,' called another voice running over the road from across the street, as Toby headed over from the gate back into the fair. As he ran, he pulled on a pair of blue latex gloves. From the opposite direction two more officers ran over. He'd called in the cavalry and I felt the relief wash over me.

'Check the other entrances. Now!' He called to the officers, taking charge, as they nodded and continued on at a sprint around the back of the building.

I took several shaky steps away from the body and sank to the ground.

CHAPTER TWENTY-TWO

The next three minutes went in slow motion. And soundless. I know it was three minutes as in the inquest this was how long it took from the moment the officers arrived, to the moment the ambulance pulled up.

Once Toby reached us, he carefully held a hand to the woman's neck, then looked up and shook his head.

He stood, and I could see him use his phone. I now know he was calling the ambulance and Derek. The ambulance simply to declare her dead, Derek to coordinate all the waiting backup needed.

I just stared at the body while Tabetha held an arm around my shoulders and then eventually stood up to talk to Toby.

It was unbelievable that, seconds before, this had been a living, breathing person just above me, and now it wasn't a person at all. A smashed vase no one could fix.

I had been relieved when I'd turned to see her

and realised it wasn't Tabetha, and yet someone was still dead.

As the sound of the ambulance started to wake me from whatever was blocking out my surroundings, I realised I did recognise the wavy hair, the slight body.

A paramedic bent down close to me. 'Are you okay, are you hurt at all?' she asked.

I shook my head and kept looking as they turned the body over, making a futile attempt to check for signs of life.

And there was her face, it had been to the side as she fell, so one half was barely recognisable, but I still knew her from what was left. Our lovely, quiet health visitor; Tilly.

I heard myself gasp and felt vomit rise in my throat.

Toby turned sharply and looked at me.

I could hear him speak to Tabetha, quietly. 'Take her away, would you? She doesn't need to see this.'

'No, it's not that,' I said, as Tabetha walked towards me. 'I know her, we know her,' I said urgently towards Tabetha.

She just nodded her head and looked down at the battered face, she obviously already knew.

'Who did this? Did you see them?' I asked, and Tabetha crouched down close to me and held my shoulders tightly like she needed me to hear what she was going to say.

'I lost a minute or so just inside the building.

She must have gone straight up the stairs while I was searching the ground floor. By the time I'd started heading up she'd have been close to the top already and then she must have...' I looked at her closely. What did she mean?

'She must have what? Fallen?' I asked, completely confused as she shook her head.

'I can only think she jumped. I called it through, like we agreed, right?' she said for reassurance to Toby. 'I called it through and didn't go out myself. But I had no idea she'd jump off.' She looked back at the body.

'I could hear her moving about up there, right until the last second. Then I heard the bang and you screaming down below. I had a choice, go up or go down and I chose down.'

I couldn't remember screaming, but she was probably right.

'What the hell is going on?' I searched into her eyes; something wasn't right.

What had made Tilly jump? Why was she here anyway? I looked back at the body. The crew from the ambulance had fallen back, there was nothing they could do. Now Toby was crouching by her with two colleagues carefully looking at the scene. He picked up the Mum's Diary and I saw something fall out and flutter through the air, lifted by a breeze. It gently settled to the floor at my feet, face up. It was obvious at once it was some sort of a letter and I recognised the rounded writing.

I know I shouldn't have let it happen, but I couldn't help myself.

These last few months have been madness, but exhilarating, and this final step has been in my mind since day one.

I can't pretend I don't know the hurt I'll leave behind. But I can't just sit silently watching everyone else from the side lines anymore.

I feel bad, of course I do, but I know I won't regret any of it.

Tilly x

Toby came and carefully retrieved the letter.

'Oh God, is this a confession, is that what this is?' I looked between Tabetha and Toby.

'How did you know her?' asked Toby softly.

'She's our health visitor, she's looked after all of us, and our babies,' I said disbelieving.

'Guv! ID here,' shouted someone coming over from the body and holding out a driving licence.

'Natalie Clare Tovey,' read Toby slowly.

We were moved from the scene almost as soon as the ID was found. Derek arrived and cleared the area, including a large group of people hanging around watching us, who obviously saw this as their next piece of entertainment after the fun of the fair. Nothing like a good death to capture the attention of a crowd. Necks craning to make sure they didn't miss a speck of blood or the possible glint of a weapon.

I was bustled into a police car with Tabetha and taken back to the local station for questioning. I desperately wanted to talk to her, to find out exactly what had led her to follow Tilly into the offices and if there was any clue from inside as to what exactly had happened, but as I rotated to speak to her, she turned away.

'No discussions until we've given our statements, I'm afraid. I don't want anything jeopardizing this case.' She looked out of the window as we sat in silence the ten or so minutes back to the station. As we drove past the front of the fair, I could see Priya and Anil talking with a police officer, as the others came over to meet them from various directions. Nina was wiping her face.

I wondered what they knew at this point, probably just that a body had been found. But that was enough. I knew Priya particularly would be kicking herself. No one wanted another death today.

I was interviewed for around three hours. It's amazing how much you can say, and ask, about an event that lasted a matter of minutes, start to finish.

I explained how I lost everybody, how I finally saw Tabetha and began to follow her. The phone calls we had and considering whether to go into the old factory building, and finally that thud.

They asked me a lot about my connection to

Tilly. It was hard to explain it really, particularly to a male officer. I had maybe met her ten times at the most. We weren't friends, but she knew me intimately. All of us new mums. The people who help you when you have a newborn are life savers. They listen to you as you cry and hold your boob as you try to latch on a screaming baby. They show you how to change a nappy and recommend ways to put them down for a nap when you're desperate to sleep.

They asked me about Tabetha too. Why had she followed Tilly? When had she arrived after the body fell? I answered everything as clearly as possible. I knew what they were getting at. It all seemed so strange, but I knew why Tabetha had followed her without thinking of her own safety. Because, like me, she needed to know what was going on, finally. I was amazed she'd held back from going out after her if I was honest. But she was right to, God only knows what would have happened if she had.

When I got home that night, I fell into Dan's arms as the door opened. I felt like I'd been up for days. I couldn't talk about it anymore. He just held me, and we watched on the news as the information started to be picked up. *The mystery of the Surrey Slayer came to a tragic conclusion today.*

They talked about a witness seeing a body fall and Dan took a big intake of breath. I knew what he was thinking, not just that it must have been awful for me but that it could have been me. He had been scared something awful would happen and he was right.

I had thought that knowing the truth would be some big relief and that I'd finally feel like I understood what the whole thing had been about, but it wasn't. And I didn't.

In the coming days Tabetha kept in touch to share snippets of information from the investigation. They'd searched Tilly's mum's house where Tilly still lived, despite being well into her thirties. Tabetha sent me a photo of Tilly's bedroom. It looked almost like the room of a teenager. Just a single bed with teddies tucked all around the pillow. By the side of the bed was a pile of baby things, probably the bits and pieces she took around with her. A couple of spare nappies, some clean muslin cloths, packs of wipes, and next to them a cardboard box with Mum's Diaries piled inside.

To anyone else that would have seemed normal for a health visitor, but they looked sinister to my eyes now. I knew that it must have been from that box that she'd taken a booklet to lay out next to poor Mama Nolan, bleeding on the floor, and then by Shelley's body after battering her on the Green, and even taken one with her for that final fall.

Then the biggest breakthrough on day three, recovering a deleted list of appointments updated weekly on her phone. All three locations matching her health visitor checks on the same days. And on the day she died, the name of the fair followed by one capitalised word FREEDOM. It seemed she'd been looking forward to that final act, to it all being over.

It was Friday before I met up with Tabetha again. She came to mine with Luca and we laid the babies on the floor together for the first time in a while.

'I still can't believe it,' I said as I poured the coffee.

'I saw her at the fair, and suddenly I wondered if she was the final target, 'T' for Tilly perhaps. But as I followed her, trying to decide if I should stop her, her actions seemed stranger and stranger. She wasn't there to go on the rides or buy candyfloss. She looked like she had a purpose.' I thought back to seeing Tabetha watching something so intently. Had that been the eureka moment?

'Then I realised,' continued Tabetha, 'rather than fitting the profile of a target, she perfectly fit the profile of the murderer. An intelligent woman, close to mothers and babies, access to the baby books, she knew Mama Nolan and Shelley. Most importantly perhaps, she knew me, my work and even my home address. So I followed her. What I was going to do I don't know, confront her maybe?' Tabetha shook her head.

'But she seemed, so, I don't know, normal,' I said.

'Well we all have our characters we put on to survive the big wide world, don't we? Her mother said that outside of work she had no real friends. She'd been desperately lonely for years. She put everything into her job and being with the mums.'

'But that's just it, why would she want to hurt any of them?'

'The picture that's building is that she was having some sort of breakdown. She had always wanted a husband, children, a family. She could see her life wasn't on the track she'd hoped. Maybe in some twisted way this plan of hers gave her a new goal, some control even.'

I tried to line this up in my mind. It must have been torture to be around us all, if that was how she felt. I thought about her visit to Tabetha's when I'd been feeling so low. When I'd opened up about how unsure I was about being a mum, had she been listening in despair at my feelings for what I had? Had she been angry even? Probably.

'I just had no idea.' I shook my head. 'She was such a small almost nondescript person. It's hard to think that so much was going on below the surface.'

'That persona probably helped her. No one would have picked out a quiet, unassuming health visitor, travelling in and out of community centres, meeting mums, even being able to get into their homes unquestioned. We know all about that, right?'

'And Shelley,' I said, understanding more now. 'She had a health visitor appointment that day, didn't she?'

Tabetha nodded. 'It looks from phone records like Tilly called her again later that day. They're thinking Tilly used that call to invite her to meet back up. Alfie hadn't been putting on weight as he should, and Shelley had been worried that day. Maybe Tilly offered extra advice or to pass on a book to borrow. I'm sure Shelley would have trusted her.'

'But why Shelley specifically? And for that matter, why involve you?' I asked.

'I wonder with Shelley if it was her ambivalence that frustrated Tilly. Like her sister said, she could be a selfish girl and saw Alfie more as an accessory than a baby.

'And me?' continued Tabetha. 'She'd said to me more than once how I was so lucky to have the whole package; the big job, the wife, the house, the baby. I felt flattered at the time,' she rolled her eyes at herself. 'I guess I had exactly what she wanted.'

Tabetha took a sip from her coffee and we sat in silence for a while before she continued.

'I'm embarrassed to say I was excited when the letters arrived; they were a welcome distraction. But they did start to drive me crazy. I think now that she probably wanted to humiliate me. Draw me in, but then prove I couldn't do it all really. She probably loved the idea of me running around all over the place with no idea who I was chasing.'

I blew out a breath, shaking my head that anyone could look at Tabetha in that way. She was still a bit of a hero to me.

'Then there's Mrs Nolan,' she went on. 'They knew each other a little, it turns out. And Tilly had stopped by to speak at a breastfeeding class at the community centre that morning before doing at-home visits around the local area that afternoon.' I listened quietly, it certainly sounded like it was all falling neatly into place. 'That woman in the flats,' continued Tabetha, 'the one we stopped by to see on that first day. She said she'd had a health visitor around that morning, didn't she? That must have been Tilly on her rounds.'

I tried to picture her, visiting the local mums, the helpful support that she always was. Seemed to be. And then heading back into the centre at the end of the day, maybe Mrs Nolan was even making her a cup of tea, bending down into the cupboard to grab the tea bags. Then Tilly smashing her over the head to kill off her first 'Mama'. It was crazy, but then this whole mess was. Maybe none of us know what will drive us over the edge, until it happens. I'd always thought that. But the reality of it was unnerving.

We sat quietly. I could hear the washing machine hum round and round, pause, then back the other way. It was comforting somehow.

Tabetha shifted in her seat and frowned. 'I wonder if the letters were really a cry for help, even if she didn't know it. Perhaps she was hoping they would have led me to her more quickly. And I'd stop her. Maybe she wanted to be stopped.' She spoke in clipped words.

'If I hadn't paused to call down for back up... But Derek had made it very clear we had to follow protocol and not to go in alone, hadn't he?' She looked up at me with a rare need for reassurance.

I usually saw her wince when people reached out to her. But this time she let me put an arm softly on her shoulder and I could feel the tension across her back. She seemed fragile. If Tilly had wanted to humiliate her, it seemed she'd done it.

'Don't over think it,' I said. The act of reassuring her felt backwards. In fact the whole solution did. But if Tabetha was satisfied, then I should be too.

'No one suspected her. No one. Who would have? You've always said that real crimes are never like the murder mysteries on the telly, but this one was even more complicated maybe. Tilly fooled everyone. Everyone.'

Even as I said it, I didn't believe it.

CHAPTER TWENTY-THREE

In the coming days I tried to push my concerns to the back of my mind and to focus on getting back to normality, whatever that might be.

I shared a few messages on our WhatsApp NCT group, when the papers covered the theory building around Tilly. But otherwise we all kept our distance. I don't think anyone had been in the right frame of mind to meet up since we'd been hunting a killer together.

It was nearly a month since the fair when Priya sent a message asking if any of us wanted to join a 'Baby Sense' class. I wasn't sure I was ready, but as I'd promised my therapist that I'd try new things to do with Nellie, I set my mind on getting back out.

I took the bus to the community centre and found the reception empty. It turned out they didn't man it anymore. Not since Mrs Nolan had been killed. Cost savings it sounded like. What a sad way to be forgotten.

Walking in felt like an act of defiance in itself. Claiming back the space for the mums again, even after one of us had been taken. I couldn't help but look again behind the counter to go back in time. I could see Tabetha and me on that illicit visit to the scene of the crime. It had felt exciting then.

A group of women broke the moment as they entered the centre chatting and giggling behind me and I took a deep breath before heading towards my own session.

It was dark when I went inside. The class started at 10am and I'd arrived only a couple of minutes early, but of course was the first to arrive. A woman in some too-tight sports leggings and a T-shirt with 'Baby Sense' emblazoned in stretched neon pink lettering across her boobs welcomed me in.

She spoke in a weird combination of jolly and hushed tones.

'Welcome, welcome, and who's this little princess?' she asked.

'I'm called Emily, ha ha,' I said, cracking what I thought was a half decent joke, but she just looked at me confused. 'Nellie,' I said, 'She's called Nellie.'

'Gorgeous! Well I'm Nadia, come on in. We'll be starting in a couple of minutes, but do get Nellie out and feed, or let her look around the room, get comfortable, whatever you're happy with.' She waved around the room at the random assortment of baby toys laid out at one end.

I doubted everyone would be here in two minutes, but she was right, suddenly about nine or ten other mums came rushing in with their buggies, frantically grabbing babies, changing nappies, sharing wipes and feeding. Chattering and flapping, like wrens on a bird table.

It was strange to hear the conversations drift past; a new place for brunch they'd discovered, where to find compostable wipes, the pros and cons of co-sleeping. It was all very lovely and a world away from most of my recent conversations.

Suddenly Nadia clapped her hands and we all sat in a circle around her, with a range of mismatched lava lamps and disco lights flashing in the darkness, presumably stimulating our babies' senses. But simultaneously giving me a headache.

'Now lay your little ones down so you can get some good eye contact, and let's start with our welcome song,' said Nadia.

As she spoke, the door opened and Fay and Priya came bustling in with their babies all wrapped up.

'Sorry, sorry – traffic!' said Priya and the two of them noisily dropped their bags and coats at the door and came to sit down next to me. Despite my reservations about coming, I was really pleased to see them. They'd started to feel like real friends now, not just useful mum sounding boards. I hated to admit it, but maybe my mum was right about making lifelong friends at NCT.

'Oops!' mouthed Fay to me and I tried not to laugh as Nadia looked less than impressed.

'Babies on floor, welcome song first,' she said, much stricter this time. I could see why the others who'd been before had made sure to get there on time.

I felt giggles rising a good few times as the session progressed. It seemed a little silly to be singing all together to our silent babies who couldn't understand a word we were saying. But Nadia was so earnest about the whole thing, and when she dangled pom-poms over the poor babies' faces, she was delighted with any reaction.

After half an hour of 'stimulation', such as putting bits of rosemary from Nadia's garden under Nellie's nose and bouncing the babies up and down to the sound of whale song, it was free-play time, when we were to let the babies direct us around the toy area. I put Nellie on the floor and she looked up at me confused, or bored, it was hard to tell which.

I picked her back up and took her over to Jack and Shay, both of whom had already started to roll over and wriggle about on their tummies like little parachutists.

'Nellie can't roll over from her back yet,' I said settling her down next to the boys.

'Don't worry, it can be up to six months they say, so you've got a good few weeks,' said Priya supportively, as she patted Shay's little head proudly. It was hard not to compare kids, and even harder not to feel smug when yours was a bit ahead.

Nellie began to squeak, and I looked at my watch. She was still feeding every four hours and it was about time. I picked her up and sat up against the wall to feed her.

'Wow, you're still going, well done,' said Priya.

I'd been really lucky, breastfeeding had been one of the things that pulled me through my lowest points. I just smiled and said: 'Well, I'm just seeing how long Nellie wants to go. Take each day as it comes.'

'You're lucky,' Fay chimed in, 'I managed three months, but it was so hard, it never settled down really and I just couldn't keep going. I wasn't sleeping, and he was so hungry all the time. But I feel so guilty.' She reached over to Jack and gently stroked his hair away from his eyes.

'Don't be silly, you need to do what's best for both of you,' I said – and I meant it.

'There are still some nights, when I just wish I could call her,' Fay whispered.

I didn't know who she meant for a second.

'Tilly, I mean,' she went on, 'I know it sounds crazy, but whatever she did, she was a great support to me.'

'God, me too, I still can't believe it really. She seemed such a loving person. It's hard to see her as this mother-hater they all write about now,' said Priya.

I was relieved the others had reservations too and was just about to launch into Tabetha's explanation about the breakdown and the jealousy when Fay spoke again.

'There was this one night, about eight weeks in, or was it ten? No, it must have been eight because it was my birthday, the twenty-first of September. I was so low. Tim was away, I'd been up every hour for the past three nights and I'd been meant to go out with my sister and her kids for a birthday meal, but I couldn't face it. I was just so tired, and Jack was screaming and screaming.'

'I remember those days,' said Priya in solidarity.

'I called Tilly up and she wasn't even meant to be covering my area that night, but she came straight over. She worked with me for half an hour maybe, before she found me a better latch that worked for Jack. I did the longest feed I'd ever managed, and he finally went into a deep sleep.'

'Poor you,' I said.

'I was panicking that she'd leave, and he would get straight back up. But she just stayed with me, pretty much all night. She even rocked him when he did stir, while I had a sleep. The sun was coming up by the time she left, bless her. It got me through that day which got me through that week which got me to the next stage when he started to sleep more. It's so strange that the same person who did that for me was also plotting to kill other women, other mums. You just never know what's happening in people's minds, do you?'

Priya shook her head and we all sat quietly.

'And back together mummies!' called Nadia, clapping her hands again to get us back to the circle.

As I cuddled Nellie and sorted out my top, my mind flipped through the rolodex of information stored away and something clicked.

I stood quickly and caught Fay's arm as she moved ahead of me.

'What date did you say is your birthday?' I asked.

'The twenty-first of September,' said Fay without missing a beat.

'And you are sure that's when she stayed at yours?'

'Yes, I know it was then because I cancelled my plans, like I said.' She looked certain.

I couldn't wait for the rest of the session to end. I made my excuses and left early, but instead of heading back to mine, went straight over to see Tabetha. She was in when I knocked, and she let me straight through; it must have been clear on my face that I had something urgent for her.

I waited until we were sitting down, and a sleeping Nellie was parked up. Baby Sense had worn her out.

'So, Fay has just let me know that Tilly spent the entire night of her birthday at her house, helping with Jack.' I said, 'The twenty-first of September, she's certain,' I finished and couldn't help giving a satisfied smile.

As with me, it took a moment for Tabetha to click.

'The evening Shelley was killed?' she asked.

'Exactly. She arrived at 5pm, spent all evening helping her feed and even stayed into the night while she got some sleep.' I slapped my hand down on the table to make my point. 'I knew something didn't add up!'

Tabetha didn't respond.

'It changes everything, right?' I prompted her.

She sat quietly, looking thoughtful. 'Well... if Fay slept some of the night, Tilly could have gone and come back? It would have been the perfect cover in many ways.'

I could tell that she was just being professional, but it irked me, nonetheless. I couldn't keep an edge from creeping into my voice.

'What, so she'd have taken Jack with her? Or left and risked a sick baby waking up and Fay seeing she'd gone?'

'Okay, so maybe Shelley was killed earlier, or even later than we thought. Or maybe there's an accomplice?'

'You don't really believe that, do you? She was a loner, even her mother said that.'

'Look, we have Tilly at each location, her

notes, the Mum's Diaries stored in her room. We even have her dead at the final crime scene with confession in hand.' Tabetha tried to persuade me as I shook my head. But she had a point. In all other ways it seemed open and shut.

'I agree though, this raises some questions,' she continued. Maybe this had piqued her interest. 'I'm not convinced we're asking *if* she did it. But maybe this is a case of revisiting *how* she did it. Just to be sure.'

'So, what first – call Derek?' I asked.

'No,' she said, still deep in thought, 'I want to be really sure something is up before we do anything like that. It would be a big step to officially open this back up again.'

I was a bit surprised, but I could tell she had a plan forming in her mind and she wouldn't want them meddling again. She seemed to come to a decision. 'We have all the information about the murders, maybe what we are missing is really understanding Tilly herself.'

'Her mum seems to be the only person who was really close to her, we could make a visit?' I asked, already standing.

We stopped by a flower shop on the way and yet again I found myself ringing the doorbell of a grieving relative.

Tilly's mum looked a bit like her daughter, small and mouse-like, with little round glasses.

She let us in with our babies, no questions asked, and took us through to her living room.

There were photos of Tilly on the wall, one in a mortar board and others from way back in school, through dodgy tinted layers, braces, spots, down to first photos at primary school with gappy grins and wonky ties.

'Was Tilly an only child?' asked Tabetha, walking along the wall of photos.

'Yes, my only one. Such a lovely little girl, always,' said Tilly's mum in a quiet voice.

'How was it you knew her again?' she asked vaguely. She seemed distracted, in a daze.

'She was our health visitor,' Tabetha answered.

'These little ones are what, five or six months?' she said, looking at the babies asleep in the slings on our fronts. 'How darling. Enjoy it, children are such a blessing.' I felt like I might cry as I watched her look along the photos herself. She mustn't have ever imagined her motherhood would end this way.

I looked down at Nellie. One day she would be Tilly's age, my age, a mother maybe. But I'd still be her mum, and she'd still be my little girl. Is that how it would always feel?

'I'm so sorry,' I said quietly. She didn't respond. What do you say?

I took a seat on a neat, hard sofa, while Tabetha sat next to me. 'Mrs Tovey, *I'm* Tabetha,' she said, looking the woman in the eye with a nod to show she was coming clean with who she was in relation to the case. But Tilly's mother didn't react.

'Yes?' she said, eventually.

'I'm Tabetha Tate. The person Tilly wrote the letters to. I'm the Detective Inspector,' clarified Tabetha, but there was still no recognition in Tilly's mum's eyes.

'Yes, they said she wrote some letters. She did like writing letters. She used to write to me every week from college...' she shook her head.

'Did she ever mention me?' Tabetha asked.

Mrs Tovey shook her head again.

'Or Luca maybe, my little boy?'

Mrs Tovey's eyes lit up. 'Oh yes, I heard about Luca. So, you're *his* mum.'

'Yes, that's right. And what about Shelley?' asked Tabetha.

'Now I did hear that name, maybe once or twice. Tilly worried about her and her baby, Alfie wasn't it? She was young. Tilly always worried most about the young ones and what would happen to them once her visits ended. Yes, she used to talk about her babies all the time. What they were doing, how they were changing, problems going on, what she was doing to help.'

'*Her* babies?' I asked.

'Well, that's how she thought of them, I think. She loved babies, she always loved babies. She knew from school she wanted to work with them, but even before that, she'd be pushing dollies around in her little pushchairs. She used to take them everywhere with her.'

'Did she want a child of her own?' Tabetha asked carefully.

'Yes,' she answered quickly, 'Well, I think so,' she continued, and didn't look so sure. 'I always thought she did, but then she never seemed to meet the right boy. I never met any boyfriends... you know.'

'Do you think she may have been gay?' asked Tabetha.

Mrs Tovey looked a little shocked, and then composed herself. 'I don't think so. Right through her teens she had all sorts of crushes on singers, and actors, and boys from school. But she was so shy around them. I don't know if it was my fault maybe, because I never had any men around as she was growing up; it was just me and her after her dad left. She would read all sorts of romance novels and watch all the films. We'd watch them together sometimes. She was a real romantic, that's what makes when it happened even sadder.'

'What do you mean?' I asked, intrigued.

'Well I thought she'd met someone; I was sure of it. She'd changed. She was more skittish, excited to go out of the house, a bit secretive, you know? She wasn't usually like that.' She looked at us with a hopeful glint in her eye for just a second. 'But I suppose that must have just been in my mind. We know why she was secretive now, don't we...?'

The glint in her eye was from the tears forming now.

'This must be such a shock,' I said. I couldn't imagine how she felt knowing that all that time her daughter was plotting to kill. That is if she was.

'Look,' Tabetha said, her voice level and calm, 'I don't want to raise your hopes, but we have reason to believe that there may be some missing information in the case. Something which raises a bit of a question about Tilly's involvement, or perhaps whether she was acting alone.'

Mrs Tovey looked up with her sad, sad eyes. 'Look dear, I loved her, I'll always love her. But I've seen the evidence. Where she was, what she wrote, how she died.' She shook her head. 'You don't need to patronise me.'

'So, you do think she did it?' asked Tabetha.

'Not in my heart. No, I don't. But,' she picked up one of the photos with Tilly smiling gap-toothed as a little girl, 'I can't see any other explanation, can you?' She looked up at us, but without a response, her shoulders drooped again, resigned.

We left soon after. I was more confused than ever. We knew that there was a question mark over one of the murders, but even her own mother couldn't see another option.

We sat quietly in town, with a coffee. Tabetha was reflective. I'd never seen her looking so unsure.

'Is it worth us opening this all up again then?'

I asked.

'I'd built up a picture in my mind of who the murderer was, and Tilly was as close as you could get to that profile... maybe once I'd spotted the fit, I just didn't look as hard as I should at whether it actually made sense.' She looked embarrassed, maybe even cross with herself.

I tried to reassure her. 'If something isn't right here, then it doesn't just sit on your shoulders. You weren't even in charge, that was Toby. It would be his fault just as much as ours.'

'No,' she shook her head. 'Toby had said I needed to keep a more open mind. I didn't listen though. If I'm honest, I liked the idea of getting it right while he got it wrong.'

I didn't know what to say to make her feel better. I'd opened this all back up, without a single suggestion for another solution. Maybe there wasn't one. Maybe we needed to accept Tilly for what she was.

'Look,' I began, 'even her mum thinks that the evidence is overwhelming. It might feel a bit uncomfortable, but you couldn't write a clearer story taking us to Tilly.' I used my fingers to count off each point on my hand. 'Her initials, the letters and the handwriting, so similar to her confession, her list of appointments lining up to the locations, her presence at the fair, her own death. Her mum said it, and she was right. If Fay hadn't mentioned what she thought happened that evening, I'd never have questioned it.

Maybe that's what we are reading too much into? Fay must be mistaken...'

We didn't stay on for long. There wasn't much more to say. Tabetha was going to take the weekend to consider whether to go to Derek and Toby with our concerns. To think through all the options.

I was surprised then, when my phone beeped on Sunday night as I sat with Dan talking things through for the millionth time, getting nowhere. If anything, our chats had convinced me even more that Tilly was the only viable suspect given the evidence. She must have either crept out, or had an accomplice, or even perhaps Fay was wrong after all.

Then, a message from Tabetha:

> Something you said made me think. I've done some digging. Need another 48hrs. Meeting Tuesday night, 6pm, T

It was a long forty-eight hours.

CHAPTER TWENTY-FOUR

It was Tabetha's idea to gather at Fay's house. It felt right. To bring everyone together again, back where it had all started. It was what all the great detectives did.

As I walked into the room with Nellie, I could see Fay, Priya, Nina and their partners had already taken seats, with Tim carefully handing out mugs of tea. Toby was standing in the far corner and gave me a small wave as I entered. I was surprised how normal things felt when I saw him now. The case had put everything else into perspective.

I found my way to the armchair I'd sat in the very day it had begun, quietly greeting people as I walked past. Fay was sitting to my left and gave my hand a squeeze as I sat down.

Everyone was quiet.

Quickly behind me came Shelley's sister, Kat, with Tom. Kat looked like she'd rather be anywhere other than here, and they bickered at the door before finally entering the room. Finally they headed to my right and took the last two of the dining chairs that had been dotted around the edges to accommodate everyone.

Clive came skulking in next and stood in the corner, watching us from the sidelines.

After a few moments, Tabetha came in from the kitchen and I was taken back in time as she walked towards me holding what looked like another letter. I raised my eyebrows in surprise. But as she got close to me, Dan walked over to join us and she folded the paper back up, putting it in her pocket as she greeted him.

'Sorry I'm late, my work call overran.' He kissed me on the forehead, did the same to Nellie, then sat on the arm of the chair as Tabetha had done all those months before.

Finally Derek entered the room, he walked directly over to Tabetha, and leant in close to her face to speak low and urgent. I could just make out her final response as he started to walk away: 'I'll explain everything, I promise'. He turned quickly, replying, 'I'll give you fifteen minutes, that's it.'

Tabetha nodded and took a breath before plastering a smile back on to her face. 'Great, we're all here now, so let's begin.' She walked to the archway into the kitchen, and it created a frame around her, like she was going to perform for us.

'Thank you everybody, I'm really grateful you've all been able to make it today.' She looked around the room at all of us, as if taking the moment in.

'As you know, everything going as we expect, Tilly will be named in the upcoming inquest as the person with sole responsibility for the deaths of two women, Mrs Nolan and Shelley Carter. And that she then took her own life.' She shook her head a little as if it hadn't yet sunk in.

'It's been an almost unbelievable case for everyone involved. I really wanted to bring you all here today to try to make some more sense of what's happened, and to share my own thoughts.' She paused, and people stirred around the room.

'What's always struck me and has been going around my head since Tilly's death, is the conflict of two ideas. That for the solution to make sense, for her to be the murderer, we needed to believe two things. One, that Tilly was a vulnerable woman, desperate and on the edge. And two, that she was a calculating murderer, skilled at laying clues of Christie-like proportions.

'I've been left asking myself, if she really was a desperate woman, angry at the world, angry at mothers, driven mad by her own female yearnings,' she rolled her eyes, 'why contrive a scheme lasting many months? Why write letters to me? Why lay clues that could, that did, lead to her detection?'

Kat spoke up. 'Well, she wanted to humiliate you, to punish you, right?'

Tabetha shook her head a little, then carried on, 'I know women like Tilly. She may have had a vulnerable side, but she was also hard-working, ambitious, loving. And I believe she was hopeful. The idea that wanting a child could be enough to push her over the edge,' Tabetha rolled her eyes again, 'well I just don't buy it and I don't know why I ever did.'

Kat huffed and looked away. It was clear some people in the room didn't want to open things up again. But Tabetha persevered.

'Let's just focus on one murder, the person pretty much all of us in this room knew: Shelley. Why would she have gone out to meet Tilly that evening?' She looked at us all in turn and I realised it wasn't a rhetorical question.

'Well, she wanted some extra advice or something, didn't she? They had met up that day and she'd been struggling, right?' jumped in Kat again.

'I can imagine the sort of person that persuades a young woman like Shelley to meet alone in a park. The sort of person she rushes to when she gets the chance to be alone, to take a break from her baby. And it's not Tilly,' said Tabetha, more directly now. 'No, we believed that because it fit with the other patterns, because someone made it fit.'

'Oh, come on!' Kat made a show of rolling her eyes, but there was a desperate edge to her voice. 'It all makes sense that it was her. She even confessed! Why are we dragging this all up again now?'

'Because despite what her work records for that day said, she actually made an urgent visit to this very house that evening,' explained Tabetha.

Now I really felt like I'd stepped into a murder mystery, as Tabetha looked over to Fay to reveal our new evidence.

'That's right,' Fay nodded. 'I was desperate. Feeding wasn't going well, Jack had been up and down all night for days, Tim was away with work and I was at my wit's end. She came over before five and she stayed basically all night. She even held him while I got some sleep.'

'How long has this information been about?' Derek barked, stepping forward to Tabetha. 'Why wasn't I told right away?'

'Just give me a chance, Derek, please,' Tabetha replied.

Toby stepped forward. 'Let's hear what she has to say Derek, what have we got to lose?' he asked.

Derek looked at his watch and sighed. 'Fine, but your time is running out, understand?'

Tabetha nodded and smiled gratefully.

'Go on then,' he said quietly. Perhaps even he was starting to get intrigued.

'Well, we know it was the same night because it was also Fay's birthday. And Tilly – who we are led to believe was a woman-hating murderer

– stayed as long as was needed, despite this not even being her patch that night. Which was why I think she didn't update the work log. She was a rule follower and she didn't want to get in trouble. We wouldn't have ever known about that visit unless Fay mentioned it,' she indicated Fay with a hand, who smiled back.

'And if Tilly couldn't have killed Shelley,' continued Tabetha, 'then why on earth did she kill Mrs Nolan? And for that matter, why would she kill herself?'

The air bristled. I could feel Dan shuffle nervously on the arm next to me.

'No, it wasn't Tilly,' she went on, 'And I don't even buy that it was a woman. Not anymore. It was when Emily said to me something quite simple the other day that I realised what was really going on. She said, *You couldn't write a clearer story taking us to Tilly.*'

She looked over to me and smiled gratefully, but I was yet to see the significance. She went on.

'The reason this all felt like walking into the middle of a BBC One drama is that this whole thing was a setup, from start to finish. A fiction quite deliberately orchestrated to lead us – to lead me – to that final conclusion when Tilly died and the whole case would be wrapped up, packed away and forgotten.'

'So, what are you saying Detective Tate?' asked Derek, using her title for the first time since I'd met him. 'Be specific.'

'I'm saying that the more I've heard about Shelley and Tilly, the more I've thought about the profile of the person who drew one into a park late at night and another up to the top of an old building, both to their deaths. I'm sure now that who we are looking for is a man.' I was surprised, this seemed quite a turn around.

She looked at the ground and shook her head. 'Of course it's a man. And the fact that I thought otherwise will be an unending shame to me.'

All eyes were on the men in the room, but it was Kat who stood up and spoke first.

'I know what you are getting at, alright, but you're wrong!' she shouted.

'Look,' Tabetha held up a hand, 'I considered Tom, of course, but I agree with you, Kat. When you seemed keen to direct us off elsewhere the day Emily visited your house I even wondered if it was you and Tom working together. But you have a different sort of relationship, don't you?'

'No, it's not like that,' said Kat defensively.

'I think it is. I'm guessing you are waiting a good amount of time before you share with your family that the two of you are together, right?'

'I don't want anyone judging us, okay?' Tom jumped in now. 'Me and Shelley had been on and off for ages, well before all this happened. I'm not even sure if Alfie's mine,' he gulped some air, 'but I love him, and I'll do what's right by him.' Kat took his hand, and he looked at her before continuing. 'The one good thing that's come out of this is me and Kat. I think we could be a good family together. Us three.' He looked back to Tabetha. 'I know what I sound like...' his voice faded.

'Guilty?' said Tabetha, 'I know. It explains the dream. You feel guilty for your relationship with Kat, but not because you had anything to do with Shelley's death.' At this Kat sat down and relief was written across her face.

'You weren't sure though, were you Kat, not one hundred percent sure that he wasn't involved?' asked Tabetha. 'That was why you tried to put us off the investigation, right?'

'I just thought, deep down, that maybe Shelley had done something or said something and then, in a moment of madness, maybe...' She looked at Tom. 'I'm sorry, I'm so sorry. But I couldn't risk it. I can't lose you too.'

'So,' Tabetha continued, 'That ruled out Tom, but that left a lot of other people in the frame. Maybe Clive really was hiding an evil streak,' she said, turning to where he stood.

He spat out a puff of air, 'Are you crazy? Of course I...'

Tabetha jumped in, 'But we couldn't find connections to Shelley. Why would you start with someone you knew, then go on to kill two completely random strangers, risking being discovered? No, it didn't make any sense. Which left me thinking about the dads that I knew. Had fatherhood pushed any of them to the edge?' she held up her hands as she posed the question.

No one else spoke.

'But that takes me back to my first point. This can't be the work simultaneously of a madman and a sane man. So why not a sane man pretending to be mad? Imagine the kick you could get out of that. What if the idea of a *serial* murder scenario was all a game, a misdirection right from the start, aimed primarily at getting my attention? Ensuring I would lead the investigation through to a watertight conclusion?' she asked.

Now I really was confused, but it was Dan who spoke.

'What do you mean? There wasn't a serial killer at all?'

'That is exactly what I mean,' she replied.

'That doesn't make any sense! The letters, they linked all three deaths from day one, right?' He looked to me, but I didn't have the answer either.

Tabetha did.

'What if three murders were committed to hide just one? A killing that had to take place. A killing that was needed to hide a secret. One death alone would be easy to follow up, to find the trail back. But three deaths, a serial killer... now that tests even the best detective.'

She paused and we all waited, trying to understand.

'Poor Shelley. She knew her killer. She trusted them. So much so, that she went out late at night to meet them in the dark with no fear, no inkling that she wouldn't come home.' Tabetha spoke slowly and carefully, to ensure we heard every word.

'I'm pretty sure I've got it all sorted in my mind now. It took a while, but it was a few things Emily said to me last week... I got there in the end.'

'I was left with one question though,' she said, her voice louder, more forceful, 'Where on earth did he first meet Shelley? That confused me.' Tabetha turned back towards us. For a second I couldn't tell who she was talking to.

Before she spoke again, she caught my eye and I could almost see an apology on her face... for me?

I looked at Dan, wondering for the first time if he wasn't who I thought he was. He'd been so kind, so patient with me. But was that a cover? When he didn't come to the fair, was that really to keep Nellie safe, or to get there ahead of me and hide up on top of the factory? To push Tilly to her death? He looked down at me and I tried to read his eyes.

Then Tabetha spoke again.

'Then of course I remembered. That camp she went to. Back at the end of the summer. And how long was that before Alfie arrived, about nine months? She was sent there to keep her safe. But it was there that she meet her killer. I'm sure of it now.'

'Is that right Toby?' her tone a command then, 'Is that where you first met Shelley?'

CHAPTER TWENTY-FIVE

Somebody gasped into the silence, and I realised it was me. I turned from Dan to where Toby was standing, leaning casually against the wall, looking down.

He looked up; his eyes wide. 'Excuse me?'

'You heard me,' she said quietly. Her eyes were like fire.

'Is this some kind of joke?' he asked, his voice high with shock. 'Because it's not very funny I can tell you that.'

Tabetha didn't answer, but neither did she move her gaze from him.

'Why would it be me? I'm investigating the bloody thing!' He turned around the room and we shared a look for half a second. His eyes were wide, like a rabbit in a trap.

'And hasn't that been just the perfect cover?' said Tabetha, taking a step towards him now.

He shook his head in disbelief and then stopped and nodded. 'Ah, I get it! Of course. You said it, Tabetha, what a perfect cover to be so closely involved, right?'

This was a standoff now and it looked like one of them might lash out at any second.

Rising from my chair, I tried to step between them.

'Keep back from her,' he said, putting out a protective arm in front of me.

'What? Keep back, from me?' said Tabetha, glancing my way, then focusing straight back on Toby.

I stayed where I was.

'I've been wondering for a little while, but I didn't want to believe it,' Toby revealed, his eyes still firmly locked on Tabetha, watching her every twitch and shift of weight. 'Those dramatic letters conveniently turning up at your house. How close you've been at every stage of the investigation. And building that profile so neatly to lead to Tilly.' He shook his head. 'But this is too much. It wasn't enough to get away with murder; you want me out of the way too. Solve the case of the decade *and* get me out of a job?'

Tabetha's mouth opened, but Toby went on.

'I bet you enjoyed performing for Emily and me.' He glanced at me for just a second and I could feel Tabetha lean in closer towards him before he looked straight back at her.

I hadn't taken a breath. Tabetha had always been enigmatic, secretive even. And Toby was right, she loved to perform, to show she was the great detective. I thought of her face as she turned up at my door with the next clue, the meetings she'd organised for us all, and even today, standing ahead of us, like Poirot, twisting his moustache and leaning on his cane as he finally reveals the solution.

Tabetha glanced my way again.

I looked her in the eyes and tried to search for what was real. I took a deep breath. Then stepped towards her.

Toby sighed and his shoulders dropped. 'You don't need to choose. But one of us is lying and I will do whatever it takes to prove that it is not me.' He looked pointedly towards Tabetha.

'You can try, but there's one thing that won't lie Toby,' spat Tabetha, now relaxing a little as I moved closer to join her.

'Oh really?' he responded.

'DNA tests are a wonderful thing, aren't they?' She held the paper up, finally revealing its contents. 'You're Alfie's father. But then you knew that.'

'I'd be careful what you say. Do remember you aren't even a DI right now, that's me, so don't overstep the mark.' Toby was quiet and controlled now, his eyes on the paper.

He tried to not look rattled, but I could see him looking closely. He was trying to work out if she was bluffing. Finally his hand shot forward like a snake to grab it. He skimmed the contents in seconds.

'So that's that then,' he said quietly, still looking at the paper. Then back up at us. His face had changed in a second, from calm and confident to defeat.

'That was always a risk of course.' He put the paper on the side, as if he didn't want to look at it, to acknowledge it was over.

'DI Bolton?' said Derek from the corner. His mouth was open, his eyes wide.

'I was in an impossible position, Derek,' Toby responded. Then he sank back to lean against the wall. The game was up, the adrenalin gone.

'What happened?' asked Tabetha, trying to keep his focus.

'I spotted her on day one at the camp. Or rather, she spotted me. But I didn't take advantage of her, not really,' he said towards Derek, as if that changed anything. 'It was a mutual attraction. And... well... it just happened. She knew I was married, though, I was honest with her from the start. We were always clear it wasn't anything more than the summer. And when the fun was over, we went our separate ways. I didn't think of her again.

'It was months later, after I'd made the move down here, that I saw her in town, and she clocked me right away. It had never crossed my mind I'd see her again. I was out with Marcia and she approached us. Her boldness surprised me.

'We had a little chat and she behaved herself at that point. She didn't say anything compromising and I foolishly hoped that things would be okay.

'But, later that afternoon, the doorbell went. She'd actually followed us back to our house and come to confront me. I knew then this wasn't going to be over quickly. She'd had a little Dutch courage by then and had obviously planned what she was going to say. She had the patter down, you know. If I didn't step up with the money she needed for the baby, she was going to tell my wife and my work that I'd taken advantage of her at the camp. But it hadn't been like that,' he shook his head.

'And you didn't want to help with the baby, was that it?' asked Tabetha.

'It wasn't that. I didn't kill her because of money,' he said, as if that would have been distasteful. 'I knew whatever I gave wouldn't be enough at some point. And even if she kept quiet, Marcia's no fool. She'd spot the cash going out the door and join the dots eventually. And, well it's not the first time I've slipped up.' I remembered back to when we'd kissed, he'd said it hadn't always been plain sailing. What had his wife put up with?

'When Marcia got pregnant, I'd promised myself that this was it. I was doing things properly this time. I wanted a clean slate here. No running away, no messing up, no more apologising after. I had to keep her quiet, I had to...' he trailed off.

'So you told Shelley what she wanted to hear,

that you'd leave Marcia to be with her,' said Tabetha, pushing him to take the story further. 'When her friends thought she was back on with Tom, it was you all along. She thought you were going to set up as a family with her.'

Toby nodded. 'She didn't mind waiting for me while I was working things out. In fact, she liked all the sneaking around, the rendezvous at different locations.' I could imagine how special she must have felt, how exciting it must have seemed. He had a way of making you feel like he was smiling just for you. I could see how dangerous that was now.

'And then, your biggest piece of luck, meeting Tilly.' Tabetha spoke quietly and calmly, she didn't want to send him off track.

He nodded a little, 'I knew I'd need a watertight solution to keep all eyes off me. And then it happened, I was at a local baby thing with Marcia. They had this stand for NCT with a few health visitors talking through local baby clubs and things. I was talking with Tilly, she got all jittery and nervous just speaking to me, you know?

'It was her that pointed out how funny it was her initials matched the NCT. Even then I could see a plan emerging. Her strange name, her proximity to women, a possible connection to Shelley. I needed a cover and it was worth exploring.

'I got enough from her that first meeting to know where she lived, where she hung out, her patch for visits. Once you get a bit of a picture of someone, it's easy to work out how to casually cross paths and strike up a conversation.' Tabetha nodded, but didn't interrupt his flow. My heart stopped for a beat, and I remembered his face coming into view in the coffee shop all those months before, when we'd bumped into one another. Had that been a set-up too?

'I took it slow with her. I told her Marcia had tricked me into the baby and that I felt trapped. She was all too happy to believe Marcia was the evil witch, Tilly the innocent princess. But she was very sweet, very... trusting. Someone was going to take advantage of her at some point.' He stopped and stood quietly for a moment, as if he was letting that sink in. Was he trying to make excuses for his actions – was he really saying it was partly her fault?

'So, she agreed to help you?' asked Tabetha.

I could feel her tension. The whole room was tension.

'Oh no, she didn't have a clue, please don't think that. No, I used to go round her house, to that funny little room of hers when her mum was out. She didn't do anything other than work, and now see me of course. And she trusted me implicitly. She had all her stuff out. Her rota of visits, that box of books. It wasn't always easy to meet up though, and keep things secret from her mum. So she started sending me these little love letters. She was like a teenager that way.'

'And that's what gave you the idea,' said Tabetha. 'The letters were the perfect way to get my attention. Whilst also distancing yourself from the case.'

'Once I had the NCT link and her letters, with that distinctive writing, so easy to replicate, it all fell into place in my mind. I would hide Shelley's death within a pattern. I've worked these sorts of cases before. You'd all be looking for a link between the first two murders and be totally distracted from me.

'I'd heard about you of course Tabetha. The guys at the station raved about you. So focused and insightful... and ambitious. I knew the letters would grab you and you wouldn't be able to let go. In fact the plan relied upon it.'

'And Mama Nolan?' asked Tabetha quietly.

'I was waiting and waiting for the N to line up with a woman's name on Tilly's rota. But weeks went by and nothing fitted. But I knew Newton Hill was on her list, and I went down to see if anything sparked a thought. That's when I met Mama Nolan in the community centre. She wasn't what I had wanted, not really, but I was on a time limit,' he said, almost matter-of-factly.

'So, Mrs Nolan was just unlucky, was she?' Derek spoke out. His usually calm tone had slipped now, and he struggled to hide his fury as his voice cracked.

'Well if the NCT pattern was going to work, I

needed an N. In a way I suppose it was better like that. She was older, she didn't have kids...' again with the excuses. It was like he thought he was doing these women a favour.

'Then to your real target, is that right?' asked Tabetha. 'You waited until Tilly had a visit with Shelley and organised to meet her later that day,' she prompted.

'Now this was the hardest one. But the plan was moving then, and I knew I had to see it through, or it would have all been for nothing. I felt a bit sorry for her when she came over to one of our usual spots in the park. We headed back into the woods and I told her I had to grab something from my bag. She was all dressed up, bless her. I told her to close her eyes and I think she was hoping for a ring.' He really did look sad about it, his eyes lowered.

'But you smashed her over the head instead, did you?' This was Kat now, the shock was beginning to wear off and the anger was kicking in. His eyes flashed and I could see the sadness disappear in a blink. It had just been for effect. He ignored her and turned back to Tabetha.

'And to your credit you had read the clues I left behind by then. You were focused on women, and you were looking for someone connected to mothers, weren't you? You didn't seem so sure Emily,' he said, looking my way and making me shiver. 'But it seemed like even if we questioned it Tabetha would push through. In fact, the more I argued against the theory, the surer she was. That was fascinating.'

I couldn't even look at Tabetha, I knew he was right.

He looked almost reflective now, his eyes up and back, thinking through what had happened. 'I suppose it was easy, really, getting all these women to trust me. And do you know what it takes? It's so simple. Listening. That's it, just listening. It's shocking how easy it is, once you realise.'

'You don't even need to *actually* be listening. Just sit, quietly and nod in silence.' Tabetha huffed at the front of the room as he spoke, starting to lose her cool.

'Don't offer a solution, don't even give an opinion...' His eyes flickered in my direction and I knew then that our conversations, all I'd shared with him. It had been a trick, and I'd fallen for it, like God knows how many before.

'And then there was Tilly,' Tabetha jumped in, saving me. 'She never had a chance, did she?' Toby shook his head in agreement.

'I didn't hold anything against her. But if it was going to work out, I couldn't leave her around,' he replied.

'How did you get her up on the roof?' The voice was mine, but it sounded distant. I needed to piece together how it had happened that day.

'We arranged to meet at 11.30 at the top of the offices in the old factory. She was starting to get a bit paranoid about the murders by now. She could see they seemed to be taking place where her visits had been and now here we were meeting at Tatten Waters. But I reassured her about coming and promised I had some big news for when we met that day and that we'd finally be able to get away together.'

FREEDOM, I thought, remembering back to her phone records for that day.

Toby continued, 'I'd copied keys for a few places over the town from various jobs. Useful little nooks for meet ups.' He took a breath before carrying on.

'I wasn't too worried about getting up there. With all the noise and crowds I was pretty sure I'd be able to break free of you guys. Then we spotted Kat and Tom, didn't we?' he looked to me properly for the first time and I nodded silently, remembering how I'd lost him in the crowd when I'd headed back to the toilet block to look for Tabetha. It must have given him at least a ten-minute head start on us.

'As soon as I could, I went straight out of the back of the park. I knew we were the only group patrolling that side of the event, and if one of the officers spotted me, they'd never question my actions. So I went straight through, no problem. I got there well before 11.30 and just waited.

'It was a bit of a shock when you called up Emily, and told me you were outside and that Tabetha had gone in. She was closer to the truth than I'd expected and was perhaps seconds behind. I knew I had to do it quickly then.'

'But I could hear the fair on the call, couldn't I?' I asked; trying to understand how I'd missed everything.

'Just the wind from the top of the building Em.' I couldn't bear to hear him call me that now. 'And some huffing and puffing on my part.'

'I put the phone down just as Tilly made it out and said she thought she'd been followed.' She was so worried about anyone finding out about us, and confused about the murders of course, that she'd tried to get ahead of them.

'She came towards me, even reached out for me. And I just lifted her up and over the edge. It was tough getting her over completely, but she didn't fight it, I don't think she really knew what was going on.' As if that made a difference, I thought. 'Then I just had to throw over the book, with that perfect letter inside. She didn't know she'd helped me out when she'd sent me that. It was meant to be a final love letter before we ran off together and left our pasts behind.'

'Then once it was done,' stepped in Tabetha, 'you just had to head back down and around the side, so we'd see you come from the direction of the fair, right?' she asked.

'That's it.' He nodded. I remembered him arriving after Tilly had fallen. While we'd been busy looking at the body, he must have run up from behind us. And I'd actually been relieved to see him. He'd called to the officers to check the other entrances. It hadn't crossed my mind that he'd come out of one of them.

'I knew I should have come out and onto the roof.' Tabetha looked pained now she'd heard the whole story. She'd failed Tilly.

'Don't beat yourself up over it. If you'd come out, I'd have had to have sent you over the edge with her too. I always had in mind that you could be the final T if really needed, but I was so relieved I didn't have to go that far. We've grown close haven't we?' He really was completely oblivious to the pain he'd caused.

'That's enough.' Derek stepped forward.

'Sorry Derek, you're right, it's all tied up by that DNA test anyway isn't it. But do you know what, you were useful the whole time. You hated the idea of Tabetha being involved, didn't you? I think if you'd shared everything with her, she may have worked it out earlier.' I could see Tabetha's shoulders crumble a little now as she turned to walk back into the kitchen and away from her little stage. The show was over.

'No more, okay? We don't want to hear any more,' said Priya, standing up and beginning to follow Tabetha out. I had been frozen in my chair, listening, realising just how wrong I could be about a person. My mouth was dry, and my heart was beating in my ears.

Derek moved towards Toby and took him by the arm to lead him away. As he started towards the door, he looked over to me and we locked eyes. They seemed dead to me now. He looked down as if composing himself, and when he looked back up, they had flickered back into life. A new face plastered on, as he tried one last time, 'You understand I had to do something, right? I couldn't lose everything over one little mistake,' he asked in my direction. He really was evil hidden in plain sight. How many men were? And I hadn't spotted it.

I looked down. I couldn't bear to look into his eyes one more second. He may have been the one heading to prison, but we hadn't won.

Tabetha was the Great Detective. I was the Gifted Amateur. Right.

EPILOGUE

It was the final week of 'Baby Sense' before the break for Christmas.

Nadia had decorated the room in a selection of old Christmas decorations and flashing lights. I anticipated trailing musty old tinsel from her attic across the babies' tummies to stimulate their senses.

I unzipped Nellie from her snuggly snowsuit and took my seat in the circle. As I sat down, Fay and Priya came bustling in, not quite late, but pushing it as always.

I lay Nellie on her back and she immediately showed off her new trick by rolling over to wriggle forward on her little round tummy. I went in to give her a kiss to congratulate her again. It's amazing how proud you can feel of the smallest thing your own child does. I couldn't imagine how it would feel when she'd learnt to read, or graduated from university, or got her first job.

'Hello Em, how are you doing?' asked Fay squeezing in next to me.

That day, at Fay's house, as soon as Derek had taken Toby down to the station, it was just us

NCT parents there and we opened some wine and talked for hours. About Mrs Nolan, about Shelley, about Tilly. And I opened up about myself too. It felt like it was the right time to be honest.

I'd gone into motherhood thinking I was ready. Ready to be a parent, ready to be a grown-up. But I'd made a lot of bad decisions. Not just the kiss, but who I'd chosen to trust and how I'd judged others, particularly the other mums. And how I'd hidden how I was feeling, from everyone.

Apart from Tabetha, everyone seemed genuinely surprised to hear how hard I'd been finding motherhood, that I'd pretty much hit rock bottom. But also, each and every one related to something I said.

Yeah, my lows had been really low, but I wasn't alone with any of my feelings. My guilt, missing my old life, my worry about how much I loved Nellie, how relentless it had all been, and how motherhood had been so different from what I had imagined. Everyone had a story to share.

So, I knew when Fay asked how I was, she didn't ask lightly. 'You know what? I'm doing really well,' I replied. 'I'm really getting to know Nellie and it's great that she interacts more now, you know?'

She nodded.

'I'm not taking anything for granted though. I could easily go backwards, so I just need to keep working at it,' I said.

It was still hard being a mum, but an amazing privilege too. One I would always struggle to understand and sometimes to enjoy, but that I would make sure I did my best at.

Well, okay, so sometimes maybe I didn't quite do my best – but at least I'd learnt to give myself a break. Just start the next day fresh and try again. And when I was rewarded, like when Nellie hit some new little milestone, I thought of Alfie and what Shelley was missing out on.

Right on cue the door opened, and Tom tentatively entered carrying Alfie. Kat came in behind with a mountain of baby stuff and sat at the side while I waved him over to sit down next to me.

He'd joined the previous week, after he'd managed to make some peace with Shelley's mum and was starting slowly to get more involved. He'd been true to his word; nothing that had happened had changed how he felt about Alfie.

'All here?' said Nadia, looking around the room to get started.

Then the door went one more time and a mum with a much smaller baby entered. It looked just a couple of months old, still so fragile. A little kitten, soft and squirming. She looked nervous – just how I'd felt when my baby had been that small.

'I'm here for a taster session,' she said, trying a smile.

'Oh of course, welcome, come and join our circle.' Nadia made a circle with her arms and indicated for her to sit.

'Marcia isn't it?' Nadia asked. I knew I recognised her. Toby's wife. I'd seen her just that one time outside my house, she'd seemed withdrawn and tired then. And he'd been just that bit short with her when she'd arrived. Back then I thought it was because I was inside. The new me knew perhaps there was more to it than that. Maybe she was tired of him, and his behaviour. Or maybe she was even scared; perhaps she'd seen a glimpse of the real him. You never know what is going on behind closed doors, behind the masks we all put on. The last few months had taught me that above all else.

Despite her nerves and all she'd been through, she looked healthier now, happier even, as she laid her tiny baby on the floor across from Tom and me. I looked at the two babies opposite one another, who were half-siblings but didn't know it.

Toby had stolen three mums from the world, Mama Nolan, Shelley Carter, and finally Tilly Tovey. She was a mum to so many babies. A great mum. I could feel it when she held my own baby close when I couldn't bear to. But looking at Marcia leaning over her tiny baby, and Kat as she smiled over at Tom and Alfie, despite everything, Toby had made two new mums. And brought Alfie and Tom together too. Maybe he hadn't won completely.

Nadia looked up sharply, as a phone beeped, and as all eyes turned in my direction, I realised with embarrassment it was mine.

'Phones off please. This is mum and baby time, remember?' she said, her ever-present smile hardly hiding her disgust.

I pulled my phone out of my pocket, frantically switching it to silent as I glanced at the message flashing on the screen.

> Drinks tonight? Got something interesting I'd love your view on, Tx

WITH THANKS

A big thank you to my friends and family who took the time to read and share their ideas on the book every step of the way. I couldn't have got here without you.

I must give a special mention to Jeff, Lynsay, Helen, Lindsey, Adrian and my mum and dad, as well as my very patient family: Pete, Gus and Olive.

Finally, thank you to my own lovely NCT group and all the mums I've met along the way. You are all doing great, I promise.

ABOUT THE AUTHOR

Holly Greenland

Murder on Maternity is Holly Greenland's debut novel. It all began in a coffee shop while she was on maternity leave herself, but thankfully she did not encounter any murderers. Holly lives with her family and seven fish just outside London.

Crosskeys, the new Emily Elliot Mystery, is due for release in 2021.

You can sign up for pre-order alerts, find out more about Holly's writing and get in touch with her on her website: www.hollygreenland.com

If you enjoyed Murder on Maternity, please consider leaving a review on amazon to let other readers know.

Printed in Poland
by Amazon Fulfillment
Poland Sp. z o.o., Wrocław